Book Two: A Story of Reighton,
Yorkshire 1709 to 1714

New Arrivals
in
Reighton

Joy Stonehouse

Acorn Independent Press

Contents

Acknowledgements

I would like to thank the staff at the Treasure House, Beverley, and the Hull History Centre; they are always helpful and both sites make research a pleasure.

A huge thank you is due to the members of the Hornsea Writers Group for continuing to offer their constructive criticism and support.

Special thanks go to Lisa Blosfelds for her transcript of the Reighton parish records which has been an invaluable aid. She has also been most helpful in loaning local history books and allowing access to her collection of documents and maps.

Last, but by no means least, thanks to Pam Williams for painting my book covers, and for continuing to help in every possible way.

For Pam

Author's note

While inspired by the parish records, I must stress that the stories in this series are works of fiction. Interested in my own family history in Reighton, I carried out extensive research into the early 18th century. Though the names of most of the characters are taken from the parish records, some are not. Any omissions and deviations from the records have been made for the sake of narrative interest.

The main characters, and those of higher social standing, speak in Standard English. Lesser characters and the older generation speak with a slight East Yorkshire accent. Although Reighton is mentioned throughout as a village, the people of the time would have called it a town.

Part One

Passions

Chapter 1

1709

It was a cold, damp and foggy November afternoon when Francis Jordan led the newly hired farmhands to Uphall. They trudged behind him up the steep street, all hoping for a fair-minded master and mistress. It would be a long year until they could find another employer at the next Martinmas hirings. Among the group, there was a young man, John Dawson, and his sister, Ellen. As they emerged from the mist and turned the corner, the house that would be their home for the next year loomed large. Its chalkstone walls gleamed in the low sunlight, and smoke from one of its chimneys, unable to disperse in the still air, flowed down over the thatch.

Francis Jordan ushered them into the kitchen where they put down their belongings. His wife stood by the fire, stirring a pot, while his two daughters laid the table with bowls and spoons. They turned to see the new girl and the lads, noticing immediately how the girl swept her eyes around the whole room.

Ellen Dawson was quick to take in her surroundings. The kitchen had a huge hearth, big enough to roast a lamb, but the only light came from the fire, a sign of cutting costs. The place was warm though and smelled of stew and onions, so there'd be a good supper for the night. There were a settle and a large chair in dark oak, almost black and highly polished through use; the Jordans had obviously been at Uphall for generations. The curtains were faded chintz. Perhaps the family were no longer prosperous enough to replace them.

Ellen's eyes scanned the walls where various kitchen and farm tools dangled from hooks. Above the hearth were an ancient-looking gun and a row of perhaps even more ancient pots and pans blackened by fire. A frying pan and kettle rested beside toasting irons, roasting spits and a griddle. Nothing had been spared regarding the cooking, a promising sign. She looked forward to seeing the pantry – if she was ever allowed into it. No doubt it was just as well-organised and full of preserves and cheeses.

Suddenly, a great cloud of smoke poured from the chimney. Ellen stepped backwards.

'Is it always this smoky i' kitchen?' she asked.

The mistress stopped stirring the pot and waved away the smoke. She glared in Ellen's direction and ignored her question.

'Tha can leave tha stuff there o' floor. This is my daughter, Jane. She'll take tha bags upstairs.'

Francis saw the look in his wife's eye and decided to lead the new servants back outside and into the yard. They could have a brief tour of the outbuildings before it grew too dark. As Ellen followed him, she thought her mistress looked as smoke-dried and wrinkled as the hams hanging above her head.

Jane gathered as many bags as she could in her arms and left the kitchen. Her other sister, Dorothy, was left alone with her mother who turned to her, hands on hips.

'That new lass 'as trouble written right across 'er fore'ead. Did thoo see way she gawped all round kitchen?'

'I certainly did. She looks full of herself. She flounced in here as if she owned the place, and then had the cheek to ask about the smoke.' They shook their heads in disbelief.

Dorothy, now an eligible seventeen-year-old, had looked forward to the new arrivals but was disturbed by Ellen Dawson. She could spot a rival a mile off. The girl was not beautiful, but something made everyone look at her. When she scrutinised any one of Ellen's features, they were too large or distorted. Ellen's eyebrows were on the thick side, her nose was large with one nostril pinched and the other

4

flared, and her eyes were enormous, as was her mouth. The attraction, Dorothy realised, must lie in the way she held herself and moved.

'I'm not sharing my bed with her,' she said.

'Nay, she can share wi' Jane. Jane won't mind.'

At supper time, Dorothy watched Ellen Dawson charm everyone around her – everyone except herself and her mother. The girl was never still for a moment and forever expressed herself with facial and bodily gestures. When the others retired to bed, Dorothy and her mother stayed behind and sat by the dwindling fire. Dorothy clicked her tongue.

'Did you see the way that girl picked up her spoon? Who does she think she is – one of Queen Anne's maids?'

Her mother rubbed her cheek in thought. 'I reckon she's goin' to 'ave all the lads after 'er. She 'as child-bearin' 'ips, and there's more bosom yet to come. Lord 'elp us.'

Dorothy gulped at the thought of Ellen growing more buxom and desirable. Her mouth turned down in a sneer. 'I've seen a corpse with more colour than she has. I've never seen anyone with a face that pale.'

'Never mind,' replied her mother, 'we'll soon sort 'er out. A bit o' good, 'onest outdoor work'll change 'er for the better, eh?'

Seeing an advantage to be had, Dorothy had an idea. 'Let's put her in charge of the geese and hens. It'll give Jane and me a rest, and then we'll see how she fares. I bet she'll not like feathers and fleas, or plucking – she'll be too high and mighty for that.'

Ellen walked into the kitchen without knocking. They were shocked, not knowing how long she'd been behind the door listening. Despite what Dorothy had said, Ellen had plenty of colour in her cheeks now. She frowned and her black eyebrows had a life of their own.

''Ow dare thoo judge me like that?' She strode towards them with tears in her eyes and they backed off. 'Thoo judges me too 'arshly.' Dorothy looked at her mother in alarm as Ellen pointed a finger. 'Thoo doesn't even know me.

Look at me,' she pleaded. She dropped her arms helplessly by her sides with palms open. 'I've only come 'ere to work 'ard an' earn me keep like anyone else. I've not 'urt anyone. I don't mean any 'arm.' She wiped her eyes and sniffed. 'Me parents are dead. I've only me brother, John, to care for me now.' She begged them, the tears streaming down her face. 'Please don't judge me so unkindly.'

They didn't know where to look. Dorothy blushed about being overhead but was annoyed to be put at such a disadvantage by this new farm servant.

Reluctantly, her mother admitted defeat. 'Don't take on so,' she said. 'We didn't mean anythin' by what we said. Ignore it. Tomorrow's a new day. We'll all start afresh.' She put an arm around Ellen's shoulders and gave them a rough squeeze. 'There now, go on up to bed. Tha knows tha's sharing wi' my daughter, Jane? Sleep well an' enjoy a good breakfast i' mornin'.'

Ellen blew her nose and dried her eyes. She bid them goodnight and retired, smiling to herself. Jane was already in bed, but had left a candle stub burning. Ellen decided the girl might be kinder than her sister; she could be a useful ally. Later that night, lying in the dark and listening to the creaks of the old wooden beams and the distant scuffle of mice, Ellen felt quite at home. She smiled once more to herself and slipped into a peaceful sleep.

In another bed, not far away, Dorothy lay alone. She didn't know what to make of that scene in the kitchen. Though suspicious of Ellen, she knew she should be more charitable. She fidgeted as she wrestled with her conscience. Her bed was uncomfortable and she couldn't get warm. For much of the night, she tossed about and had very little sleep.

In the morning, Dorothy was irritable and tired. She glowered at the sight of Ellen and Jane, looking so fresh and lively at breakfast. Every day now she'd have to face them, and already they were looking as if they'd been friends for life. Yet there was some consolation – Ellen's brother, John. Though he'd kept himself in the background, she'd noticed his dark good looks and, as luck would have it, they were the same age.

Over the breakfast table, Ellen ignored the smoke puffing from the hearth and began to tell everyone how good a worker her brother was.

''E's so skilful with a plough. Thoo should see 'im make a straight furrow. An' 'e can 'andle any oxen.'

John didn't even look up. He said nothing and carried on spooning in his mess of fatty bacon and potato. No one answered Ellen.

Dorothy looked at her mother and father. Both ate their breakfast as if they were deaf, and so did her brothers and the other workers. She looked at John, being as shy as his sister was forward. She noted the soft down on his upper lip where soon he'd need to shave. His black hair curled on his forehead like a young ox.

Tom, the only permanent hired lad, noticed her ogling John Dawson and grinned at her. She stuck her tongue out at him and suggested he worked with John today. Her father, however, had already planned the week's work for the newly hired servants and proceeded to tell everyone where they'd be working, who with, and what was expected of them. There was no argument.

'Ellen,' he announced, 'will be working wi' poultry. Jane – thoo'd better 'elp until Ellen can manage by 'erself.'

Dorothy looked down at the table to hide her smile. She'd now be able to stay indoors all winter and help her mother in the kitchen.

Word soon went round Reighton of the charming new girl working at Uphall for the Jordans. Matthew Smith, a widower for years, listened eagerly and confided in the vicar, George Gurwood. The two men stood by the church wall looking northwards across Filey Bay. They gazed at the choppy sea as the east wind blew the last of the leaves off the nearby trees. Matthew put his hands deep into his coat pockets and began what he'd rehearsed.

'It's been five years now since I've abstained from women. And I've worked hard on building up my herd. I've attended church even when I lost my faith. Yes,' he nodded his head, 'it's true – I blamed God for Margaret's death. But listen – I've found purpose in making my land more profitable.' Matthew looked at his feet and poked a toe through the newly fallen leaves. The vicar waited patiently for Matthew to get to the point.

'I'm thirty years old now,' Matthew resumed with a sigh, thinking of all the talk about Ellen. 'I wonder if there should be more to my life than work.'

Chapter 2

One fine winter's morning, Matthew Smith sauntered in the direction of Uphall. The frost still lay on the ground sparkling in the sunshine and, as he approached, the Jordans' geese spotted him. They charged as a group, honking loudly. When he ignored them and carried on walking through the yard, they turned as one and retreated in single file to the kitchen door. There Ellen had appeared with some scraps. This was Matthew's first proper sight of her. At once, he was besotted. She looked so full of life as she scattered the food; her hips swayed as she stepped between the geese, and she chattered away as if she knew each goose individually. Not wanting to spoil the moment, he stood some way off to watch at leisure. She began to sing to herself. It was all so charming.

He was surprised that he liked her so much since she was nothing like his wife had been. This young woman was striking and, no doubt, a challenge. His wife had been quiet, submissive and gentle with mousey-coloured hair. He'd grown to love her; Margaret's character and loving devotion had won him over. Damn devotion, he thought as his eyes lingered on Ellen's hips. He'd missed having a woman in his bed, and made an instant decision to court her and get her to marry him. He was past the freshness of youth. His hair was beginning to thin on top but he was still handsome, he reckoned, and certainly a good catch. With this in mind, he strode towards her, lifted his hat and bowed in a gallant fashion.

'Good morning,' he said as he straightened up with a radiant smile. 'You must be Ellen, the new girl.' When she nodded with her head coyly to one side, he added, 'You have plenty of geese to look after.'

'Not just geese – 'ens too,' she replied. 'I'm goin' to see if any of 'em 'ave laid. We 'ave some pullets. They 'aven't moulted so they're still layin'. Come an' see where I think some eggs might be.' He followed her and she led him into the barn. 'They don't all like to lay in 'en 'ouse. Some 'ens prefer it in 'ere. Maybe it's warmer. Look out! Mind where thoo puts tha feet. There's an egg down there.'

'I'm sorry. My big feet are always in the way.' He gazed at where she was pointing and noticed the egg among the straw.

She picked it up delicately. 'It's still warm.' She held it next to his cheek and blushed. Her huge eyes glistened and she looked like a child in her excitement on finding the egg. There was a tiny streak of blood on the white shell. She put a finger to her mouth, licked it and then rubbed away the mark. The sight of her darting tongue took his breath away.

'I'd best be goin' back,' she said quickly. 'I've a lot to do.'

'Yes, of course,' he replied. 'Please – I'm stopping you from getting on.' As they walked back out into the bright sunlight, he found himself asking if he could walk her to church on Sunday.

'If thoo wishes,' she smiled, lowering her eyes, and then picked up her skirt and rushed back to the house.

Matthew walked home like a new man. Now full of hope for the future, he relished the cold sea air and lifted his face to the pale blue sky. Perhaps God did move in mysterious ways after all and had mapped out his life. At that moment, the sun's rays shot out from behind a cloud and a patch of sea was caught in the light. Humbled by this vision, he said a prayer for the first time since his wife's death.

Each Sunday Matthew walked Ellen to church. They could never sit together; she had to find room on the bench at the back with the other hired servants while he sat in the Smiths' pew towards the front. He thought that, after a few months of this Sunday walking lark, he might be able to see her indoors at Uphall – on her own if he could.

Matthew wasn't the only one smitten with Ellen. Jane Jordan, fourteen years old, thought Ellen was everything a woman could be. She wanted her own hair to look as shiny and healthy, and thought her own body would never fill out in the right places. Ellen was as perfect as she herself was lacking. Even Jane's nose was boring – a small snub of a thing with no character at all.

Jane's affection for Ellen soon became a passion. She was the most intimate with Ellen, shared her bed and listened to her secrets. All day Jane looked forward to the time when they'd light the candle stump and get ready for bed. It was her special time alone with Ellen. There was her sister, Dorothy, and all the other female servants in the same chamber but, once the candles were out, she could lie next to Ellen in the dark, feel her warm body against hers and they could whisper to each other. She didn't mind if Matthew was courting her. Courting could take a long time, and Ellen had already hinted that she hoped to stay and work at Uphall for many years.

Jane knew that Ellen was a flirt. She'd seen her notice Matthew the first time he'd come in the yard, and seen her snatch the food and rush outside to feed the geese. She didn't mind. She'd never been so happy. She loved showing Ellen around the house and the outbuildings, introducing her to people in the village and taking her on Sunday walks, arm in arm, on the cliff top. She told her all about the trouble between Robert Storey and his wife, about their lack of children, about the scandal of Susan Jordan, and the drunken abuses at the Huskisson house. On being questioned, she also informed Ellen of the likes and dislikes of Matthew Smith.

Ellen was quite aware of Jane's feelings for her and was mindful to keep Jane on her side. She was also well aware that Uphall was one of those places where, if you once got on the wrong side of the master's family, you'd never be happy and would have to leave. Her brother had settled very well to his work there and, as she now had her eyes set on Matthew Smith, Jane was an essential ally – for the time being.

As part of her plan to keep Jane sweet on her, Ellen began to give Jane a goodnight kiss. She kissed Jane lightly on the cheek before getting into bed. This was quite in keeping with their friendship and Jane did not think it unusual. However, one night, after they'd talked for a while in bed in the dark, there came a moment when the whispering stopped and they prepared to sleep. It was then that Ellen put an arm around Jane, pulled her towards her and kissed her on the mouth. Ellen knew what she was doing, but did not anticipate the excitement she would arouse in her young bed mate. Jane was breathless. She couldn't believe her luck.

Once Jane knew she could expect the same kiss each night, she trembled as they whispered in bed, waiting for that soft arm to pull her head towards Ellen's lips. Jane thought about it all day and feasted her eyes on Ellen whenever in her company. She could spend a lifetime gazing at Ellen's features – five years on each eye, five on her nose, ten on her lips, five on each breast, a couple of years on her ears, her toes, her ankles, her knees, not to mention her wonderful body. She'd never tire of her, ever, and often whispered this to Ellen in the dark.

When alone in her work, Jane daydreamed about Ellen, recalling their intimate private conversations and the softness of Ellen's lips. The servants at Uphall would see Jane go off into one of her trances, and they'd nudge each other and grin. Jane was oblivious to it all. It was the best winter of her life, the short days and long dark nights providing the perfect conditions for a growing passion. It was only her mother who looked grim and tight-lipped about her behaviour, biding her time.

Chapter 3

1709-10

In the middle of December, the Jordan family had a christening to celebrate. William, the eldest son, had moved back to Uphall as soon as the baby was born. Though he regretted this time away from his wife Mary and the children, he knew she needed the month with her women helpers to recuperate from the birth. There were compensations at Uphall. Almost straight away, he noticed the new servant, Ellen. He watched her eat her breakfast. She wasn't like the others. While there was the clatter of spoons and dishes all around and everyone else rushed their food, Ellen was like the still eye of a storm. She spooned in her porridge as if each mouthful was to be savoured, and held it for a while before swallowing. There was a moment when William's younger brothers and the hired hands looked up from their porridge; on seeing Ellen eat her food with such calm, they all stopped, spoons in mid-air. Then, without a word being said, they began to slow down in their eating. William saw her throat move as she swallowed. No wonder his friend, Matthew, was so smitten.

On the morning of the christening, William had other concerns than Ellen Dawson. He fretted about the weather and his mother didn't help.

'Middle o' December's not best time for a bairn to be taken outside,' she warned. He already knew that. Just lately his mother had been as cold as winter. He guessed it was something to do with his sisters and the new hands, but he was not interested enough to find out. He scraped the ice from the kitchen window and peered out. Reighton was white over with snow. It certainly was not a day for a christening.

When William and his family left for church, there was no warmth in the sun. The village lay silent in a frozen wasteland and, in the churchyard, only the odd tall spike of grass poked through. William left his family at the church gate and carried on walking down the hill to his home on St Helen's Lane. His heart beat faster as he rapped on the door. The servant girl, Kate, was expecting him and let him in, shutting the door quickly behind so as not to let any heat escape.

'Mary's i' parlour,' she said. 'Don't go puttin' tha cold 'ands on 'er or the bairn. We've already got tha daughter wrapped up warm wi' extra shawls so she should be all right. An' tha mother sent the christenin' sheet yesterday.'

He entered the parlour where his wife was sitting up in bed, the baby beside her and the toddler, Francis, kneeling on the floor. William ruffled his hair.

'Now then, Francis, what do you think to your sister?' The boy didn't answer but stood up and tried to see the baby's face. 'You'll see her better after the christening. It's bitterly cold outside. I hope Kate's got your boots and coat warming by the fire.'

'Kate's been such a help,' Mary said and smiled at her servant. Then she looked at William, her eyes glistening with tears. 'I hope your month away won't seem too long.' He swallowed hard, wishing he could take his wife in his arms and hold her tight.

'Here,' she said, 'take your daughter.' A large bundle of swaddling and fleece was passed over. He could only see the tiniest part of his daughter's face – her nose and her neatly defined dark eyebrows. She was perfect.

'Little Mary,' he whispered. 'You're going to be named after your mother.'

After the usual Sunday service, it was time for the christening. William and the godparents left their box pews and followed the vicar to the font that stood near the entrance. A cold draught blew under the door as William took the sleeping baby from Kate's arms. They looked at the vicar and nodded that they were ready. George Gurwood began, his breath steaming in the icy air.

'Almighty and everlasting God, which of thy great mercy didst save Noah and his family in the ark from perishing by water, and also didst safely lead the children of Israel, thy people, through the Red Sea, figuring thereby thy holy baptism: and by the baptism of thy well-beloved son Jesus Christ, didst sanctify the flood Jordan, and all other waters, to the mystical washing away of sin.'

William smiled and winked at Matthew; he never tired of hearing his family name, Jordan, spoken in the services. Normally Matthew shrugged as if he didn't care. Today he returned the smile and looked back into the church where Ellen had her head turned towards him. The other godparents, Matthew's sister, Elizabeth, and William's sister, Dorothy, noticed what was going on. Dorothy narrowed her eyes and glanced at Elizabeth with a knowing look.

Elizabeth gave nothing away; she wanted her brother to be happy. To avoid Dorothy's stare, she cast her eyes down to the font. The lone candle flickering in the draught cast strange shadows onto the stone carvings. The side facing her was full of circles, lines and swirls of unknown meaning. All around the top, a stone rope was carved. Once more, she didn't know what it signified. Looking up again, she faced the peeling whitewash on the damp walls. The church was bare. It was too early for the Christmas greenery. She shivered and contemplated the baby in her woollen christening sheet. If the baby died within the month, the sheet would become her shroud. As the vicar continued to read aloud from his book and baptise the child, she prayed that the young Mary would live and that Matthew would find a new wife. Above all, she prayed that she and her husband, Robert Storey, might have a child of their own.

As everyone left the church and passed on their good wishes to William, Kate leant over and whispered, 'Let's 'ope she's as easy to look after as 'er brother, Francis.'

Young Mary wasn't easy. She was just the opposite. She screamed when Mary pulled her off the nipple and didn't stop until her mouth fastened onto the other breast. While Francis had slept well after feeding, this little girl always wanted more to drink. William blamed his wife's milk, thinking she wasn't providing enough, and the way that the baby arched her back and struggled against the swaddling bands made Sarah Ezard diagnose convulsions.

'All that frantic kickin' 'll distort tha bairn's bones. I'll fetch some medicine for 'er. It's made from cow dung an' preserved roses.'

When this didn't help, Sarah advised Mary to swaddle the girl tightly to a board to stop her writhing so much. Later, she suggested a remedy in case colic was the problem.

'I've kept a piece o' tha navel string,' she told Mary. 'I'll make it into a ring. Tha must wear it o' tha finger.'

None of Sarah's methods worked for long and the New Year was heralded in by sleepless nights. When Mary was too tired, William took over the nursing of the baby. During those long winter evenings, he grew ever more attached to his small daughter. He paced up and down the room in the dark, her hot damp face against his neck. In time, she'd relax and grow limp in his arms and he could lay her down once more in the old crib.

They hoped for an improvement in the spring but, as the girl grew older, she asserted herself more. It wasn't long before she could pull herself up in the crib, grab hold of the ornamental knobs on each side and rock it till it nearly tipped over. All the while she'd scream for attention like an animal trapped in a cage. The lives of everyone nearby were disrupted by the various choking cries coming from William's house. It sounded as if the baby was being murdered. No one could believe that one little girl could make so much of a racket.

Chapter 4

1710

Mary's sister, Elizabeth, had her own troubles. The dark winter months had strained her relationship with Robert as he'd refused, whenever alone with his wife, to talk about his feelings. Instead, he'd chosen to read the Bible. Elizabeth gave up the battle. Having failed in her attempts to be agreeable with him and continue the one-sided 'conversations', she began to spend more time over at William and Mary's house.

Young Mary always seemed hungry and, as the year progressed, both Elizabeth and Mary reasoned that she might need something more solid than milk. As soon as the harvest was over, Mary attempted to wean her daughter earlier than was expected. When her mother-in-law heard of her weaning the baby in October, she marched straight round to say what she thought.

'Thoo young uns don't know owt these days. Why's thoo wantin' to wean yon bairn now?' Mary explained patiently enough the reason for it, but Dorothy answered back with a smug look on her face. 'Well! Thoo'll soon know why. Be it on thy 'ead lass. It's not so far wrong what they say – wean a bairn now an' tha'll end up wi' a restless child.' Mary was shaken. 'Aye,' continued Dorothy, 'thoo'll soon find out.'

The next day, Mary discussed it with her sister.

'What rot,' said Elizabeth. 'Don't pay any attention to such old wives' tales. Besides, young Mary's restless enough already. I think she'll calm down as soon as she's fed more – don't you think?' Mary hoped so. When the baby cried less during the day she believed her sister was right.

'You're the one that should have had children, not me,' she said one day.

'Please don't start that again. It's obviously not meant to be.'

'How is Robert?'

'The same – no need to ask.'

'It can't go on. Tell him. Tell him you've had enough of his silences and his moods.'

'He can't help it. I know he's unhappy.'

Mary couldn't understand how long-suffering her sister could be. 'If it was me he was ignoring I'd do something.' Elizabeth sighed as Mary went on. 'Have you tried talking to George Gurwood about him?' Elizabeth's jaw dropped. 'Robert might listen to the vicar.'

'But that's the problem,' said Elizabeth, 'I think Robert's having trouble with his faith.' When Mary raised her eyebrows in surprise her sister explained. 'You see he reads the Bible all the time, but it gives him no comfort. He sits for hours frowning over it and then gazes into the fire. He looks so lost at times but, if I interrupt his thoughts, he glares at me as if I've hit him.' Elizabeth was close to tears so Mary apologised for pushing her too far.

'No,' Elizabeth said as she blew her nose, 'it's not your fault. Maybe you're right. Maybe I should approach the vicar. Oh, I don't know. It's so hard to know what to do.'

'Don't make any decisions just now,' suggested Mary, 'not when you're upset.'

'Alright, but can I spend more time here if things get worse?'

'Please do. Kate used to be such a good servant. Now, just lately, she's being rather difficult. I could do with more help and some better company.'

Kate overheard all their conversation as she played with Francis in the kitchen.

'Difficult?' she muttered to young Francis. 'Difficult – when I'm one 'as to look after animals as well as look after thoo, 'elp with all kitchen work, an' then be kept awake by tha baby sister every night?' She paused and thought. 'It's true I 'ave complained to tha mother more than usual. But if that's bein' difficult,' she chuntered away to Francis, 'then Mary 'as a lot to learn.'

The boy concentrated on building his tower of wooden blocks. She began to help him again and soon they were taking turns happily when Mary marched in and stopped their game.

'It's time he had his sleep. Put him to bed Kate, and then see to dinner.'

Kate obeyed but gave Mary a cold stare as she left the room. She remembered that, years ago, before Francis was born, when Mary had lost two babies, they'd got on really well together. Mary had needed her then. They'd spent hours together in the milkhouse and become good friends. Since Francis had been born, it was Elizabeth who was always around to help make cheese and butter while she, the servant, was banished to the kitchen. Now, after the birth of a daughter, Elizabeth would call round even more. It was time to think of moving on. She almost wished the baby girl *would* continue to be a handful – then they'd be sorry they'd treated her so shabbily. More for the sake of Francis, she decided to stay on at least until next Easter.

Elizabeth did go to see George Gurwood. He was shocked to hear of Robert's possible loss of faith but didn't know how to help him without betraying Elizabeth's confidence.

'He must not know I've told anyone,' she kept repeating.

The vicar understood and decided to visit Robert and coax him into better behaviour at home with his wife. After all, Robert was his brother-in-law. As George Gurwood set off down the hill towards Robert's house, he was deep in thought and almost bumped into old Ben coming the other way.

'Now then, vicar,' Ben said as he removed his pipe from the gap between his teeth. 'Is owt wrong?'

George looked up, surprised to see Ben standing in front of him. 'No, not really.' Then, on second thoughts, he added, 'You've known Robert longer than me, known him since he was a lad. Tell me, do you think he's changed of late?'

Ben scratched his grey, stubbly chin. 'Well now,' he replied and sighed at the enormity of the question. 'Where do I start wi' young Robert? He's always been diff'rent.'

'I'm aware of that,' said the vicar, 'but this last year, do you think he's changed?'

'I think 'e stays inside over much if that's any 'elp. 'E needs to be out more working on tha glebe lands. That's 'is job, not stoppin' at 'ome doin' nowt but readin'. Over much thinkin' I reckon's 'is problem.'

'You think there is a problem then?'

'I'm only sayin' what I feel i' me bones is right or wrong. I'm not one for book learnin'. I've always said – an ounce o' wit is worth a pound o' learnin'.' Warming to his theme, he cleared his throat and spat on the ground. 'If tha stops indoors an' never gets any proper outdoor work done, then anyone's goin' to get low i' spirits. Man weren't meant to be cooped up bent over books an' thinkin' all time. Robert should be outside wi' others, out i' God's fresh air. 'E needs to feel sun an' wind on 'is face an' a good, 'onest ache in 'is back when day is done.'

'Well, if that's his only problem, it could be sorted out. I was afraid …' George stopped before admitting that Robert may have lost his faith.

'Afraid what?' Ben asked, curious to know any secrets.

'No, it's nothing,' the vicar mumbled. Then, thinking that Ben could be trusted, he added, 'It's just that I was afraid, probably unnecessarily, of course, that Robert …' He took a deep breath. 'Robert may not be as steady in his faith as he was.'

Ben stepped back in horror. 'Robert? Our Robert? Never!' The vicar was relieved by Ben's reaction. 'Steady?' continued Ben. 'Steady? 'E 's as steady as yon 'ills. Never doubt Robert o' that score.' Ben shook his head as if to rid his ears of some evil, crawling thing that might have wormed its way into his head.

'Ben, I'm sorry I mentioned it.'

'Nay, vicar, that's tha job. I don't blame thee for thinkin' it. Robert's a strange one that's for sure. Who really knows what goes on in 'is 'ead. I still reckon all 'e needs is to be out workin'.'

George Gurwood thanked Ben for his help and continued on his way. Robert answered the door and invited the vicar to sit in the parlour. They were alone as Elizabeth was at Mary's house helping with the children. George noticed there was a gaunt look to Robert's face. No doubt he'd been fasting again. The Bible lay open on the table.

'It's natural to look for solace in the good book,' he said, 'but there comes a time when we need to take more note of things around us, take more note perhaps of those closest to us.'

'We need to consider our souls,' growled Robert. 'Our lives here on Earth, as you well know, are so insignificant – nothing but a speck.' He snapped his fingers to demonstrate his point. 'We can't be wasting our lives on petty worries, women's affairs and babies, if that's what you mean. You want me to do that? You want me to risk my soul and diminish my love for God by spending my time on lesser matters?'

George was chastened, but Robert's way was not for him. His loving wife and large family had brought him closer to God rather than enticed him away. He didn't know what to say. His brother-in-law should perhaps have become a man of the cloth rather than him. He tried a different approach.

'I was speaking to Ben just now. I bumped into him on the way. He thinks it's fresh air and outdoor labour that's good for us, makes us happy and healthy. You know Ben's never been overly fond himself of being indoors.'

Robert smiled but was not giving in. 'Ben can do what Ben thinks best. I'll do what I think. Listen, George, all my life I've fought the temptations of the flesh. Being married changes nothing. I don't mean to give up the battle now, and I'm surprised at you even thinking I might. What would be the point of me striding round the hills and fields – to have deep and meaningful talks with the hired lads? No – leave me alone with my books and the Bible. They're my true friends and guides. I need no one and nothing else.'

George now realised that, in Robert's mind, his love for Elizabeth had been his one lapse and it had led to distress for both parties. The marriage, as George knew from Elizabeth, had become increasingly platonic. He could understand some of what Robert was suffering. As a young man, he himself had been torn between the flesh and the spirit, and it had been his marriage that had helped him reconcile the two sides of his nature. George had long since ceased to worry that his physical needs and pleasures were an obstacle to his love of God. Now he could empathise better with his flock and be of greater assistance. Robert though was a different challenge. When he tried to explain the benefits of married life to his brother-in-law, Robert squirmed on his chair. George hoped he'd not made things worse. The look of disgust on Robert's face put a stop to further details.

Robert pointed to the open Bible at his side. 'You know what the Bible says. Jesus didn't marry, and he told his disciples to leave their homes and follow him. I'm thinking more and more that it's the only way to be.'

'But you're a married man now, Robert. You have a duty to your wife. You can't let Elizabeth suffer for your beliefs. Just think! What has she done to deserve a hermit and a scholar for a husband?' As Robert sighed and looked away, George wondered if he'd ever fathom him out.

After a long pause, Robert broke the silence. 'Do *you* think I spend too much time indoors reading?'

George nodded slowly. 'Yes, I do think, in the circumstances, it would be good for you to get out and be with other people.'

'Then I will. Does that satisfy you?' In a flash, he closed the Bible. It was like a door being slammed. George was startled, as much by this gesture as by Robert's submission.

'It's not a failure, Robert, to show you care for people. We're all different. We all find God in our own way. Try not to judge others as harshly as you do yourself. Get out in the sunshine. Don't just supervise the men on my glebe land, work with them. Tire your body in healthy ways. And visit us. Susanna would love to see you more.' Robert agreed to do his best.

When George got up to leave, he put an arm around Robert and said he'd pray for him. As soon as George left the house, Robert leant wearily against the door, relieved that he'd got off so lightly.

Over the next few months, Robert did go out more. He worked in the fields and was often seen walking alone along the sands when the tide was out, or on the cliff top, walking towards Filey and back. The mere act of walking with a certain rhythm cheered him. What he hadn't expected to see was two young women lying in the grass kissing and cuddling. One of them he knew to be Jane Jordan.

Chapter 5

1711

At Uphall, in the new year, Jane Jordan's mother kept a close eye on her daughter and Ellen. She didn't like what she saw.

'They're shameless,' she whispered in bed one night to her husband. She spooned her body round his back and explained. 'It's bad enough them 'oldin' 'ands i' front of everyone but Jane's forever fondlin' Ellen's fingers.' She'd noticed the girls with their hands under the kitchen table, clasping and then unlocking their hands just to re-entwine them in more intimate ways. 'The sight makes me sick.'

Her husband sighed and rolled onto his back. He thought nothing of it – surmised it was just women's fond ways.

'But it's not natural,' she argued.

'Leave lasses alone,' he said. 'There's nowt wrong with a bit o' fondlin'.' He, like all the other men at Uphall, found Ellen very becoming and enjoyed her presence. His home was the happiest it had been since his daughter, Anna, had died.

'Who's i' charge o' lasses?' Dorothy demanded. 'Thee or me?'

'Thoo,' he sighed, knowing she wouldn't give up. She didn't interfere with his ploughing and fencing and he, as a rule, didn't question her decisions around the house. Yet he felt sorry for the girls.

'Be easy on 'em, Dorothy. They're still young. Jane's just fifteen. They don't mean owt by a bit o' kissin' an' walkin' round arm in arm together.'

Dorothy sniffed and turned away from him. She determined to have the last word and muttered, 'It's only a matter o' time before I'm proved right. Thoo'll see.'

Two days later, she caught them kissing behind the milkhouse door – not just a peck on the cheek, but a prolonged kiss on the mouth. She coughed to show her presence and the two girls leapt apart as if stung. She gave them her stoniest glare and stormed out. They were left red-faced, wondering if there'd be consequences.

Many times Dorothy thought of changing the girls' sleeping arrangements, but each time she came to the same conclusion. There was just the one chamber for all the maids and her two daughters to share, and a limited number of beds. Only her daughter, Dorothy, had a bed to herself. The obvious answer was to put both her daughters in one bed but she knew they'd argue and fight. More to the point, if she did separate Jane and Ellen, it would arouse suspicion. There'd be gossip and Ellen, she knew, could make trouble. No, there was no easy solution. She could only nag at Jane and hope the fascination with Ellen would burn itself out.

Despite her mother's chastisements, nothing could stem Jane's passion. She found places to be alone with Ellen, and there was always the night time to make up for any lost opportunities. As the days of spring lengthened, the girls were busier, and the chances of catching a few moments of intimacy grew scarce. Ellen was given extra duties in the milkhouse while Jane was confined to the kitchen. When the two girls did fall into bed at night, they, like everyone else, were worn out and knew that they'd be up at dawn for another arduous day.

Jane became tense and watchful, but Ellen didn't seem to mind or even be aware that she was seeing less of her. When Ellen did have free time on a Sunday, instead of going for a walk with Jane as before, she now met Matthew Smith and walked out with him. It was flattering to be so admired by a wealthy, eligible yeoman, especially one that looked healthy and strong and had no children. When Jane questioned her motives, Ellen was quite clear.

'I like it 'ere i' Reighton. I could do a lot worse than marry 'im.'

The following Sunday, Matthew Smith found Ellen more charming than ever. The spring weather had put colour in her cheeks and her lips were as red as rosehips. Together they gathered violets and then ran down the hill behind the church, zigzagging in and out of the clumps of gorse. When they both tripped over a root, they rolled down the hill one on top of the other like a barrel. On finally coming to a halt, Matthew lay on his back and laughed. He gazed at the blue sky, his head still spinning, and then stared at the giggling heap of beauty at his side. He felt years younger and was convinced that spring had arrived early that year. The hawthorn buds were a brighter green, the lambs were bigger and healthier, and the new grass was thick and lush. He was more than content with the progress of his courting; now whenever he walked out with Ellen, they would hold hands.

For Ellen, the Sunday walks with Matthew were a welcome relief from her chores and also from Jane, who was now always demanding her time and company. She was beginning to tire of Jane's cloying persistence and couldn't understand why their sleeping together was not enough. The more she avoided her, the more Jane nagged for attention.

For Jane, the Sundays were turning into a dark muddle of jealous imaginings. She could hardly follow the courting couple, but she tracked them in her mind, which was worse. While Ellen and Matthew might only be indulging in one, slightly intimate and innocent exchange, Jane would be conjuring up a nightmarish sequence of events where the couple ended up in a passionate embrace. Sundays became almost unbearable. Sometimes she paced up and down the hayloft, or walked in the opposite direction to Ellen and Matthew – anywhere so long as she didn't have to sit still. On Sunday evenings, she'd be so full of pent-up jealousy that she'd ignore Ellen and sulk. As soon as they were in bed, she'd start questioning her, whispering viciously in the dark. She'd demand to know where Ellen and Matthew had been, what they'd spoken about and what they'd done. Though Ellen would patiently tell her, Jane could never bring herself to believe it. She was out of control, as if possessed. She heard herself say the most heartless things.

'I reckon your mother didn't die. I think you killed her. You just wanted to get away. You only care about yourself and your precious brother.' Light-headed, her heart thumping wildly, she'd speak out of breath, her mouth dry.

'And I don't know why you think Matthew will marry *you*. He won't. He's just having a bit of fun. Do you think for a moment he'll stoop to have a serving girl like you for a wife? Never!'

Ellen knew it was jealousy on Jane's part; it didn't affect her own life too much but it was certainly poisoning Jane's.

Things came to a head late one Sunday afternoon as Matthew gave Ellen a goodbye kiss, not on the cheek or hand as usual, but on the lips. Jane was just returning from a solitary, anxious walk and saw them together. All her worst fears were realised. She couldn't face the sight of someone else kissing Ellen. And Ellen was enjoying it. They looked to be in love. How could she bear that? As soon as Matthew had left and was out of sight, Jane ran up to Ellen who was still gazing fondly into the distance. She grabbed her shoulder and spun her round.

'What in God's name do you think you're doing?' she cried through gritted teeth. Ellen looked surprised. Jane was short of breath but managed to spit out, 'You and him. How could you, Ellen?' When Ellen shrugged casually as if she didn't care, this provoked Jane to demand an answer to the most important question.

'You love me still? You still love me, eh? Ellen? Ellen? Tell me.'

Ellen looked at her with no feeling in her eyes. 'I don't know. I don't know anymore.' And she turned and went indoors, leaving Jane standing in the yard as if turned to stone. Jane looked about the yard and at her Uphall home. The walls seemed to be melting like wax – nothing was substantial anymore. The yard she stood on began to slant and quiver and then turn to sand. Somehow, she pulled herself together, determined to correct the horror that Ellen had so suddenly introduced. Ellen must love her, or it was the end of everything she'd ever held to be good and true. Her one thought now was to make sure that Ellen loved her again – she could not carry on living otherwise. With this in mind, she held herself in check until bedtime.

That night, in the darkness, Jane forced herself on Ellen, believing that she would soon be won over. At first, Ellen lay unresponsive beneath her but did eventually warm a little to Jane's kisses. Jane realised how her life hung by a thread. She had a vision of a lone, bright star in a black sky dangling on a long golden chain – but such a thin, delicate and beautiful chain. She clung onto that image, hoping to repair the day's damage, yet she knew in her heart that Ellen's feelings for her had changed for good.

For the next few weeks, Jane did not pester Ellen anymore, thinking that a little freedom might win her back. As a result, Ellen barely noticed Jane in the daytime and returned the bedtime kisses with indifference. Jane soon fell ill with the worry of it all. She hardly ate at mealtimes and went for long walks alone whenever she could. Often she looked as if she'd been crying, but her mother did not intervene, letting things take their course.

After weeks of being a nervous wreck, an instinctive desire for a better life began to assert itself. Jane decided to treat herself as an invalid in need of care and attention. She planned to take small, gradual steps to recovery. First, she ate larger portions of food and chewed them well so as to make her meals last, and then she allowed herself a tiny treat from the larder as a reward for getting through yet another day.

One morning, Jane was up at dawn as usual and went to fetch water from the cistern. As she heaved the wooden bucket onto the ledge, she was aware of her surroundings in a totally new way. The sun lit up part of the yard and a cobweb, perfect in construction, was loaded with droplets of dew and trembled in the breeze. A snail had left a silver trail across the ground, and the nearby trees were full of tight, green buds. She broke down in tears, so glad to be alive that it hurt. There was more to life than Ellen.

As Jane began to value life again and be more like her old self, Ellen suddenly rekindled the passion. Matthew Smith was often away on family business and Ellen was bored. Jane knew it was suicidal for her new-found health and yet jumped at the chance of enjoying Ellen's favours again. Once more she threw herself wholeheartedly into the romance and realised how deeply she was in love with Ellen.

Early one evening, Jane was tempted to buy herself more time alone with Ellen by helping her shut the chickens up for the night. She rushed around with her, trying to shoo all the hens into their huts, and let drop all the pop-holes. Then they sneaked off to the hayloft. In their hurry to be together, the girls did not bother to count the hens. While they were enjoying themselves, a number of chickens found they were locked out of their huts for the night.

In the morning, when Ellen went out to feed the poultry, she found a scene of carnage. A fox had been on a killing spree. Nine chickens lay headless or maimed in various parts of the yard and the nearby field. The chickens, she realised, must have run around all night trying desperately to find somewhere to hide. The fox had killed for pleasure, satisfying some bloodlust. Ellen was sickened. It was her fault and she'd have to report it to Jane's mother.

When Dorothy Jordan saw the extent of the damage she was speechless. Her mouth tightened into a thin line at the loss of the hens, and she took out her anger, not on Ellen, but on her daughter Jane, who, she said, ought to know better. She refused to say any more, barged past the two girls and marched around collecting up all the hens. Then she fetched a stool and a large basket and sat by the kitchen door. She grabbed one of the dead, limp chickens and proceeded to pluck it, muttering to herself and taking out her wrath on each fistful of feathers. The more she plucked and the more her back and fingers ached, the more determined she became to do something about Jane and Ellen. This cruel loss of the hens was the last straw. She didn't stop working until the basket was brimming with grey and brown feathers. There were nine skinny, white bodies by her side. Downy fluff stuck to her hands and, as she wiped away angry tears, bits of fluff stuck to her cheeks. Red in the face and exhausted, she strode into the kitchen.

'Jane!' she shouted. 'This isn't first time thoo an' Ellen 'ave scuttled off together. Don't think I 'aven't seen. Thoo can't fool me, I'm tha mother. Never mind what tha father says, I've 'ad enough.'

Jane knew better than to attempt to explain or interrupt.

'Well, summat's goin' to be done. This can't go on. I've 'ad it up to 'ere today.' She pointed to the top of her forehead and feathers floated off her fingernails. In other circumstances, it would have been funny, Jane thought, but she was very afraid of what her mother might decide. She might send Ellen away, or try to keep them apart, or alter the sleeping arrangements.

Her mother saw the frightened look on Jane's face but said no more. She didn't have a fully-worked out plan as yet and would need to talk it through with her husband. 'Just leave me alone,' she said. 'Leave me to think. I've enough to deal with without *thy* sad face all day an' night.'

That evening, Dorothy and her husband discussed the problem. He was adamant not to lose Ellen's brother, John. If Ellen was sent away, then John would go with her, and he wasn't going to lose one of the best ploughing lads he'd ever had. Keeping the girls apart was not going to work – there'd always be opportunities for them to see each other even if they slept in different rooms.

A solution presented itself a few days later when their son, William, reported the chaos in his own home. Kate and Mary had fallen out again and Kate had finally decided to leave at Easter. Mary couldn't manage very well on her own with two young children; she needed a girl to help out with the chores. Dorothy Jordan saw her chance. The very next morning she informed Jane of her decision.

'Tha can move out at Easter an' go an' live wi' William an' Mary.' Jane went pale. She didn't know what to say.

'An' there's no point goin' to tha father. 'E's of same mind as me. Think thassen lucky. Work 'ard an' forget Ellen – she'll ruin thee for marriage, that she will.' She rubbed Jane's arm. 'We only want thee to settle down one day an' be 'appy.'

Jane couldn't speak or move. The thought of not sleeping anymore with Ellen gave her physical pain as if she'd been run over by a heavy cart. In a daze she staggered away from her mother and out into the yard. Ellen was there feeding the chickens – what was left of them. She told Ellen the news, as if relating some improbable event that was happening to someone else. Ellen held her close and kissed her forehead.

'Don't worry. We can still see each other.'

'When though?' asked Jane, beginning to see the enormity of the problem if she was living down St Helen's Lane and Ellen was at Uphall.

'We'll find a way.'

Jane was not convinced. Ellen didn't seem to be taking the news too badly at all, but then she had Matthew Smith. Jane had only Ellen.

Chapter 6

1711

Easter came and Mary's servant, Kate, paid her farewells. Although she'd not been happy in Mary's house for over a year, she was very attached to the three-year-old boy and knew he'd miss her. She'd spent more time with him than his own mother had. Alone for a moment in the kitchen with Francis, she picked him up for a last cuddle.

'I don't know what's to become of us,' she whispered into his hair. 'I'm not sure Jane is up to it. She's only fifteen. 'Ow can she 'andle tha baby sister as well as look after thee – an' do all 'ousework at same time?' She held him a bit longer before kissing the top of his head and putting him down. 'Never mind, Francis, you be a good boy.'

When Mary walked into the kitchen, Kate held out her hand. 'Goodbye then. I did enjoy makin' cheese wi' thee. I'm sorry to go.'

Mary shook her hand formally, but then gave Kate a kiss on the cheek. 'I hope you settle down soon and have a family of your own. You deserve to be happy.'

With that, Kate grabbed her bag of belongings. She left by the front door to make her way home to Hunmanby.

At the same time, William walked down the hill from Uphall carrying a small chest of Jane's clothes. It was a cold April morning and Jane trudged sullenly behind him, conscious that each step was taking her further away from her life with Ellen. She was exhausted and almost numb after a night of crying and clinging onto Ellen in desperation, trying to imprint on her memory every last touch and smell.

All William's attempts at conversation were ignored. As they approached the house, he hoped she wasn't going to be as moody as his wife had been of late. Women, he thought, were sometimes more trouble than they were worth.

Mary met them at the door, shocked to see Jane's drawn, white face and puffy red eyes.

'Oh Jane, you do look cold. Come on in and sit by the fire. I'll make you a hot drink.' As she warmed up the ale, she wondered how it would be to have William's sister as a servant. It would be strange giving her orders, and she didn't want her mother-in-law to descend on her and complain of mistreatment. Looking at the poor girl shivering by the fire, she wasn't sure if they'd ever get along. At least Jane was submissive for now.

For many weeks, Jane lacked energy and did as she was told with little interest. All her thoughts were concentrated on Ellen. Exiled from Uphall, she indulged in both yearning and despair. She'd have crawled gladly on her bare knees to Filey and back if it had meant she could be with Ellen again and have her just to herself. In her bed in the loft, she speculated whether she'd give her right arm, but thought this rather stupid as you wouldn't be able to enjoy your lover the same with only one arm. Certainly, she decided, she'd have given up a few fingers on her left hand.

At Uphall, in the absence of Jane, Ellen flirted freely with everyone, whether male or female. All were bombarded with her charm, and all succumbed in varying degrees. Even the two Dorothy Jordans began to appreciate the effect she had on life at the farm, though they'd never admit it.

Matthew Smith, while busy sowing the fields like everyone else, always found time to be at Uphall at sunset. He made a habit of sitting with Ellen and the flock of geese to watch the sun go down. Late one afternoon, he held her hand, and they listened to the blackbirds singing their last songs of the day. As the sky darkened, the birds, now hidden in the bushes, began making their chink-chink noise. In the distance, a dog barked and set off all the others for miles around, as if they each wanted to have the last bark. He smiled at the geese. They amused him.

They were always manoeuvring, muttering and grumbling to each other.

'I don't know how you tell them apart,' he said. 'They all look the same to me.'

'Nay, they're all diff'rent,' Ellen began to explain. 'They might all 'ave same white bodies but, if thoo looks close thoo'll see each goose 'as a diff'rent pattern o' grey feathers on its wing.'

He grinned. 'I can see one that's easy to recognise.' He gestured towards one with his thumb. 'That poor bird has a damaged wing. It sticks out at an angle and trails on the ground.'

'Now look at lead goose,' she said, pointing to the one standing apart from the others. 'It 'as an odd grey patch on its neck.'

As she spoke, it stretched its wings. It was on guard and held its neck high and stiff, its eyes on the lookout for danger.

'They're always at war,' she said. 'They'll chase any chickens an' cats. They look for trouble.' She nestled up to him so that he could put an arm around. 'Even when our cats an' kittens are dozin' all quiet o' back doorstep, an' enjoyin' last rays o' sun, them geese'll get together, as if o' command, an' open up their wings an' attack.'

'I suppose they fight for territory,' he murmured as the sun went behind the hill. They watched the geese wander off, in almost military formation, to their resting place, taking last pecks at the short grass by the walls as they went. This was the cue for a goodbye kiss before Ellen went in for supper. As they lingered, they both knew the courting was going very well. They also wished it would progress a bit faster.

A few weeks before Whitsuntide, Francis Jordan stood in the yard and called William over. He had an idea to put before him and guessed his son wouldn't approve.

'Tha knows there's always a day off work an' some fun goin' on at Whit?' he asked with a sly grin. 'Well, I'm thinkin' o' ploughin' up some of our cattle pasture o' Land Moor.'

William stepped back and shook his head.

'Now, wait,' said his father, 'I 'aven't finished. I've seen Matthew Smith about it and he's happy with it. Me idea is that *we* don't plough it – well, not like thoo thinks anyways. We'll 'ave a ploughin' match. We'll invite lads from Speeton an' they can compete.'

William was speechless for a moment. He soon found flaws in the plan. 'It's too far to bring their ploughs. They won't do it. And I bet you haven't spoken to Dickon – he'll hate to see any change to that pasture.'

'Well, let's see, shall we? Dickon'll 'ave to do as I say. 'E's only foreman, not master.' He rubbed his hands together. 'I reckon there'll be some keen competition. I'll send Dickon or maybe Tom round with all details, rules an' such, an' I'll get vicar to announce it i' both churches.'

William shook his head again, this time in admiration. 'You've really thought this out, haven't you? That land's had cattle or sheep on it all my life. It'll be as tough as anything. And now you even get others to help plough it!'

His father smiled. 'Me gran'father once 'ad crops o' that same land. Tha must 'ave wondered why it was all ridge an' furrow. I 'aven't decided yet whether to sow wheat or barley there come next year.'

William scratched his head and thought about it. 'I don't suppose we'll miss that pasture,' he concluded. 'It's Matthew with his herd of cattle who needs more grazing. We can concentrate more on corn.'

His father slapped him on the back. 'So, it's agreed then. We'll ave a ploughin' match, an' I'll get them Gurwood lasses to make up some fancy ribbons or summat for prizes.'

Francis Jordan was right about the local lads wanting to compete. For the next few weeks, they bragged about their chances. They were full of bravado, especially if they'd drunk any ale, and boasts of their ploughing skills often led to fights. The vicar questioned the sense of the competition, but Francis assured him all would be well.

At Uphall, on the day of the match, Dickon, the foreman, and Tom rose before dawn to make sure the oxen were looking their best and do a final check of the traces and ploughs. They knew that William and his brother, John, would compete and be joined by Ellen's brother. The other farmhands came down to breakfast in clean shirts and breeches, and pulled on boots which had been well-cleaned, brushed and oiled the night before. They discussed their chances and put wagers on the likely winners. The Jordan brothers had the best ploughs while John Dawson had to make do with an older, much heavier one that was still in use. They'd seen the brothers in action many times before, seen how William and John paused at the end of each furrow to look back on their work. Then, if the furrow wasn't perfect, they had enough pride to redo it. Hardly any lads backed John Dawson, not because he wasn't skilful, but because they didn't want him to get ideas above his station. They also reckoned he'd have more trouble with the older plough. He'd find it difficult to make the first split and control the depth of the furrow.

Dickon strolled in with Tom, late for breakfast, and caught the end of the lads' conversation.

'It's not just a matter o' ploughin' a straight furrow,' he told them. 'Its depth 'as to suit condition o' soil. I 'ope, for John Dawson's sake, judges take into account state o' plough an' oxen used, an' way oxen are led. An' don't forget, winner also 'as to finish ploughin' in a given time.' As he ate his bread and bacon, he thought John Dawson looked confident in his usual quiet way. He noticed William's sister, Dorothy, gazing at him again.

She was admiring his broad shoulders and sunburnt arms. His hair was thick, black and shiny, tight little curls falling over his forehead like a strong, young bull. And his eyes were such a remarkable blue.

Tom grinned at her across the table and winked. She blushed and turned her head away. Her father saved further embarrassment by giving out instructions for the morning. He stood up and clapped his hands before clearing his throat.

'Dickon an' Tom'll see to ploughs, carts an' sledges. Tom – 'as tha fed oxen yet? They need at least a couple of hours to digest their food before bein' set to work.'

'Why aye. Fed 'em a while back.' He didn't know why he was being asked. He wasn't daft.

'Good, that's all right then.' Francis Jordan wiped his greasy hands down his breeches and cleared his throat once more. 'We'll draw lots when we're up o' Land Moor. I reckon we 'ave some fierce competition from Speeton this year.'

There was a roar of disbelief from the lads and they started banging their bowls on the table. They were not hushed. Dorothy smiled at her father. Today the lads could show off and make as much noise as they liked. If they played their parts well, they'd be welcomed back like heroes.

Chapter 7

While the men and lads followed the oxen to the field, the women at Uphall carried the food to the barn for the feast. They hurried so they could join the rest of the village and watch the ploughing. The Uphall teams were the first to reach the field and waited there. They heard the jangle of chains that heralded the arrival of the Speeton lot. Matthew Smith turned up, eager to enter the contest and keen to impress Ellen. He wore his new grey breeches bought recently at Bridlington and a new red neckerchief. His white shirt was of superior quality. Everything about him, his upright stance and confident teasing of the other ploughmen, spoke of the rising fortunes of the Smiths. The other contestants sat around putting on their leather spatterdashes.

'Come on, Matthew,' shouted William. 'Get yours on.' He gave his friend a cheeky grin. 'You won't want to hurt your legs, and I'm sure you won't want those precious stockings getting mucky.'

Matthew ignored him. He did not put his leg protectors on until the last moment. Ellen had not arrived yet, and he wanted to be seen at his best.

William was amused to see his friend looking so clean and smart. 'Just look at you!' he said. 'Mind out – I thought I saw a speck of dirt land on your shirt. No – you're still spotless.' He pretended to slap him on the back but withdrew his hand in time. 'Don't worry! I wouldn't dare spoil your shirt with my calloused hands.'

Just then, Ellen and a crowd of other villagers arrived at the edge of the field.

'Come on, Matt,' shouted old Ben. 'Get tha gamashers on. Thoo looks as if thoo's dressed for a weddin', not a ploughin'.'

And so began a day of teasing.

The weather stayed fine for the match – sunny, with just the occasional, pure white cloud drifting high in a brilliant blue sky. Being so early in the day, the field was still damp enough for the sods to turn over cleanly, and there was a fresh breeze off the sea to make the day pleasant for working.

Mary stood watching with her young son, Francis; he was bewildered by all the noise and movement around him. He clung onto his mother's gown, shy in the company of so many people and terrified by the oxen. He stepped forward to watch the proceedings only when his Aunt Elizabeth joined them. Mary nudged her sister and winked.

'Matthew's rather grand today, what do *you* reckon?'

Elizabeth assessed her brother. 'Yes,' she agreed. 'He looks wonderful. I'm glad. He deserves to win this match – even if it's just as best turned-out ploughman.'

'I don't think they give prizes for that,' Mary replied with a smile.

'Pity though,' said Elizabeth. 'He's so handsome today. Look at Ellen gawping at him.'

'But do you think she's good enough for him?' Mary asked, hoping Elizabeth would collude with her and gossip about Ellen. Elizabeth's response surprised her.

'I think she's perfect for him. Just look at the way she stands and watches his every move. They're in love. Since Margaret died, all he's done is work, work, work. Now he's met Ellen, he's more like his old self.'

'You mean the annoying brother I remember? The brother who made my life a misery with his jokes and teasing?'

'Yes, but look at him now. How can you not be happy to see him like this? Believe me, Mary, we're only in our prime once. Let Matt take his chance of happiness – and God bless him.'

Mary thought she saw a tear in her sister's eye. Instantly, she felt guilty and mean-spirited; Elizabeth often made her feel less worthy. How could Elizabeth be so pleasant all the time? She had to live with Robert Storey, still had no children, and yet she could be so generous about others.

Ashamed, Mary tried to shake off her animosity towards Ellen. She wondered what it was about the girl that she disliked so much.

Jane Jordan was absent from the onlookers. She'd been made to stay in the house with young Mary. 'Jane, you look after the girl,' Mary had instructed. 'She's always wanting to walk everywhere now and she'll be nothing but trouble up at the field.' Jane was glad of the excuse not to attend. She wouldn't have to face Ellen in a field full of watchful villagers.

While Jane scrubbed the kitchen table with more rigour than usual, Ellen appreciated the sunshine and the easy atmosphere of the village enjoying a break in routine. She realised that Jane was not at the ploughing match and felt relieved. There would be no embarrassing scenes.

George Gurwood arrived with his wife and all eight of his daughters, followed by the rest of the spectators. He found the younger Jordan boys, aged between eight and thirteen, mesmerised by the scene. Over a hundred people had turned out to watch and were wearing their brightest neckerchiefs and best hats. All agreed the ploughing match had been a great idea. George wanted to check the rules, but Francis Jordan was taking the chance to discuss farming with folk from Speeton. He was arguing about the relative merits of oxen and horses. George waited beside him. He knew some folk prided themselves on their horses and believed they were the animals of the future. Robert Read, an up-and-coming young farmer from Speeton, was such a man. He stood in front of Francis with his feet planted wide apart and argued that a horse was faster than an ox and more versatile.

'Also,' Robert said, 'a horse is cheaper to buy – its meat is of little or no value. And a horse has more stamina than an ox. It can work for at least a couple more hours every day.'

Francis pointed out that it was fine if the land you worked had light soils, but in some parts of the Reighton fields, the horses could get bogged down. Dickon overheard the conversation and butted in.

'Why aye,' he added, 'an' their 'ooves get soft in all our cold an' wet weather. Before long they'd be as lame as lame.'

'Aye,' added Francis, 'an' we all know 'ow much grain an 'orse needs. Why, I reckon an' 'orse is four times price o' feedin' an ox. Hay an' grass'll do for an ox.'

Tom was eager to join in too. 'Thoo can't beat an ox o' clarty soil after teemin' rain.'

'Aye, lad, thoo's right,' said Dickon, proud of the lad. 'An ox is far better when land is tough.'

'They pull nice an' steady like,' continued Francis, 'not wi' jerks like 'orses. Gi' me an ox any day.'

'Slow but sure, eh?' said Dickon. 'That's always been our way at Up'all.'

'And yet,' argued Robert Read, 'an ox is not so good on a steep slope. I've found the plough slips a bit at their slower speeds.'

Francis eyed the well-spoken man with suspicion. 'Aye,' he retaliated, 'but goin' up a steep road an' pullin' a load – they're like sheet anchors, is oxen. They'll not slide back'ards. An ox'll stand 'is ground when an 'orse'll skitter about an' slip.'

'There's something in what you say,' admitted Robert Read.

'Thoo's still young yet,' said Francis. 'Thoo 'as a lot to learn. Don't forget – when 'is workin' days is over, an 'orse is worth next to nowt whereas, come Martinmas, tha can 'ave good meat on tha table with an ox.' Robert Read had to agree.

They turned to see that all the plots had now been marked out in the field. It was time for Francis to pass the bag of straws round the competitors and, once this was done, the ploughs were moved onto the respective plots drawn. A lad from each team ran out to fix markers for their ploughmen so they had points to aim at. Suddenly, Ellen dashed forward waving a handful of pink and green ribbons at her brother.

'John, wait!' she cried out. 'Keep 'old of oxen while I fix on these ribbons.' She made sure that Matthew was looking before she leant over and tied the ribbons onto the horns.

John Dawson was hardly aware of the honour. He was focussed on the task of making the first split with his plough, the crucial beginning of the first furrow. He knew how much depended on the start and the first few yards.

The oxen stood harnessed and ready, and the ploughmen lined up to begin. Last instructions were shouted to the goaders, and the ploughmen kept their eyes on George Gurwood who'd give the signal to start. The vicar checked with Francis Jordan that everyone was ready. The crowd then went quiet as Francis reiterated the basic rules.

'Only three sightin' poles to be used. Nobody is to touch ploughs except ploughman. No tamperin' wi' clods or furrow with 'ands or any other tool. Furrows must be left clean as they leave mouldboard. Furrows to be at least four inches deep – usual width apart.'

He gave a nod to the vicar who raised his arm, a white neckerchief dangling between his finger and thumb. When he dropped his arm, a great cheer from the crowd mixed with the shouts of the ploughmen and the goaders as they urged the oxen through those difficult first steps.

John Dawson had a good understanding with his goader, a robust lad who led the oxen well. He trusted him to keep the beasts moving with a steady action. His plough, heavier than the rest, lurched forwards and bit deeply. Then it jerked to a halt and rose a little before he could control it again. William's sister, Dorothy, grew nervous on his behalf. Soon though, as the oxen got back into their stride, John managed to keep the furrow straight and the depth even.

After those first few yards, all the goaders stopped the oxen. Each ploughman turned to inspect their furrow. They were to be judged partly on this first 'striking out'. Two yeomen from each village stepped forward to inspect the work. They measured the depths carefully with marked sticks. George Gurwood recorded the outcome.

All had begun better than John Dawson, but he wasn't discouraged. Dorothy thought he looked so strong and brave; there was an air of the hero about him. She wondered if David in the Bible story had such an intense and confident aura when he strode out to meet Goliath. If she hadn't known it before, she knew it now – she was very much in love with him.

The ploughmen now began the major part of the work, concentrating hard on their markers at the end of the field. The crowd stood round the edges and cheered or jeered, depending on which ploughmen they wanted to encourage or distract. It was fair game to taunt them and shout anything that might take their attention for a moment. Robert Read cursed as his plough hit a large lump of chalk or maybe flint, and veered off course. It took all his strength to correct the furrow as he moved further into the field. All the time he was afraid the sharp ploughshare would leap up without warning.

To Robert Read's left, William and his brother John had settled into a steady rhythm. Unlike Robert, they both knew the field well, but William had the disadvantage of drawing the plot towards the edge. His goader had to turn the oxen round on the rougher ground in the corner, and it was harder for William to turn the plough. He tried to ignore the crowd's calls and whistles and trust in his skill and patience. For another two hours, they ploughed on, stopping at the end of each long furrow to stretch their backs and have a drink of beer.

By midday, there was hardly any difference in the amount of land ploughed by each man. The goaders saw that the oxen were watered and replaced with fresh beasts while the ploughmen joined the villagers for bread and cheese and more beer. Ellen sat with her brother and was soon joined by Matthew. Seated between the two of them, Ellen was in her element. Both were handsome, and Matthew was the most eligible man in Reighton. John said very little as usual – he was still thinking of nothing but furrows. Matthew and Ellen did all the chatting and laughed when Tom got the young Jordan boys to pretend to be oxen and have him as their ploughman.

When Dickon had finished eating, he led the Jordan boys over to William's furrows.

'Look there. If thoo wants to be a good ploughman, tha can do worse than follow i' William's shoes. That's as straight a furrow as thoo'll ever see.' Young Thomas Jordan let out a whistle. It was his ambition to be as good as his elder brother.

Dickon grinned. 'I reckon soil, not blood, runs i' tha veins.' He ruffled Thomas's hair. 'Thoo's a proper Jordan.'

William had been watching. He hoped his own son, Francis, would be as keen on the land. As for Matthew Smith, well, his friend had a lot of catching up to do – he hadn't even remarried yet, let alone had a son.

Matthew and Ellen, still sitting to one side, looked very comfortable together. Matthew didn't care whether he won the match or not since he could tell by her eyes that she adored him. She was so lovely; he couldn't bear to wait much longer. Tonight, at the feast, he'd ask her to be his wife.

Chapter 8

Dorothy Jordan sat with her mother and father waiting for the ploughing match to restart. She looked around at the various young men still eating, and wondered which one she'd end up marrying. She had plenty of cousins and half cousins, but they were all a good bit older than her, and she preferred someone outside the family. There was always John Gurwood. Now aged twenty, he was very eligible. She often speculated on what had really happened between him and her cousin Susan, and thought he'd been cruel to her sister, Anna. Perhaps he just brought bad luck. As for John Dawson, though the most desirable, he was only a hired lad and was either shy or didn't even notice her or the other girls. She questioned her ability to catch his attention, but hoped he'd win the ploughing match. Maybe then her father would keep him at Uphall for another year at least. When she finished eating, she wiped her hands on the grass and crossed her fingers.

Her father stood up and stretched himself, beginning to realise he was getting too old to sit on damp grass. He called everyone to attention.

'It's time to plough again!' he shouted. 'An' remember, it's quality, not quantity that'll be judged.'

For the next two hours, the ploughmen struggled on in the heat of the afternoon. Dorothy should have been watching her two brothers, but her eyes kept returning to John Dawson. As he came nearer she saw how his curls were matted with sweat and stuck to his forehead. His face was dark with effort. When he turned to go up the field again she was thrilled to see how his white shirt, drenched in sweat, revealed his shoulder muscles and tapering waist.

John Dawson had no idea who was watching or how the others were doing. He was concentrating on the pull of the oxen and on steering the iron coulter through the ground. His ears were popping and the noise of the crowd was distant and unreal. Suddenly, he felt Dickon's arm on his shoulder.

'Time's up. Thoo's finished, lad. It's all done.' John was dazed and couldn't hear clearly what was being said. His legs trembled from exhaustion. 'Come on lad,' Dickon said gently. 'Leave plough an' sit down.' He led John towards the crowd who cheered him as he approached. Dorothy wanted to run up and be the first to give him a drink but held back. Instead, it was Ellen who passed him a jug of beer which he gulped down in one go.

No one knew who'd won. The judges had yet to make their final inspections of the furrows. Dickon thought that John Dawson deserved something for his efforts. He was proud of the youngster. John had been a thoughtful, hard-working lad all year, and had always listened to advice. Yet Dickon reckoned that the experience of the older ploughmen would tell.

The judges returned to report to George Gurwood. Their comments were added to the initial marks given for the 'striking out'. George then walked over to Francis with the final decision. The villagers, who till then had been quite raucous, fell silent. The standard of ploughing had been very high and it would be a close match. First, Francis announced the winner of the best-looking oxen.

'To Robert Read o' Speeton,' he shouted, 'cleanest an' most scar-free beasts.' He shook the man's hand while the vicar's eldest daughter, Jane, came forward to present the coloured ribbons. Robert Read took her hand and kissed it while the other contestants clapped politely, thinking their own oxen were better.

'Best goader today,' Francis continued, 'is John Dawson's lad.' Loud cheers followed this popular victory for Uphall. The lad waited to receive his set of ribbons from Cecilia Gurwood. She made her way through the crowd, grinning and curtseying and thoroughly enjoying being the centre of attention.

'An' now … best ploughman o' day … wi' furrows so straight tha could see a mouse run up 'em all way to end …

young John Dawson!' There was a hushed moment before the crowd cheered. William was the first to slap him hard on the back and congratulate him.

Dorothy was breathless with excitement. Her wish was granted. Now, surely, John would be kept at Uphall. Her father shook his hand firmly and passed him the home-made tasselled badge to wear on his hat.

'Thoo deserves this lad,' said Francis. 'That's some o' best ploughin' I've ever seen. Well done. An' if ever any o' them other yeomen want thee to work elsewhere an' leave Up'all, then see me first. I'll see tha wages is right, don't worry.' Dorothy couldn't believe her luck.

John Dawson was carried back to Uphall on the shoulders of William and his father, followed closely by the rest. Dickon and Tom stayed behind to see that the oxen and ploughs were returned in good order. They watered the oxen and cleaned the ploughs and leather traces before they joined the others. By the time they got to the barn, the feast was well underway and John Gurwood was playing his fiddle. Some had even left the food to get up and dance.

Dickon nudged Tom. 'Thoo'd better find a lass an' dance. It's a while since tha's 'ad such a chance – what wi' village not 'avin' a weddin' nor a decent 'arvest feast for so long.'

Tom chose to eat first and drink plenty of ale before asking any of the girls. John Dawson didn't dance, but Dorothy managed to sit near him on the same bench for a while. She kept serving him food and drink until her mother warned her he might burst.

Robert Read stayed until late. He liked the look of Jane Gurwood and made a point of befriending the whole Gurwood family. Being in need of a wife, and finding no one that appealed to him in Speeton, he thought that a family possessing three eligible daughters would provide ample opportunity. Accordingly, he danced with each girl – even the four-year-old Mary who now thought the world of 'Wobert Wead'.

Matthew Smith also took advantage of the evening. He danced with Ellen until they were out of breath and then he pulled her close and whispered into her ear.

47

'I want to make you my wife. Will you consent to be Mistress Smith?'

'So soon?' She asked with a coy smile, absolutely delighted.

'As soon as you like. I'm ready when you are.'

'Then 'ow about December? I don't 'ave to ask anyone.'

It was that simple. Within minutes, a wedding date was fixed with the vicar, and Matthew and Ellen strolled casually up to various people to tell them the news.

Dorothy Jordan's heart thumped when she heard. She didn't know whether to be pleased or worried. Ellen's brother would most likely stay in Reighton, but he might leave Uphall to work on Matthew's place. She spent the rest of the evening doing her utmost to make John feel a welcome addition to the Uphall family. The other hired lads were highly amused. One of them winked at him and made a crude gesture with his fist.

'Thoo's well i' there wi' Dorothy,' he remarked. 'When's tha goin' to be *right* in?' Tom saw John's embarrassment and came to his rescue. He dragged him away to sit with Dickon and his wife. He knew the elderly couple had liked the new lad from the start, and treated him like a son in much the same way they'd treated him as a new hand.

John was relieved. Finally, he could sit in peace and watch the reckless behaviour of the rest of the villagers as they sang and danced and drank themselves into oblivion.

Dorothy watched him from across the barn. At least he wasn't with any other girls.

The feast allowed William and his wife some leisure time together. It seemed ages since they'd enjoyed themselves properly, and Mary was glad Jane had taken the children home to be put to bed. Of late, there'd always been too much work to do or something to worry about – the weather, the crops, the livestock – it never ended. Mary recalled her mother-in-law's words about being a farmer's wife – nowt but a lot o' liftin', standin' an' worryin'. She'd thought at the time that William's mother was just being her usual miserable self, but now she knew better. She sighed, half-drunk, and leant against William's shoulder.

'I do love you, Will,' she murmured.

'I know lass. Are you ready to go home?' She was in a good mood for once and he didn't want to miss his chance.

Chapter 9

1711

William reckoned it was the night of the feast that he and Mary started another child. By the end of June, his wife was nauseous at the smell of new bread and, as summer progressed, she was often dizzy and faint. More and more she relied upon Jane. All summer, she was tired and listless. When she should have been out helping with the weeding, she preferred to stay indoors where it was cool, and sent Jane to work in the fields with Francis instead.

His daughter, Mary, was becoming quite a handful – quite unlike the placid Francis. The little girl had enough energy for three children, had a huge appetite, and still didn't settle down to sleep without screaming for attention. It was often William who sat by her, holding her hand and singing lullabies softly so as not to disturb Francis. Just as he thought she'd gone to sleep, he'd try and ease his fingers from her clutch and tiptoe away. Always, just as he thought he'd escaped, she'd raise her curly head and call out for him – and he'd have to begin the process all over again.

'I'd sort 'er out,' declared his mother when she knew what was going on. 'I'd break 'er spirit. Bairns is born wi' devil in 'em, an' need 'im beatin' out. Thoo's over soft by 'alf.'

William thought he'd like to see *her* try and master young Mary, but daren't let her interfere. He didn't really want to break the girl's spirit, and wished only that Francis could be more like her, or that Mary had been a boy. She was never still for a moment, forever curious and into everything. There was a sparkle of intelligence in her eyes. She was already talking well and could recite simple rhymes, which Francis seemed reluctant to do. Yet he had to admit it was a lot easier to look after Francis who stayed where he was put. Francis could even help with the simpler jobs. He knew that one day, Jane had been driven to tie the girl to a chair just so she could get on with the cooking.

Since Easter, Jane had avoided people, especially Ellen, but a day came when she found herself weeding in the same field. Her heart thudded the moment she saw Ellen. She didn't hoe properly because her eyes were on Ellen's moving body.

Her father was supervising the work from a distance. 'Look out there!' he shouted. 'Mind tha keeps i' line. Jane – never mind what others are doin'. Keep i' line!'

Up and down the rows the women and girls tramped, trying to keep pace with each other, but often distracted by some gossip overheard from another row. Francis Jordan stood on the grass at the edge and half-closed his eyes to get a better idea of their movement through the field. He saw a crooked line of straw bonnets bobbing up and down among the crop and heard the hoes as they scuffled through the dry earth. There was the constant murmur of the women's voices like a distant sea. Women's chatter, he thought, was like a windmill turning with no brake – it just went on and on, never grinding to a halt. When they all stopped work for their allowance time, the chatter only increased.

For Jane it was painful, yet also exciting, to sit so near to Ellen. It was frustrating not to be able to touch her or talk in private. Ellen winked at her once, and Jane's stomach lurched. She realised she'd always want Ellen, no matter what.

In late summer, as the barley was ripening, Jane found herself once more in the same field as Ellen. This time, they and the other women walked through the field wild-oating. As well as the usual straw bonnets, the women wore protective arm covers from their elbows to their wrists. They sauntered through the barley with a bag over their shoulders for the unwanted oat plants. It was a scorching hot day.

Young Francis accompanied Jane and found himself walking through tunnels of dry, pale stalks and hairy, ginger bristles. He didn't want to lag behind but felt lost in the sea of barley. His feet kept stumbling on the uneven, baked ground and he felt sick with keeping his eyes fixed on the back of Jane's boots. As Jane plodded on, he was vaguely aware that she was not thinking about him. Her mind was elsewhere. He'd become accustomed to her day-dreaming and, without understanding why, he connected Jane's sudden changes of mood with the appearance of Ellen. He liked Ellen, but didn't like the way that Jane ignored him whenever Ellen was there.

When they all stopped at noon, Francis crept into the cool shade of the barley. The women untied their bonnets for a while to feel the light breeze now coming off the sea. The conversation turned to marriage and to likely matches. Now that Ellen was going to wed Matthew Smith, the other girls could forget him and begin to consider other suitors. Dorothy Jordan was of an age to begin courting.

Ellen teased her. ''Ow about my brother, John, eh? Don't tell me thoo's not taken with 'im.'

'He's too young yet,' answered Dorothy.

'Maybe 'e'll do for Jane then.' Dorothy thought that was cruel.

Much to her surprise, Jane found the notion pleasing and, for the rest of the day, imagined what it might be like to love the brother of Ellen. It would bring her the closest she could ever be. He was of the same flesh and blood and had similar features – perhaps he would smell and feel the same in the dark. It was certainly worth thinking about.

As the women ended their day's work, young Francis sighed and looked up at Jane. He could tell by her eyes that she was miles away. Some beards of barley had got inside his clothes and were scratching him. With a hangdog expression he followed her home. He was hot, itchy and uncomfortable.

When the barley was ready for harvest, the weather remained sunny for days. The whole field was scythed and put into sheaves to dry. Every tenth sheaf was allotted for the tithe-gatherer, and they'd made sure it was not as packed as the others. The wheat was already safely stored, tithes given or paid, and everyone was optimistic. On the day when the barley sheaves were to be brought in, Matthew Smith and William Jordan both arrived at Dike Field with their wains. Tom was one of the chief loaders, and William and the lads forked the sheaves up to him. Matthew stood on top loading another wain. The women busied themselves raking up the loose grains.

By the end of the day, the sheaves were piled dangerously high and needed roping down before being moved to the yards. At the last moment, Matthew called for Ellen to sit on top with him and be taken back in style. Her brother gave her a leg up, and Matthew hauled her over the sides and up onto the sheaves as if landing a giant fish. Then, with a cheer, Matthew pulled off her bonnet, took some coloured ribbons from his pocket and tied them in her hair. As the wains journeyed slowly back to the yard, everyone walking behind chanted.

''Ere we come at our town end,
A pint o' beer an' a crown to spend;
'Ere we come, as tight as nip,
An' never fell over but once in a grip.'

They took pride in balancing the loads and kept a close eye on the piled-up sheaves; it would be a disgrace if they toppled off. Back at Uphall, Francis Jordan gave his orders and the sheaves were laid down very precisely onto wooden frames close to the barn. They stood on top of cobblestones; no rats were going to get at his grain.

'Don't make ricks over big,' he shouted. 'I want 'em size of a day's threshin' that's all.'

The rest of the day was spent thatching the ricks. Francis Jordan kept looking at the sky. It grew ominously dark as if a storm was coming. As the work finished, an eerie silence descended, as if the air was stretched on tenterhooks. They heard the first rumble of thunder, and heavy drops of rain began to fall onto the dry dust of the yard. Everyone ran with their heads down to the barn or the farmhouse – everyone except Matthew and Ellen.

He seized his chance and pulled her underneath the wain where it was dry. He took off his neckerchief and laid it down for their heads and, lying side by side, they settled down to watch the storm. Every few moments sheet lightning lit up the yard and then fork lightning zigzagged through the sky, followed by tremendous claps of thunder. A grey curtain of rain rattled down onto the planks above their head, and it wasn't long before water began to drip through. Ellen clung onto Matthew, pretending to be afraid of the storm. He felt her nipples pressed against his chest. They were safe there and he was certain no one was going to venture out to look for them. She smelled faintly of dry earth and barley. Her skin was soft, and her shifting body disturbed him, not in an unpleasant way. The storm lasted for over an hour.

From that day on they were eager lovers, and made many plans to meet each other alone and unseen. Ellen reckoned she'd been made for this life and, whether it was due to her being with child or not, folk noticed how she blossomed that autumn. She contrived to keep her secret but did tell Matthew who, in turn, confided in William who then told Mary.

Elizabeth soon heard the news. She was genuinely pleased that Matthew was to have a child at last, but couldn't hide her own disappointment. She was still childless.

Jane also found out. Despite being sick and tired of feeling jealous, and yet still craving Ellen, she was also excited at the prospect of Ellen having a child.

It was a bitterly cold day in mid-December when Matthew and Ellen were wed. Light flurries of snow blew over the cliff top towards the church, and the distant horizon was lost in a dark, grey blur. More snow was on the way. The ceremony was a rushed affair due to the cold and, by the time the congregation emerged for the wedding feast, large snowflakes were whirling around and settling. Outside, small coins were thrown for the children to run and grab. The feathers shot from Francis Jordan's gun fluttered about and mingled with the snow as the newly-weds almost ran up the hill to Uphall, closely followed by the guests.

Since Ellen was an orphan, Francis and Dorothy Jordan were acting as parents. When the couple reached the door, the kitchen maid passed Ellen the bridal cake, cut into small pieces. Ellen grabbed a tiny piece with her gloved hands and then let Matthew throw the rest of the cake, plate and all, over his head. As the plate broke on the frozen ground, everyone clapped – the marriage would be a happy one.

Jane watched from across the yard. She was looking after young Francis and Mary, but did manage to worm her way closer to Ellen, kiss her on the cheek and wish her well. She felt a strange kind of pleasure in acting the martyr, the generous lover forgiving all.

'Thoo can call on us whenever tha likes,' said Ellen. 'She can, can't she, Matthew?' He smiled. Jane knew they were just being polite.

During the feast, Jane often gazed at Ellen's brother. She was now serious in her intent to attract his attention. She was quite aware of her sister's liking for him, but there was no love lost between her and Dorothy. Besides, she thought, there were no rules in love and war.

John Dawson, if he'd known of the girls' intentions, would have run a mile.

Chapter 10

1712

As Matthew and Ellen settled into their new life together on the Smiths' farm, the girls in Reighton had only one thing on their minds – their likely sweethearts, whoever they might be. John Dawson would stay at Uphall at least until the next Martinmas hirings, so Dorothy and Jane Jordan had nearly a year to work on his affections.

It was January and almost St. Agnes's Eve. The girls became obsessed with the idea of finding out, by way of sorcery or white magic, who their future husbands would be. If they fasted all day, their husbands might appear in a dream that night. Dorothy Jordan discovered a far more interesting method from Sarah Ezard.

She went to the vicarage at once and told the Gurwood girls, knowing that Jane Gurwood had taken a fancy to Robert Read. It was such an odd set of instructions that they were both shocked and excited. They thought it must work and yet, as daughters of the vicar, Jane and Cecilia felt they should shun such superstition. Nevertheless, as January 21st approached, the Gurwood girls found themselves unable to resist.

The first priority was that two young, unmarried girls had to sit together alone in a room from midnight until one o'clock in the morning, and without speaking. This was easy for the Gurwood girls, but Dorothy and Jane Jordan lived apart now. Jane said she'd sneak out of the house and meet Dorothy at Uphall where they might use the parlour without interruption.

On the appointed evening, they retired to bed early as usual. It had been a cold, dark day but, by evening, the clouds had vanished and, when Jane left for Uphall, the moon was high in the sky. She'd never been out alone at night before and was glad of the moonlight to show her the way up the hill. As she hurried past the church, the hairs on the back of her neck prickled. Her eyes widened with fear. The few trees by the vicarage seemed to sway towards her and watch her pass by. With a thumping heart she wondered if the Gurwood girls would really carry out the same plan, or would they panic at the last moment. The thought of their cowardice gave her strength and she marched quickly on.

As she eased open the kitchen door, she saw the dogs curled up asleep by the last embers of the fire. One of the hounds lifted its head and sniffed. Recognising Jane, it lurched up and rushed to her, wagging its tail.

'Whisht,' she whispered as she stroked its ears. 'There's a good boy, Jack. Go back to sleep.' Jane wondered what reason she could give for being in Uphall if she was found in the kitchen. Perhaps medicine was needed for young Mary – that would be a good excuse. She petted the dog once more and managed to settle it down again by the fire. Then she tiptoed silently towards the parlour. The door creaked as she entered.

'Hush, for God's sake,' whispered Dorothy who was sitting huddled in the corner beside a candle, her only source of warmth. 'It's nearly time. Remember what we have to do? Once it's midnight, we mustn't speak.'

Jane nodded and sat by her sister, trusting that everything was ready. They waited until the candle burnt lower and reached the mark that Dorothy had made. Then Dorothy put her finger on her lips and touched her head. This was the signal for them to pull some hairs from their heads – one for each year of their age. It was fine to pull one or two out, but quite painful to pull out nearly twenty. They bit their lips to avoid crying out. By the time they'd finished, their eyes were watering. They lined up the hairs on a linen cloth along with some true-love herb. Dorothy pointed to the candle where there was another mark. They had to wait in silence now for an hour.

The only sound was the draught whistling gently under the door. Many times during that long hour Jane was tempted to say something, but Dorothy guessed her intention each time and frowned angrily and shook her head. They stared wide-eyed as the candle flame flickered. Jane shivered in the cold room and wished she'd never come.

When the candle finally burnt down to the next mark, Dorothy took one hair at a time and burnt it in the small, dancing flame. Jane copied her actions, hoping the smell of burning hair wouldn't linger. Dorothy whispered the all-important words.

'I offer this my sacrifice to him most precious in my eyes.' Another hair sizzled in the flame. 'I charge thee now come forth to me that this minute I may thee see.'

Jane repeated the words as all the hairs were burnt. They glanced nervously about the dimly lit parlour, hoping to see a vision of their future husbands, but fearing it just the same. All of a sudden, Dorothy gasped and went as white as a ghost. She clutched her sister's arm.

'Did you see someone?' she hissed.

'No. I didn't see anything.' They both knew they could only see their own intended. Jane wasn't sure if Dorothy was pretending to have seen something or someone. Her sister's hand was shaking as she blew out the candle.

'We'd best get to bed,' Dorothy announced, her lips tight. 'Thank you for coming.'

'That's all right,' Jane shrugged. 'I'd better get back.' It was very disappointing. It was all over and she'd seen nothing. She shivered again as she got up to leave, dreading the walk back to the bottom of the village and along St Helen's Lane.

On the threshold, she paused and peered out. The air smelled of snow though none had fallen yet, and there was not a glimpse of moonlight. Appalled by the total dark, she stepped back.

'I can't go,' she whispered in panic. 'It's black out there. I can't see a thing. Lend me the lantern.'

'No,' answered Dorothy, 'they'll need it in the morning when they see to the stock. There'll be trouble if it's missing.'

'Please,' begged Jane.

'No!' Dorothy hustled her back into the doorway. 'Get out there – and be brave.' She pushed her through and shut the door.

Jane stood on the step. The night closed round her, engulfing her like the black pelt of some gigantic creature. She pulled up her hood and took a few deep breaths to summon the courage to move forwards. Feeling her way along the walls, she crossed warily to the cottages opposite. It was almost easier to see with her eyes closed. She concentrated on counting the different dwellings until she touched the vicarage wall. All she need do now was head down the hill. Afraid of ghosts and evil spirits that might lurk behind the hedges, she stretched her arms out in front and took one fearful step at a time. At last, the hill levelled out and she was able to turn up the lane and find William and Mary's house. She began to breathe more freely although she still shivered, as much from the cold as from fear. When she reached the door, she knew she'd never get warmed up again, even in bed. She was cold to the marrow, and all to no purpose.

When morning came, both Jane and Dorothy were eager to hear news from the Gurwood girls. Dorothy called round to see them. Yes, they had attempted it and got as far as the burning of the hairs before their brother John had caught them. No, he wasn't going to tell their father, although he'd been appalled by their unchristian behaviour. Their main concern was that they were now in John's debt and, no doubt, he'd have them running after him all the while. Dorothy lied and informed them that it hadn't worked anyway. She was afraid that if she told them what she'd seen, it would fail to come true.

Part Two

Mary

Chapter II

1712

Married life suited Matthew. His body responded eagerly to Ellen's presence and he felt like a man again. He regretted the years he'd spent ignoring women and most human beings for that matter. Old Ben found him at the forge one afternoon.

'Now then, Matt. Thoo looks skippity these days.' He winked at the blacksmith. 'Mus' be that lass Ellen 'as put new life i' thee.'

Phineas Wrench looked up from his anvil and grinned at them. As he began to hammer again, he beat out a rhythm to accompany the old saying.

'Once i' mornin' an' twice at night, keeps a man 'ealthy, wealthy an' bright.'

It was true, Matthew thought. Despite Ellen's swelling womb, her desire for him had increased, and they always found time to enjoy one another.

Mary's next child was born at the end of February. Ellen was invited to the birth, to the embarrassment of Jane, who was now acting as a servant rather than a relative. All had gone smoothly and Mary was grateful to have another healthy son. She hoped to call him William. He was quite long with very large eyes and a wide, thin mouth; he reminded her of a baby bird.

For some reason, as soon as he was born, Mary had a splitting headache. It had been the same with the birth of Francis. Perhaps, she wondered, delivering boys just made you feel unwell. The headache did not shift though and, rather than feed and nurse the new child, she wanted to rest in the dark and be left alone. Instead, she was surrounded by fussing friends and relatives. They meant well but, already, Mary was looking forward to the end of her lying-in period when they'd all leave her and let her get on with things by herself.

William spent his month away ploughing and preparing for the spring crop with John Dawson. He had no idea that Mary was unhappy. When he visited her she was cheerful enough, almost nonchalant, boasting about the way her milk was coming through and how the baby was feeding well. Everything seemed fine.

William's father spent his time thinking, not of babies, but of fields and fences. Francis Jordan reflected on his grandfather's experiment with hedging. Hawthorns had been planted down the short eastern side of one of their old pastures on Land Moor. His father had convinced him that a well-tended hedge was better than fencing. It gave shelter from the winds off the sea, it saved using wood, and there was always some old hawthorn you could use for fuel. Now that spring was on its way, he was itching to walk over his pasture with Dickon and discuss what needed to be done.

It was a cold morning in early March when the two men set out in their thickest coats. They pulled their collars up high and were almost bent double as they leant into the biting east wind. Every inch of the banked hedge was inspected. Dickon sucked his breath through his teeth when he saw signs of a shoddy repair job.

'Look there,' he said with horror. 'These gaps 'ave been stuffed wi' briars an' whins.'

'Aye,' Francis shuddered as he replied, 'an' they're stoppin' all proper growth. Them gaps'll only get bigger. It'd be no good 'avin' sheep in 'ere. What sheep can see through, they'll go through.'

They continued the hedge inspection and decided, after some argument, where to prune and where to set new hedging.

Once back at Uphall, Dickon loaded a sledge with stakes and fetched the wooden mallet. Tom coaxed out the reluctant mule and harnessed it to the load.

'Come on Tom, look lively. We'll get a good few hours work in before it grows too cold.' He was, in truth, thinking that he'd rather be patching up fences. His master might be saving wood, but he wasn't saving on their labour.

Dickon could wear his fustian trousers for the job, but Tom had to make do with layers of sacking wound about his knees. While Tom had an old, worn-out pair of hedging mittens, he noted that Dickon had a left-hand leather mitten for grabbing onto thorns, and a right-hand glove for wielding the bill hook. He also had a piece of old sheepskin to kneel on. He split the hawthorn stems almost to the ground, and then laid the stems flat in a line while Tom hammered in stakes every two feet. Dickon then wove the stems in and out of the stakes. Always, after finishing a length, he trimmed it and made it look tidy. His master would be out to inspect the work.

They'd been hard at it for a couple of hours before Dickon noticed how cold and miserable Tom looked.

'What's up wi' thoo?' he asked.

'Nowt.'

'Well, summat's up.' Tom had his hands rammed under his armpits in a futile attempt to warm them. His mittens lay on the wet grass. 'Thoo needs better mittens,' Dickon said. 'Them's no good at all. Let's see tha fingers.' Tom pulled out his hands. They were not just swollen and red, they were badly chapped. Dickon sighed and shook his head. 'I reckon us both could do with a rest an' a warm up. Come wi' me for a while. We can finish rest o' field later.'

They walked back to the village quicker than they'd gone out, both longing for a hot drink and some warm food. As soon as Dickon opened his cottage door, they could smell the broth that his wife was stirring over the fire. After being outside in the cold, they found the small kitchen stuffy and hot. Tom felt faint and had to sit down quickly on the bench. He rested his elbows on the old pine table and held his head in his hands. He closed his eyes to stop the room spinning. Dickon saw that his wife was worried.

'Isabel, don't fret. There's nowt wrong but what a bowl o' broth can remedy. Dish us some up, there's a good lass.'

She leant over the pot and ladled out the pale, greasy liquid into wooden bowls. She fished out some beans and the odd lump of mutton lurking at the bottom. Tom watched her and envied Dickon. It must be very pleasant, he thought, to come back to your own home every night and be welcomed with a caring smile and a hot meal. He'd given up the idea of courting long ago. Anna Jordan used to make him feel special and welcome but, since her death, he'd never met anyone like her. He was resigned to being a loyal and permanent fixture at Uphall. Though he spent a lot of time teaching the young Jordan boys, he'd always be Tom the hired hand, never a real part of the family.

Isabel eyed him as he ate his broth. He looked so forlorn and could hardly hold the spoon, his fingers were that swollen. All her maternal instincts were aroused.

'Dickon,' she said, and nodded towards Tom's hands, 'it's been such a raw day – does tha need any ointment?'

'Aye, what a good idea. Tom – tha'll 'ave to try Isabel's recipe for chapped 'ands.'

'Aye, Tom,' she said. 'It'll do thee good. I'll just fetch it an' warm it up a bit by fireside.'

She went to a tiny closet and brought out an earthenware pot which she placed near the hearth. As Tom ate his broth, he saw that she turned the pot round every now and again to melt it evenly. The firelight made her hair look blonde though he knew it was turning grey. She was still a fine woman with an ample bosom, and always looked cleaner and healthier than most. Whenever he thought of Isabel he was reminded of clean linen and newly-baked bread. She interrupted his thoughts by taking the lid off the pot and placing the ointment beside his bowl.

'There,' she said gently, 'rub some o' that salve in an' feel diff'rence.'

Tom peered into the pot. 'It looks a good deal better than stuff we get at Up'all,' he said. 'I'm given nowt but ol' goose-grease there.'

'Tha'll like this then. Try it,' urged Isabel.

Tom dipped a finger into the pale, yellow cream and scooped some out. Dickon beamed with pride and couldn't resist explaining the recipe.

'Isabel whisks some lard till it's light an' fluffy like.'

'Aye,' she added, 'an' then in goes some 'oney an' egg yolk. An' then I sprinkle in some oatmeal – very finely ground, mind.'

'It sounds good enough to eat. What's that lovely smell?' Tom asked. He put his nose to the cream, and then to his finger, sniffing to try and identify it.

'Rosewater. That's what it is,' Isabel declared, smug in the knowledge that even Sarah Ezard's ointment was not so scented.

Tom smoothed the delicately perfumed cream into his sore, reddened hands. 'Mmmm,' he murmured. 'They feel better already. I don't know 'ow to thank thee.'

'If tha doesn't want to be seen comin' 'ere for ointment, tha can always go to Sarah Ezard. She 'as summat made up o' parsley an' chicken fat. Or tha can get kitchen maid at Up'all to pour boilin' water on some groundsel – freshly picked. Swab that on, an' it'll get rid of any roughness.' She put a hand on his arm to add a warning. 'Don't let on to them at Up'all about me soothin' cream.'

Tom understood. He winked at her and smiled. 'Tha secret's safe wi' me.'

Once they'd been fed and looked after, Dickon was impatient to finish hedging while the weather held and it was still light. He didn't want his master to know that he'd been at home wasting valuable time. The two of them worked in silence for a while, weaving the hawthorn stems in and out of the stakes. At the end of the row, they stood up to admire their work. Dickon put his arm around Tom's shoulder. He spoke of the blessing of having a woman at home. He hoped that Tom would appreciate and enjoy a wife of his own one day as he had done for nearly thirty years.

'There's nowt like it,' he said. 'I wouldn't exchange me life for nobody. Isabel 'as been a perfect wife, an' I only 'ope I'm 'alf as good to 'er as she's been to me.'

As they strolled back to the village, Tom wondered about Jane Jordan; she might grow up to be more like her sister, Anna. He had plenty of time. He'd be in Reighton for years. He could wait.

Chapter 12

1712

By the end of March, Mary's lying-in period was over. She still had headaches and was often nervous and tearful, but kept herself busy looking after the baby. She felt obliged to help Jane as much as she could and, though determined to be outside now and do the planting and weeding, she did not enjoy the gardening. She did not enjoy the baby either. She fed him and cleaned him and, if he didn't sleep at night, fed him again – and again. After a couple of months, the baby resembled a fat piglet. No one said anything; it was obviously better to have a plump child than a skinny one. Mary continued to force milk down him, thinking he was just lazy if he fell asleep half-way through a feed. He was so different from his sister. Young Mary used to scream when pulled off a nipple, and bawl loud enough to wake the dead until her mouth fastened onto the other breast. This boy, on the other hand, could be removed mid-way through a feed and be laid in the crib. In the daytime, he would lie there quite content and wait, without crying, until he was picked up and fed again.

Mary couldn't relax as she tried to be the perfect mother and wife. She began to get up earlier in the morning, often before dawn, to get a good start on all the jobs to be done. Even with Jane's help, there was so much to do in the house, out in the garden, or in the fields. She didn't think she was overdoing it and yet was always tired and harassed. The food was just as good and always ready when needed, but her time in bed with William became a duty. When she thought of all her daily chores, loving William was the last one. Every night she'd try and get it done quickly just so she could go to sleep. Her nights were broken by the baby's feeding times and any sleep she did achieve was brief and light.

She might have fared better if her daughter had not been so full of life, but young Mary was never still and had to be watched constantly. Maybe the young girl was jealous of the new baby but, whatever it was, she was ever more lively and uncontrollable. She bullied her older brother, chased the chickens round the garden, disobeyed both her mother and Jane, and wouldn't go to sleep at bedtime. The constant fight with young Mary and the never-ending workload began to tell on Mary's face. At the end of April, when she arrived at her parents' farm for the birth of Ellen's first child, she looked years older.

By contrast, Ellen was in the full bloom of youth. In the candle-lit room, her complexion glowed. She looked younger than her twenty years. Following her mother-in-law's orders, any knots in the house had been untied so that Ellen might have an easy time, and a piece of ash had been fastened to the bed for luck. Ellen was even told to keep her shoes on until the baby was born. She now lay basking in the attention of the women around her, blissfully unaware of the agony to come.

'Keep sippin' that raspberry leaf tea I've brought,' said Sarah Ezard. 'It'll make for an easy delivery.'

Ellen's labour pains had come and gone for two days before settling into a regular pattern. When, at last, Ellen's 'silver water' spilt out, Sarah Ezard pronounced it wouldn't be long. As the labour pains increased in both intensity and frequency, Sarah moved Ellen onto her right side and told her to push when she felt the urge. Ellen gritted her teeth, squeezed her eyes tightly shut and pressed her feet against the bottom of the bed. Without too much effort, the top of the baby's head appeared and the worst was over.

'Well done, Ellen,' said Sarah. 'Now, go steady. Don't worry though – tha bairn's only small.'

The tiny girl shot out, slippery as a bar of wet soap, onto the waiting cloth. She had a full head of dark hair and a perfectly proportioned body and limbs. The onlookers all swore they could see the likeness of Matthew. As soon as the baby was cleaned up, she was swaddled and put to the breast. They all agreed it was one of the easiest births they'd ever seen.

Ellen's luck continued and the afterbirth came away without any problem. It was immediately wrapped in an old rag and taken to the kitchen where it was burnt on the fire amid plenty of spitting. Sarah then made a suppository of cotton soaked in turpentine and cleansed Ellen inside. Mary watched with some envy as the new mother didn't even appear tired; she still looked beautiful in the candlelight.

Sarah went into the kitchen and returned with a small bottle. 'I must give bairn a drop o' this ash-sap to drink. It'll make 'er 'ave good 'ealth an' a long life.' She took the baby from Ellen and managed to wet the lips before depositing her gently in a drawer to sleep.

The women left Ellen alone to rest in peace and quiet. They trooped into the kitchen to celebrate and sat by the fire drinking toasts of warm, spiced ale to Ellen and the child. Mary gazed into the flames, still envious of her brother's wife and all her luck. Ellen was made for motherhood. No amount of blood and mess diminished her beauty but rather enhanced her feminine charm. Mary could see that her sister, Elizabeth, was delighted and, like their mother, was wiping a tear from her eye.

'I'm glad I didn't miss this,' Elizabeth said. 'It's been a real privilege to see that baby born.' Mary said nothing.

Matthew was out harrowing in one of the top fields when Elizabeth ran to tell him the good news. He made the goader stop the oxen when he caught sight of her waving her arms about at the end of the field. On hearing of the successful birth, he went pale.

'And Ellen?' he asked anxiously. 'How is Ellen? Is she all right?'

'She's fine ... really well, in fact. Hardly tired.'

'Thank God,' he managed to say. As Elizabeth left him and returned to the farmhouse, he walked unsteadily to the edge of the field. Alone there, he sobbed with relief and noticed a faint rainbow appear in the west. He looked down towards the church tower, and then glanced again at the rainbow, full of gratitude for the gift of a daughter and a lovely wife. Wiping tears away with his jacket sleeve, he strode back to the oxen and carried on with his work.

While Ellen relaxed and made the most of her lying-in period, Mary became tense. Lack of sleep, coupled with the outdoor jobs she insisted on doing, was affecting her health. She was on a treadmill; her work never ended. When her mother-in-law heard that she'd been up before dawn in order to plant onions before the children woke up, she didn't think anything wrong. As a busy farmer's wife with lots of children, she'd have done the same.

Mary's children gave her no joy. The last baby was just another load of work added to the great pile already stacked up. Overwhelmed by it all, she didn't know if she had the physical or mental stamina to cope. At times, she was afraid of losing her mind.

William did not, or could not help. It was one of the busiest times of the year and his father had him working all hours. When he did eventually return home for supper, he just wanted to rest. If he talked to Mary he spoke only of his work, and was too tired to play with the children or listen to Mary's account of her day. It wasn't long before they settled into a routine of eating in silence. There was tension in the air as Mary strove to keep the children quiet so their father could have a bit of peace. The couple became more distant, their regular time together in bed spent without love at the end of a long day.

Mary began to see William as her worst enemy. He expected her to work all day and night and could not understand or sympathise with her complaints about the children's behaviour. She envied him being out in the fields doing one job at a time while she had to do all her tasks with young children hanging around and getting in the way.

'I can hardly even use the chamber pot,' she complained one evening. 'There's always one of the children wanting me.'

'It's all part of a mother's life,' he replied. 'And you do have Jane to help out.'

'And a lot of good she is. I might as well have done the work myself by the time I've shown her how to do it.'

'Then let *her* look after the children – if you think *you* can't manage.' This accusation was a knife in her heart. Of course she could manage.

'No,' she spat out. 'I'll see to them. Jane can't deal with young Mary like I can.'

'Well then?' William shrugged.

It was the end of the discussion. Mary's complaints had fallen on deaf ears as usual. She didn't know what to do next, but knew she could not go on like this for much longer.

Chapter 13

Mary's housework and her gardening jobs were done on time but at a cost. She lost her temper daily, and William and Jane had to watch their step. Her children were especially wary. Though the look of fear and uncertainty in their eyes broke her heart, it only provoked her more. She could hear herself ranting on, nagging and scolding them for the slightest thing. She could not control the surges of anger.

The goings-on in Mary's household became the talk of the village. Many heard her screaming at the children or learnt about it from neighbours. Some even thought the devil had crept into the household. Old Ben hated the rumours going about and, concerned for Mary, was keen to speak his mind.

'We're all made diff'rent,' he told them all. 'It's no use expectin' everyone to act i' same way. Folks is complicated, 'ard to fathom. None of us can 'elp 'ow we're made.'

Dickon's wife, who'd never had children of her own, helped Mary by taking her pies and bread. More important was the kindness that she brought with the food, and Mary began to look forward to the visits. Isabel never gave advice or wore her out with chatter. She sensed instinctively Mary's need for love and understanding, joined in whatever Mary was doing, and did not pressure her to talk. Most importantly, Isabel put Mary first. When others came, they only paid attention to Mary's children, and the conversation drifted into talk about childhood ailments and behaviour. When Isabel was there, she listened properly to whatever Mary said.

When Isabel left, she always held Mary close and kissed her on the cheek – a lingering, soft kiss that showed her love and concern. Mary wished that Isabel had been her mother – then perhaps everything wouldn't have got into such a mess. Her own mother was now wrapped up in Ellen, Matthew and the new baby. That was another thorn in Mary's side – Matthew and Ellen had decided to name the baby Ann. There was nothing wrong in naming the child after the grandmother, but they were ignoring the fact that Mary's lost daughter had also been called Ann. When she told William and tried to arouse his sympathy, he just shrugged, turned away and said he didn't see anything to complain about.

Towards the end of May, things deteriorated. Mary had not had a decent night's sleep for weeks. The light evenings had energised her daughter and, instead of being out gardening in the evenings, Mary was compelled to stay indoors and see to her. Jane and William were never around to help – they were always out gardening together or helping out at Uphall. On some of the loveliest evenings of the year, Mary was left alone inside, craving to be outside, away from the children. Even when everyone was in bed there was no peace. Young Mary kept waking up which meant that both mother and daughter were bad-tempered the next day. A vicious circle began where tiredness led to Mary screaming at her daughter who then would become more unsettled and sleep even less.

William ignored it as best he could, but he dreaded coming home. Also, he didn't like the effect it all had on his time in bed with Mary; any loving had stopped altogether as Mary's only thought was to get some sleep.

The day came when Mary was pushed to the limit. She was worried about their food supplies which, with two growing children, were running low. One item she could rely on was the daily cow's milk. Francis, as usual, had gone out to work with Jane somewhere. Mary had just got the baby to sleep when young Mary picked up the large jug of milk, staggered towards the crib, tripped and sent the whole lot over the baby. The little girl had not meant any harm, but Mary lost all control. She slammed her daughter up against the wall with a thud, her hands round the girl's throat, and screamed at her.

'For God's sake! What *is* the matter with you? Can't you do *any*thing right?'

The look of puzzled fear in the girl's eyes brought Mary to her senses. She let the child go and ran out into the garden crying. She leant with both hands on the apple tree, and then banged her head against the rough bark. Hearing a high-pitched moaning, as if an animal was in pain, she realised the noise was her own voice. She kept seeing her daughter's face; that look of surprise and fear haunted her. Children were supposed to be comforted and protected by their parents. What kind of a mother was she? How could she have done that to her own child? Full of guilt, she pulled herself together and went inside to look for the girl. She was desperate to see how her daughter would react. She found young Mary sitting quietly, trying to mop up the milk with an old cloth in one hand, and rock the baby back to sleep with the other.

'Come here, Mary. Mother's sorry.'

The little girl looked up with a blank expression. She let her mother hug her and then she walked out to play in the garden.

Mary's hands shook as she cleaned up the mess. She hoped her daughter would forget what had happened. After all, she was only two and a half years old.

Later the same day, there was another incident – trivial, William thought – that proved to be the last straw. They'd all just sat down to supper. Mary was very tired, having prepared the food after being on her feet all day. She was glad of the chance to sit down and have a moment's peace while they were all eating. Young Mary, however, left her chair to use the chamber pot. She toddled back to the table carrying the pot in her arms.

'No, Mary!' shouted her mother. 'Set it down, quickly, there's a good girl.'

Too late. The pot slipped from her hands and broke in two. The contents splashed everywhere – up against their legs, spilling over the reeds on the floor and running under the table. William saw his wife shudder and go pale.

The reeds could not be renewed for weeks yet. She held her hands tightly to her head and sobbed.

'Why can't you leave me in peace!' she screamed at her daughter.

'She was only doing what she's been taught to do,' said William. 'Come here, lass,' he said to young Mary as she stood bemused by the mess. 'You just wanted to show us what a clever girl you were.' She nodded and climbed onto his knee to be comforted.

At the sight of them together like that, something inside Mary snapped. She realised in an instant that she could not go on any longer. She heard herself announcing, quite calmly, that she'd had enough.

'That's it,' she said. 'That's it. I can't do anymore. I'm going to bed. You and Jane see to the children. Fetch my mother or Elizabeth. I'm not doing anymore.'

She walked out of the kitchen and retired to bed. William couldn't believe that she really meant it. They got on with their suppers and Jane cleared up the mess. When William ventured to ask Mary about breastfeeding the baby, she just shook her head.

'Take him away,' she said. 'Mother can look after him.'

William was speechless. He'd never heard of a mother giving up on feeding her own child. He couldn't understand his wife at all. He and Jane could not possibly manage everything so he went straight to the Smiths' farm before it got too dark.

The contrast between his home and the Smiths' came as a shock. Matthew and Ellen were sitting contentedly together in the inglenook with their new baby while Matthew's mother knitted quietly in her chair. Matthew's father sat watching them from the other side of the fire, smoking his pipe. All was calm. William gulped; his errand would be a great intrusion.

'I'm very sorry to trouble you so late but …'

'What's up, Will?' asked Matthew.

'It's Mary.'

'Is she ill?'

76

'No. Well ... it's difficult to say. Yes, she is ill. She's gone to bed and can't look after the children. Can you help? I'm too busy – I can't leave off working, not just now.' They all glanced at each other. Matthew's mother spoke first.

'Well, we need to think,' she answered carefully. She was dreading having young Mary to stay – the girl was so lively. 'It's not suitable to bring all tha bairns 'ere.'

'I could feed young William,' offered Ellen. 'I've enough milk, I'm sure.'

'Nay, lass,' interrupted her mother-in-law. 'Thoo mustn't tire thassen wi' feedin' others. William – go an' see Elizabeth. See if she'll look after bairns.'

'Yes,' said Matthew. 'That's the best idea. Elizabeth's always wanting to be with the children. She'd be pleased. Ask her.'

William borrowed a lantern and trudged wearily up the hill to Elizabeth's house. Her husband, Robert, was aghast at the idea. He closed the book he was reading, and hoped his wife would show some common sense.

'How on earth are you going to feed the baby?' he asked.

Elizabeth was undeterred. 'William can give him sugared water for tonight. Then tomorrow I'll see Sarah Ezard – see if she can help.' She turned to William and smiled. 'Bring the children in the morning, as soon as you like. I'll be up.' She ignored Robert's groan.

'I'll just bring young Mary and the baby. Jane can manage Francis – he's no bother. Mary can have a few days' rest and then I'm sure she'll be ready to have them back again.'

As William left the house, Elizabeth's eyes shone with excitement. She couldn't wait to play the role of mother. Robert said nothing, quietly horrified.

It turned out to be weeks rather than days before Mary recovered. Ellen again offered to be a wet nurse, but Mary couldn't bear the idea of her baby on Ellen's breast. She felt inadequate enough without Ellen's maternal success being flaunted in her face. Instead, the baby was given diluted cow's milk. Sarah Ezard got a cow horn and sewed two parchment tips over the hole she'd made in the narrow end. The baby could suck the milk through the stitches. It was not ideal, but Elizabeth fed him bread soaked in milk if he was not satisfied.

Mary hadn't reckoned on another problem; her body still produced milk. At first, she expressed as much as she could. She soon realised that the more she did this, the more milk would come. She knew she could have put her own milk into a bottle to give to Elizabeth, but the very idea made her feel sick. She didn't want anything more to do with feeding babies. Her painful, swollen breasts served to remind her that she'd neglected her baby and was a bad mother.

When Mary complained to Sarah Ezard of her tender breasts, Sarah brought some horseradish to slow the milk flow. Despite this, an infection set in. Sarah then brought cabbage leaves to cool and soothe her breasts. Old Ben turned up at the same time. He'd heard of the trouble and brought a mixture of his beeswax mixed with turpentine. He proceeded to melt it over the fire.

'Dip cloths i' this,' he told Sarah, 'an' wrap 'em over 'er breasts.'

Mary could not stand the smell and chose to use the cabbage leaves. When Sarah and Ben had gone, she lay alone in bed in the darkened parlour. Her forehead was burning while her breasts were as cool as a tomb. She didn't know what had happened to her. One minute she'd been a busy wife and mother, the next minute she'd lost it all. The milk did stop coming at last, but she thought the top of her head might burst. She wanted desperately to sleep and feel nothing. Instead, she heard the front door open.

Elizabeth had called round, thinking Mary would like some company and would want to see the children. When she popped her head round the parlour door she got short shrift.

'Leave me alone,' Mary said immediately. 'Just go. I don't care where.' It was an effort to speak. It took all her concentration to stay sane. 'Please,' she begged with her eyes shut. 'Just leave me.' She really thought she might lose her mind at any moment. Elizabeth shrugged, unaware of Mary's struggle, and took the children out into the garden.

Mary could hear them laughing and talking happily. She clutched the edge of the bed with both hands and thought that, if she could get through this day, then she might be all right. She counted her intakes of breath and calmed down a little. Hearing the birds singing, she imagined she was in the sky with them, free to fly away, but was pulled back constantly by other sounds outside – young Mary knocking over an empty bucket, men shouting from the distant fields, the chickens squawking as they laid their eggs. Eventually, she fell asleep.

When she woke it was late afternoon. Her head felt a little easier and she was not so afraid. She lay perfectly still, listening to the sheep bleating on the moor and the cows lowing to be milked. She hardly dared to believe that a turning point had been reached. With new hope, she got out of bed and thought to have a walk in the garden.

Elizabeth was surprised to see Mary appear in the kitchen doorway. The children were sitting by the outhouse having a cool drink of milk. When their mother approached, they looked up at her as if she was a stranger. Mary smiled weakly and walked straight past them into the garden. She sat on the log by the apple tree, coming over rather faint in the bright sunlight. It was wonderful to be outside.

From that day on, her health improved slowly. She began to look after her children again, though with Elizabeth's help. Whenever afraid of losing control, she trained her mind to think of pleasant things. It also helped to focus well on whatever task was in hand, no matter how simple or menial. To outward appearances, Mary was well again, but it was a fine line between control and another collapse.

Chapter 14

Elizabeth had really enjoyed the few weeks she spent with young Mary and baby William. She couldn't have been happier feeding the baby and nursing him to sleep, loving his warm smell and the feel of his soft cheek against hers. She even appreciated the little girl's company. In the calmer atmosphere of the Storeys' house, young Mary had fewer accidents and slept at night for longer periods. Even Robert had begun to hold some affection for the girl, and often sat her on his knee to tell her stories.

Elizabeth told Mary of the change in her daughter and offered to take young Mary off her hands more often. So, all through summer, at least once a week, Elizabeth called for the little girl and took her out for the day. It gave Mary a chance to be quiet with the baby and get on with some butter and cheese-making, or whatever else she needed to do.

On a hot and sunny day in June, Elizabeth called for young Mary. They began their morning with the usual stroll around the village, stopping to talk to people as they went. The girl liked to walk ahead independently and, being such a good talker for her age, she received lots of attention. Old Ben, in particular, looked out for her coming to his cottage, and always had a present to give or some curiosity to show off. That morning it was a small beeswax candle he'd made.

'Now then, little Miss Fidget,' he said. 'What would tha like to see today?' He knew she loved his attempts at making weatherproof headwear.

'Hats! Hats!' she shouted. 'See your hats.' She jumped up and down as he rummaged in his chest to find something. She chose a hat that was far too big for her and staggered blindly round his garden with the hat over her face. The visit ended when, at last, she tripped over her petticoat. Elizabeth persuaded Mary to leave Ben in peace. They could go and see Dickon's wife next.

They strolled up the main street and knocked on Isabel's door. She was expecting them and had a bowl of raspberries and cream ready. The two women could chat while the girl ate her treat. Isabel had always been fond of Elizabeth and was quite aware of the lonely and unfulfilled life she led with Robert. She was surprised to hear that Robert was taking an interest in young Mary.

'Yes, Robert's teaching her to read,' Elizabeth said proudly.

'What? She's far too young for that, isn't she?'

'No – she loves it. She can already pick out some words in the Bible.'

'Well, I never! I knew she was sharp, but ...'

'When we go round to the Gurwoods, she stands on a stool and recites the rhymes she's learnt. And they've taught her some songs. John was playing his fiddle for her last week, and she danced round him singing one of her own made-up songs. You should've seen her. John said they broke the mould when *she* was made.'

'Well, I've never seen a young lass wi' such 'igh spirits. No wonder 'er mother's worn out.'

Their next call was to the blacksmith's, but Elizabeth urged Mary to hurry past the forge. It was hot and dirty in there and she deemed the men's language to be unsuitable. Instead, she led Mary into the adjoining buttery to see the blacksmith's wife and daughters. Each month, the women brewed a different beer depending on the flavouring in season – nettles or dandelions or the bitter-tasting bog-bean leaves. Young Mary ran her hands along the wooden barrels and sniffed the yeasty smells.

'She ought to be at Sarah Ezard's if she likes smells,' Martha Wrench said as she stirred the mash tub. 'There's enough stink at Sarah's to keep 'er nose busy for months.'

'Sarah's never in these days,' Elizabeth said. 'She's always outside looking for herbs and whatnot. She says it's her best time to make ointments for cuts and scalds. Come on, Mary, we'll just say hello to Bart Huskisson, the carpenter, and then we'll see your grandmother Jordan at Uphall.'

Young Mary linked each person and place in the village with their unique smells. Uphall meant bacon and beeswax polish and her grandfather's tobacco. Dickon's cottage was lavender and fresh linen. Old Ben's smells varied according to the job he was doing; she might find him tarring his breeches, or he might be brewing up a medicine for his aching legs, or he might reek of apples and honey after standing over a pot of mead. Bart Huskisson's shed always had such a sharp scent of pine and oak that it stung her throat.

Bart was busy working so Elizabeth led young Mary round the back to the garden. The family was sitting there shelling peas. Mary was told she could help so long as she didn't eat too many. For over half an hour she tried to press the bright green pods in just the right place to make a popping sound, but her hands were too small. More often than not, the pods came apart in stringy pieces and the peas rolled onto the ground. Elizabeth saw that the girl was growing frustrated.

'Come on, Mary,' she said. 'Leave those pods now. I think you've done enough. We'll go to Uphall.'

As soon as Mary entered the yard and saw that no one was about, she let go of Elizabeth's hand and chased after the geese. Having done that, she crept round the side of the hayrick where she knew the cats often dozed in the sun. To her disappointment, the new batch of kittens was not there. Elizabeth took her hand and led her towards the pigs. There she balanced the girl on the gate, and held on tight so that Mary could reach down and scratch the pigs' ears. Then they went to see the calves and stroke them before it was time to collect scraps from the kitchen and feed the chickens.

There was no sign of Dorothy Jordan, the girl's grandmother, or her Aunt Dorothy. This didn't surprise Elizabeth. They'd probably seen young Mary running about in the yard and made themselves scarce. The kitchen maid asked them if they'd like to take the men's food up to the field instead. Young Mary's eyes lit up in excitement. A trip to the fields was much better than feeding chickens. As soon as they were handed the basket, she toddled on ahead, shouting at the top of her voice.

'Your grub's coming! Dickon! Tom! Your grub's coming.'

Everyone in the far field heard the girl's voice and laid down their tools. Once Elizabeth had set down the basket, she saw that young Mary had already found Tom and Dickon and had squeezed herself between them on the grass. When Dickon got his food, he pretended to produce a hardboiled egg from her ear, and when she tried to take a bite of their cheese, Tom rolled her over and started to tickle her. She loved and hated it at the same time.

'Stop! Stop! Don't!' she cried, squirming from him.

'Alright,' he said. 'Does thoo want a shoulder ride?' He lifted her up with one swing. Immediately, she knocked off his hat and grabbed his hair to hold on.

'Can tha see Filey yet?' he asked, spinning her round. 'Can tha see any cobles out? Sit still an' tell me all. Mary, Mary – what can tha see?'

She began to list everything around her, much to everyone's amusement, and pointed out a man pissing behind a tree, and a lad stealing a kiss. The more they laughed, the more Mary pointed her finger until Elizabeth called a halt and told Tom to put her down. The workers groaned with disappointment. It was time anyway to get back to work. It was also time for young Mary to be taken home.

On the slow walk back to St Helen's Lane, the girl recited nursery rhymes happily but, as she neared her home, she grew quiet. She did not want to return to the place where she always did something wrong.

Elizabeth assumed her sister would be in a good mood, having enjoyed a useful day in the milkhouse. This was not the case.

Chapter 15

Mary had entered the milkhouse that morning and gazed around at all the utensils. Her heart had sunk. The pancheon, the ladles and skimmer, the churn, the tubs and bowls, the cheese moulds – they'd all once filled her with pleasure. Now they only made her despondent. Lacking both energy and confidence, she thought she'd never be able to make butter or cheese as she'd done before. After walking around the room and stroking the churn, she returned to the house.

As the summer wore on, Mary did regain some strength but, when harvest time approached, she felt no excitement at all, no lifting of her spirits. Something was wrong. Her body was weary and yet tense at the same time; she could not have relaxed to save her life. It was as if a bar of iron lay just below her ribs which would not go away. It was there as she stood kneading bread in the kitchen. It was there as she stirred the cooking pot. It was there as she stood talking to people, and it was there when she lay down to sleep. She found William unsympathetic; he'd taken just about all he could of his wife's complaints.

Dickon's wife was kinder. Isabel listened to Mary's worries and made her marigold tea to try and lighten her moods. Mary tried to explain how she felt.

'Imagine a mist has come down, but this mist is just around *you* – not everywhere. And it cuts you off. Somehow you can't feel things the same.' Isabel didn't interrupt. She poured out more tea. 'Or it's like someone has painted a layer of varnish over me. I'm still there. People can see me and I can see them, but I can't feel them through the varnish. There's this hard, clear wall round me.'

Isabel had never experienced anything like this. She knew Mary was suffering and, unbeknown to anyone, she confided later in the vicar.

George Gurwood was concerned. He believed that Mary's soul, despite all the outward appearance of her changed character and behaviour, was still intact, unspoilt. His task was to reunite her with her soul, help her find herself. He began to visit so that she could be more open and see him as a true friend. He offered advice.

'If you can, find some time to be alone. Take time for some calm quiet reflection.' When she raised her hands in despair, he was quick to add, 'I know you're rushing around doing a hundred and one chores, but you need to be still at times.'

They were sitting at her kitchen table. The baby was asleep in his crib. William was out harvesting with Jane and Francis, and Elizabeth had taken young Mary out. It was a rare moment of peace.

'You'll not be happy unless you're fulfilling your true nature,' he went on. 'If I know you, you need to be busy outside or learning new skills. You need to be with other women, working together. I remember how happy you were with Kate in your milkhouse.'

Mary realised she'd hardly had time for the jobs she used to enjoy. All her time was taken up with essentials for the house and children. She hadn't tried anything new in her cooking for ages.

'Thank you for your advice,' she said politely though without any real hope. 'It seems a bit confusing – to try and be calm and still, and also be busy working with others. I'll try.'

When George Gurwood left, he marched straight to Uphall. He'd done all he could for Mary and was now keen to see others. Mary's mother-in-law, Dorothy Jordan, was first on his mental list. He knew how ungenerous she could be with anyone she deemed to be idle or feigning illness but, to his mind, the strong were obliged to help the weak. He found her sewing in the parlour. They talked for a while about the harvest before Dorothy started on Mary.

'That daughter-in-law o' mine is next to useless,' she complained. 'She shows no interest in nowt but 'erself. All she does is grumble. If thoo asks me, it's just laziness.'

'No one in their right mind would be as miserable as Mary,' he answered. 'She has a good husband and three healthy children – she obviously can't help being the way she is.'

'Nay,' muttered Dorothy, putting down her sewing, 'that lass – I've seen it before – she's spoilt rotten, demandin' attention when she should be gettin' on with 'er jobs. I've 'ad eleven bairns – aye, an' lost a few. Don't tell me about misery.' She sniffed with contempt. 'That lass, Mary, 'as always been above 'erself.'

The vicar stretched out his hand and placed it gently on her arm. He looked her straight in the eye. 'Dorothy, thee and me shall not live forever. We must do all the good we can – while we can.'

She turned her head, stood up swiftly and moved to the window. 'It looks like rain,' she pronounced. 'I've jobs to do an' thoo'd best get back to vicarage before it starts.'

George Gurwood left. He knew when he was beaten.

Early one morning Old Ben found Sarah Ezard rummaging for herbs among the hedgerow by his cottage. He called her over and they began to discuss Mary's unhappiness. Both saw it as an illness to be cured. Ben recalled how Mary had tried to heal herself as long ago as Easter.

'As I remembers right,' he said, 'she dried an' grated 'er Good Friday bread an' ate it up i' good faith.'

'Aye,' agreed Sarah. 'That didn't work. An' she was brave enough to try all me purges. They just made 'er weak though. I wished I'd never got 'er to drink 'em, poor lass. I did reckon she might be short o' blood, so I made 'er drink me dandelion tea.'

'Did that do any good?'

Sarah shook her head. 'Nay. I tried givin' 'er seeds an' roots o' knapweed all crushed up wi' pepper. It was to try an' get 'er appetite back. Nowt worked.'

They stood for a while in silence listening to the blackbirds flicking leaves in the undergrowth. Ben knew she hated it if her cures failed.

'There's nowt for it then,' he concluded warily, avoiding her eye. 'William'll 'ave to buy summat from market.'

Sarah baulked at this suggestion but then held up a finger and began to smile. 'There's one special tonic Mary 'asn't tried yet. I'll ask William to fetch all I need an' I'll make some up.'

William was so fed up with Mary's cold efficiency in all her wifely and motherly duties that, as soon as he heard of the ingredients required for a tonic, he went to the market. He returned with ginger, Spanish juice and hops.

Sarah set to work at once to make enough tonic for the whole village. She boiled up field gentian, horehound and burdock with the new ingredients in a huge cauldron that held four gallons of water. She let it ferment for a full day and night before pouring it off into various containers. Mary gulped it down dutifully each morning. She thought it wasn't love that made her world go round, it was guilt.

Chapter 16

At harvest time everyone was busy, and Mary went for days without seeing Dickon's wife. She missed the unconditional love that Isabel gave. One evening she decided to leave the children with William and Jane; they could have supper by themselves while she visited Isabel. When she knocked on the door and walked straight into the kitchen, she forgot that Dickon would also be at home and having his supper. The couple were sitting side by side at the table near the fire. They looked cosy and peaceful.

'Oh, I'm sorry,' Mary mumbled.

'What's up lass?' asked Isabel.

'Nothing. I just wanted to see you. I haven't seen or spoken to you for days.' She stood by the door unsure whether to walk back out or sit down.

Dickon saw her discomfort and grinned. 'Is thoo stoppin' or what? Sit thassen down an' 'ave some o' this bread an' drippin'.'

'Aye,' said Isabel. 'We've been married an' eatin' supper, just two of us, for near on thirty year. A bit o' company on a night won't 'urt.'

Dickon put his arm around his wife and kissed her. 'There's not a supper goes by but what I doesn't count meself lucky to 'ave a wife like thee. Thirty year 'ave gone by like that.' He clicked his fingers.

Mary sat opposite them, comforted by their love and, as she ate the slices of bread they offered, she listened to them recount the early days of their courtship.

'We were amazed at our good fortune,' said Isabel. 'We were both besotted.'

'It's true, I swear it,' Dickon agreed. 'I could've gazed at Isabel all day an' night an' never tired of it. I loved every bit of 'er. An' once we were wed, it only got better.'

He recalled the night of the storm nine years ago when he'd been laid up in bed for a week. Despite his cracked ribs, he'd enjoyed his time at home with Isabel – a whole week of her company. He remembered how she'd often got into bed with him when it got cold, how they'd fallen in love all over again.

Mary felt privileged to be with the couple. They'd spent so many years together and yet they still listened to one another. Mary knew how other couples had ways of pretending to listen, continuing to think their own thoughts while waiting all the time for a gap to speak themselves. Dickon and Isabel were exceptional. Their eyes held such respect for each other. It was with reluctance that she left them and returned to her family.

When Mary arrived back home, Jane was busy putting the children to bed so she had the chance to sit alone with William. It was unusual to have time to talk. She told him about Dickon and Isabel. To her disappointment, he didn't respond in the way she had hoped.

'Dickon's getting soft in his old age. I've noticed he's slowed down of late – getting too old for the work, I suppose. He's that steady, do you know what the lads at Uphall call him? 'Alf speed Dickon.' Mary could imagine Dickon working at a slower pace and stopping for frequent rests to pass on advice to Tom.

'I've seen him,' William went on, relighting his pipe and stretching his legs towards the dying fire, 'seen him leaning for ages on his scythe or his spade, just staring into the distance. Then he rubs his back and his knees and pretends he's stopped to feel how sharp his tools are. Either that or he says he's keeping an eye on the weather.'

'Well,' interrupted Mary, 'if he has a bad back he'll need to be careful and pace himself. It's no good him charging about for just the first hour or two like some of them.'

'It's true,' he admitted, 'he gets as much work done in the end. And I have to say his jobs are neater, and his repairs last longer.' He sucked away at his pipe thinking of all the wisdom that Dickon had to offer. The foreman's words rose slowly, like weeds in a still pond. Once they were out, they stayed in the mind, difficult to dislodge. 'If February brings no rain, tis neither good for grass nor grain.' A more useful saying was one he'd heard from Ben, ''Ope for best, but prepare for worst.'

When William and Mary retired to bed, they both fell asleep reflecting on the calming influence of Dickon and Isabel. The elderly couple gave some reassurance that all would be well in the end.

When the harvest was almost done, Isabel confided in Mary. 'I've been bleedin' such a lot each month. It's me age, I reckon. Me body'll sort itself out, no doubt. Maybe it just takes time.'

The bouts of heavy bleeding became more prolonged though, and Dickon was frightened by the sheer amount of blood lost each month. He hated to see his wife sitting still, not daring to move in case she flooded again. Isabel had never needed a physician in her life. She'd always relied on Sarah's advice or her own common sense. At last, Dickon mentioned it to William.

'Tha knows Isabel is none too good?'

'Isabel? Why, she's usually as fit as a flea. What's up with her? You haven't been wearing her out with kisses?'

'Nay, it's women's troubles. An' I don't know what to do. She won't 'ave a physic.'

'Has Sarah seen her?'

'Aye, Sarah knows all about it.'

'Why don't you take Isabel to the apothecary up at Hunmanby?'

'She'll never go there.'

'Well, let me have a word with my mother. She's fond of you and Isabel. I'm sure she'll want to help.'

Dorothy Jordan visited Isabel the next day and acquainted herself with the facts. She then told William what to ask for at Hunmanby. He returned with some large, evil-looking pills and his mother went round immediately to Isabel's cottage. She found Isabel immobile on a chair in the parlour, not daring to get up to welcome her in.

90

'Oh, it's a sorry state thoo's got thassen in,' Dorothy said, shaking her head.

'I'll be fine. I'll be blithe as a linnet before long.'

'Well, these should 'elp.' Dorothy plonked the bottle of pills down onto the pine table. She couldn't help noticing that the cottage, once clean and tidy, was looking rather neglected, and Isabel was looking pasty; her once shiny hair was now dull and lifeless. A sickly sweet, metallic smell pervaded the room and, when Dorothy went for some water, she noticed buckets in the corner full of clothes that had been left to soak. The water was red with blood.

She came back with a mug of water. 'There now,' she said brightly. 'Wash one o' these pills down. Apothecary says tha's to 'ave one i' forenoon before tha breaks tha fast an' one when tha retires to bed. An' he says a long rest is what's wanted.'

'But Sarah told me to keep movin' whenever I can.'

'Well, apothecary should know.' She couldn't get the sight of the buckets out of her mind. 'I'll get one o' me lasses to 'elp. She'll do what tha tells 'er an' then tha can rest a bit more. I'll come an' visit again in a few days.'

'Nay, I'll be all right. Don't worry. Don't send anyone. I'll be fine.'

'I'm sendin' young Dorothy round, so whisht. It's nowt. I can manage without 'er for a few days. Thoo's always been very loyal to Up'all, now let me 'elp i' return.'

Next day, young Dorothy arrived to do Isabel's washing and cooking. She tried to mask the smell of blood with sprigs of rosemary stuffed in various pots. Luckily, the weather was warm and breezy so she could stretch all the linen and clothes out on the hedge to dry. She fetched water twice and fed the pig and chickens.

When Dickon came home in the evening he was relieved to see Isabel resting and showing more interest in sewing and knitting again. He began to hope she was on the mend and, because he was so pleased, he told folk how well she was doing.

Sarah Ezard got to hear about the pills and the advice about resting. She marched straight to Isabel's cottage.

'Thoo's lookin' a bit better,' she conceded.

'Aye, I feel better, but I 'ate to see young Dorothy doin' ev'rythin' I should be doin'.'

'I told thee. Rest only while blood's comin'. Move about when tha can.'

'Dorothy says apothecary prescribed a long rest. That's what's needed, she said. So that's what I'm doin' ... 'appen just for a week.'

'I can't persuade thee to get up an' 'ave a little walk then?'

Isabel shook her head. 'Nay, I'll be all right.'

Two days later, while Dickon was at Uphall sorting out the lads' jobs, Isabel felt a sharp pain in her heart. A clot of blood had travelled from her leg and lodged itself there. Dorothy hadn't arrived yet for the day, and Mary had intended visiting later. Isabel died alone in her chair. When Sarah heard the news she complained.

'Isabel might 'ave survived if she'd kept movin'.'

Chapter 17

Dickon was in the barn tidying the sheaves with Tom when Dorothy Jordan brought the news of his wife's death. He couldn't believe it. She'd been looking better. She seemed to be on the mend. The sheaf in his arms dropped to the floor. Tom stood beside him, his eyes wide in shock. There was nothing he could do or say that would help. In a panic, Dickon pushed both Tom and Dorothy aside. He almost ran down the hill and didn't leave his house again that day.

The news shot round the village. Everyone was appalled, especially Mary. She felt as if she'd been punched in the stomach. Dickon and Isabel were the kindest and most loving couple she'd ever known. They were true Christians, so why had God let this happen? She peered out of the window. It was a beautiful day. What did that matter anymore? She turned back to look at her kitchen. Everything was in its place as before, and the baby was asleep in his crib, but it wasn't the same. Her eyes filled with tears. The morning chores still had to be done. The water had to be fetched, the dinner prepared, the onions strung up ... All the days ahead now looked so bleak. God only knew how Dickon would cope.

That evening, once the children were asleep, Mary sat alone with William in the kitchen. She held her hands out to warm them by the dying fire and tried to explain how she felt.

'They were such a devoted couple. Why is it, as soon as I think something's perfect, it all goes wrong? They cared for each other so much. Dickon will be lost without her.'

'I know,' he sighed. He knocked his pipe out against the hearth. 'Sarah's gone to wash the body and my sister's gone round to do a last tidy up. Mother said she'd get the food ready for later.'

Mary stood up, her eyes full of tears again. 'I must go to him.'

He grabbed her arm. 'There's no need – Tom's gone round to sit with him. He'll stay all night and keep a vigil.'

She sat down again. 'How soon will they bury her? The days are still warm.'

'I don't know. Everyone's busy, but you're right. We'll have to make on. I'll go and see the vicar tomorrow, first thing, and find out.'

Mary sat quietly for a moment and then, all of a sudden, she added, 'Do you know what's really annoying me? I know it's daft, but it chokes me to think of the skin penny to be paid. Isabel's lived here all her life. She's tended anyone in need. She's not missed church once. If anyone has the right to be buried in her own churchyard it's her.' When William didn't answer she shook him. 'Will! Something should be done about it. Speak to the vicar. I bet he'll agree. It's bad enough to be burying someone you love.'

'There's no need to take on so. It's been on the vicar's mind for some time. I think he's going to speak to Osbaldeston about it.'

'Osbaldeston!' she spat out. '*He* won't help. It's a waste of time.' She was losing her temper and William was so calm.

He couldn't understand why she was getting so upset. 'Leave it, Mary. Leave it to the vicar for now. There's nothing *we* can do. Just be thankful we have our family.' What he said next, he soon wished he hadn't. 'You know, you don't enjoy your own children enough.' There was an ominous pause before Mary leapt up.

'What? What? How dare you say that! You've no idea how hard it is to look after young William, feed him and keep him clean, while Mary's running off and getting into all sorts of trouble. She's getting more like a lad every day the way she climbs about. You don't know half! I'm worn out with the fetching and carrying and worrying.' She flung her arm in the direction of the door. 'You're out in them fields all day while I'm stuck in here looking after the bairns. And this is all the thanks I get. I don't enjoy them enough? Ha!'

94

She marched into the parlour and slammed the door. The noise woke the baby. After soothing him she undressed and got into bed, still shaking with anger.

As soon as William thought enough time had passed for her to calm down, he joined her. They never spoke. She faced away from him pretending to be asleep. He knew she was awake, but slid under the covers carefully and hoped she'd be better tomorrow. He lay awake in the dark for quite a while, thinking how miserable his home life had become. It was a long time since Mary had been happy with him or welcomed him in bed. Even when her other babies had died she'd kept her hopes up, and he'd always been loved and wanted. Now it was as if everything he did or said was misunderstood. There were days when it was like walking on eggshells. Tired of thinking about it all, he fell asleep. His snoring kept Mary awake for most of the night.

In the morning, William got up early as usual and went out without disturbing her. He thought she'd rather be left asleep since the baby often kept her awake. He was wrong.

She heard him leave the house. What she wanted from him were some kind words to help her through the day. She wanted to be held tight and comforted. She sighed. Everything she said served only to drive him further away.

Instead of going to Uphall, William knocked on the vicar's door and asked to be allowed in on urgent business. He was led into the kitchen. The vicar was having his breakfast and was surprised to see him.

'Is something the matter?' he asked.

'It's Dickon's wife, Isabel. In this muggy weather, she really ought to be buried soon. I'll dig the grave myself if needs be. But she ought to be buried before too long.'

'You're right. I'll get Ben to do the digging. Do you think he'll be up to it?'

'I'm sure he'll be only too willing. If you like I'll call on him.'

'Yes, you do that. And would you let Dickon know we'll bury Isabel first thing in the morning?'

William nodded. 'And there's another thing,' he whispered. 'Can you forget the skin penny? Just this once?'

'Now there's a man after my own heart. I wish I could, but you don't know Richard Osbaldeston. He won't give an inch and he's quite within his rights. Hunmanby *is* our mother church and, for the privilege of burying our dead in our own churchyard, we have to pay. I promise I'll try to reason with him again. Don't get your hopes up.'

'I'll be off then.' As he left, William turned at the door to add, 'Tom wants to help carry Isabel to the churchyard.'

When William walked back down the hill, the sun struggled to appear from behind a thick mist. By the time old Ben had dug the grave, the haze had lifted and a hot sun burned down. It was as well that Isabel would be buried as soon as possible.

The next morning all the villagers turned out for the funeral. They huddled miserably by the churchyard gate, waiting for the coffin to arrive. It was early and there was little warmth yet from the sun. A cool breeze blew in from the sea. Mary had left her children with Jane so that she could pay her last respects. She stood alongside Elizabeth and Robert. No one had much to say. They were all still in shock.

When Dickon arrived he looked dazed. He shuffled along behind the coffin with his head down. Tom helped to carry Isabel with Francis Jordan and his two eldest sons, William and John. The coffin rested between them, hip-height, suspended on lengths of cloth.

Each toll of the church bells struck Mary as if it was meant for her. All she could think of was death and decay, loss and unending loneliness. She noticed her hands were shaking. It was thanks to Isabel that her strength and taste for life was returning. Now she was plunged back into a weak and nervy state. Whatever she felt would be as nothing compared to Dickon's grief. She watched him as they lowered Isabel into her grave. No one could console him.

Chapter 18

All September Mary tried to be more optimistic. She thought that working in the milkhouse might help. With Jane minding the children, she walked around the room, caressing each utensil but without any enthusiasm. She sat down on an upturned tub and stared at the cold, white walls. It wasn't long before she began to cry. She missed Isabel's kind face and longed for her comforting kiss. This is no good, she decided. I need to be active. She left the milkhouse and ambled up the lane to fetch water. As she trudged back with the heavy bucket, she stopped to lick her knuckles. She'd caught them yet again on the iron bar of the pulley. She was often clumsy these days; the backs of her hands and arms had half-healed burn marks, and her elbows were sore from various knocks.

William noticed a pattern in Mary's behaviour. A week before her monthly bleeding, she'd always lose her temper over nothing and be quite argumentative. It was as if she made up new rules and then dared her family to break them. He looked back upon the past year and realised that Mary had never been right since the last child was born. It was such a shame that seven bad months could obliterate the happy years of their marriage. Now, his family was locked in a round of shouting and arguing. He knew Mary was sorry after an angry outburst, but it was all getting too repetitive.

One morning, on the spur of the moment, William decided to get away, have a day out and take the children with him. They needed to have some fun, and the Michaelmas Fair was on in Bridlington. He reckoned his mother would not approve. You went to Bridlington on business, not for pleasure. The whole village would think he was out of his mind to take a little girl, who was not quite three years old, to such a raucous place as a fair. He knew he'd have a hard time justifying the trip to his wife.

'How are you going to take her all that way?' Mary asked with arms folded.

'She can sit in front of me on Prince. John said he'd come too. Young Francis can sit behind him on Samson.'

'Well, you've thought it all out, haven't you!' she snapped. She'd never been to the fair and would have loved to go. She knew she could have left the baby with Elizabeth or Jane and gone with them, yet anger and resentment prevented her from asking. Instead, she nourished her bitterness and found fault with William's plans.

'And how are you going to stop young Mary from slipping off the horse? You can't hold her all the time.'

'I've thought of that. I'm going to strap her onto me. We're leaving very early in the morning, and she can be wrapped in a blanket.'

'Do what you like then,' she grumbled. 'Some of us have too much work to do. We can't all be traipsing about enjoying ourselves.' She turned her back on him and pretended to be busy at the hearth.

At dawn the next day, William left his wife alone with the baby and walked to Uphall with his two children. John had the horses all saddled up ready. William soon had young Mary hoisted up to sit in front of him with a strap to secure her. With Francis sitting awkwardly behind his Uncle John, they made their way out of the village. It was the first time either of the children had been beyond Reighton Hill. Despite the excitement, the slow, rhythmical pace of the horse soon lulled Mary to sleep, and she missed most of the sights on the way to Bridlington.

Francis stayed wide awake and took note of the various fields, the sheep and cattle. His uncle tried to engage him in conversation, but he remained silent for most of the way. Having spent the greater part of his life with women, Francis was shy and ill at ease with men.

It was still early morning when they neared Bridlington. Even from a distance, they could hear a cacophony of squawking poultry, sheep bleating in panic and dogs barking. Men and women were shouting, children were shrieking and laughing and they could also pick out a background beat of trumpets and drums. It was an alarming contrast to the quiet of Reighton. Francis clung on more tightly to his uncle and wished he was back at home.

They dismounted at the bottom of Green Dragon Lane and left their horses there for the day. As soon as young Mary was put down, William had a job holding on to her; she kept pulling and tugging at his hand, impatient to be off and join the crowds. He decided to sit her on his shoulders out of harm's way.

It was from a height, above everyone else, that Mary had her first experience of a fair – a whole new world full of colour and sound. Her senses were bombarded as they wormed their way through the mob to the rows of stalls. One moment her nose was full of the smell of gingerbread, and then she'd get a whiff of roasted chestnuts. They passed baskets of apples, pears and plums, all ripe and ready for eating. Some stalls had toys, whistles, drums and rag dolls for sale. Mary screwed her neck round to gaze at them for as long as possible before her father squeezed between people and moved on.

'Sit still up there,' William warned. 'We're going to Church Green. I want to see what livestock they've got. You can see the toys again later.'

Mary's brother, Francis, had quite a different experience walking at ground level. Apart from the worry of being elbowed in the face, he hated the stench of the refuse trodden into the streets. His feet slid on over-ripe plum skins, offal and fish guts. As they neared the Green, the rich mixture of animal smells hit him. He couldn't see why it was called a Green – there was nothing between the gate and the church except mud. Any grass had been completely churned up by the numerous feet of cattle, sheep, pigs and horses. Various worn-out hacks were being paraded up and down in one area. Pitiful as they looked, they were as nothing compared to the horrors on display by the pond. He saw a calf with a hind leg growing from its neck, and a donkey limping about with deformed hooves. He could tell his sister was fascinated but, luckily, she wanted to be back among the stalls. She pestered their father so much he eventually gave in.

As they wandered back, Francis kept a tight hold of his uncle's hand. He pressed closer to him whenever jostled by the crowd, or whenever a particularly ugly or large man approached. The walk to the Green and back had been an ordeal, and he wondered what people saw in fairs; there was just noise and stench. The only good part was when his father bought him and Mary a special pastry each, shaped like a pig and stuffed with currants. They even had currants for eyes. Mary gobbled hers down in no time, but he wanted to save his to take home and show his mother and Aunt Elizabeth. It wasn't easy protecting this pastry against the push of bodies. Francis was relieved when it was time to set off back to Reighton, yet there was one more ordeal to face.

On their way back to the stables, they came across a large group of people gathered in a circle. In the middle were two men stripped to the waist, fighting with bare fists. William still had young Mary on his shoulders. He didn't want her to see, and yet daren't set her down. When he tried to push ahead through the crowd, she shouted for him to stop. She wanted to see the fight. Trapped by the throng of shouting men and women, they had no choice but to stay and watch. She squirmed on his shoulders to get a better view.

'Stop wriggling or you'll fall,' he warned. It was like holding down a piglet.

Excited by the men tearing into each other and dancing apart, she knocked his hat over his eyes and grabbed his hair to stop herself sliding off.

When she shouted to encourage the men, he was ashamed. He tried again to push through the crowd and escape, but she gripped his neck with her legs and almost choked him.

'Father!' she yelled above the racket. 'His tooth came out! Did you see? He punched him.'

He hadn't seen it, more intent on finding a way out. Francis had seen it though and retched, sickened by the blood. William straightened his hat and held onto Mary's knees.

'That's enough!' he shouted. 'We're leaving.'

All the way home, Francis was haunted by the sight of the fighter's face, almost a pulp, with blood oozing from above one eye. He kept seeing the tooth and the bloody spittle lying there on the street. Sitting behind his uncle, he held the pastry pig safely under his jacket and stroked it from time to time.

His sister had fallen asleep, snuggled in the blanket and tied securely once again to her father. She dreamed of rewarding the winning fighter with gifts of gingerbread and plums.

It was after supper time when they arrived home. Jane had already gone to bed, but Mary had waited up. William untied his sleeping daughter and passed her down carefully to John. He then carried her indoors, trying not to wake her. Francis followed, very tired and rubbing his eyes. As soon as he saw his mother he ran forward and pulled out his pastry pig.

'What's this you've been wasting money on?' she demanded.

'Let him be,' said William. 'It wasn't much – and *I've* brought you something as well.'

'You needn't have bothered.'

William put his daughter down beside the hearth and took out a cloth parcel. He opened it to reveal a thin slab of gingerbread, moulded like a ship in full sail. It had a backing of silver paper. She thought it was beautiful and yet couldn't bring herself to show much gratitude.

'Thank you,' she mumbled, 'but God knows when we'll eat it. It's too fancy.' Just then, young Mary woke up.

'Mother!' she cried. 'I saw a fight and a funny lady.' William flinched. There was no telling what his daughter would say. He didn't know half of what she'd seen.

The girl went on. 'She had whiskers all over her chin and here and here.' Young Mary pointed to her cheeks and neck. 'Mother – she had a *beard*!' Her eyes were wide with excitement.

Not to be outdone, Francis joined in. 'And we saw a lamb with two heads.' His mother shuddered.

'And the men were fighting,' his sister continued. 'He hit his tooth out. Like this.' To her mother's horror, she imitated the swing of the punch.

'Right, young lady, it's time you were in bed! And you, Francis. God knows what your father's been doing with you today.'

William thought the less said the better. While his wife fed the children and put them to bed, he sat by the fire and smoked his pipe. He couldn't help being rather pleased with himself. He'd enjoyed the day out with his brother and the children, and nothing that his wife could do or say was going to spoil it.

When Mary had settled the children down for the night she returned to William in the kitchen. He looked relaxed, even happy. Annoyed that he'd had a good day with the children, she stood over him and complained.

'Mary stinks of the fair. It's all in her clothes and her hair. What were you thinking of – taking them there of all places? God knows what she'll be telling your mother. We'll be the talk of the village. I won't be able to look folk in the eye on Sunday.'

William stood up slowly, knocked his pipe out against the wall and turned to face her.

'I'm going to bed. I have a hard day tomorrow.' And he went.

Mary was left alone in the kitchen, knowing she was in the wrong and yet incapable of changing her mood. When she joined him in bed they faced away from each other and tried not to let their bodies touch. He was soon asleep, worn out after his day at the fair. Mary lay awake for most of the night. Unable to calm down, she dreaded hearing what else her daughter might relate.

Chapter 19

As autumn progressed into winter, the fair became a distant memory. The Jordan family concerned themselves more with the plight of Dickon. Since his wife's death, he'd slowed down noticeably. His heart was no longer in his work, and he looked and acted much older than his years. Only Tom knew the full extent of the change and tried to disguise Dickon's lapses at work and his poor memory. It was fine when Tom could work alongside him, but this was not always feasible. By December, Tom could no longer keep the newly hired lads in check; they'd never known Dickon in his prime and they either mocked or ignored him. Tom did his best to shield Dickon from the worst outrages and asked Francis Jordan to find more work for him indoors. Dickon couldn't care less where he was put.

One afternoon, Dickon sat alone in his garden with a half-eaten apple in his hand. A piece was in his mouth, resting on his tongue as if he didn't know what to do with it. He kept looking up at the sky, then back down at himself. He gazed at his breeches and boots as if he'd never seen them before. Slowly, as if waking from a dream, he began to chew the piece of apple. When he heard someone approach, he raised his head, hoping it was Isabel. When he saw it was just Tom, his head sank further into his shoulders and he began to cry.

Tom did not know how to deal with Dickon anymore. He already helped him to shave and trimmed his hair. He darned his stockings and cooked his supper. Short of sleeping with him, he did everything a wife would have done.

It soon became apparent to Francis Jordan that Dickon was never going to get any better and that changes must be made. After a brief discussion with Tom, it was agreed that Dickon would be better off living at Uphall. That way, Tom could get more work done and also keep a better eye on the new lads. Dickon would have female company at Uphall, would be fed regularly and wouldn't have any worries. His cottage would no doubt come in useful for one of the Jordan boys, whoever married next.

Dickon was moved to Uphall during the slack Christmas period so that he'd be settled in before the January ploughing began. He wasn't fit to work outside, so was given jobs in the stable instead. It was there that young Mary and Elizabeth often found him on their weekly walks. The girl still wanted to see Dickon and didn't mind his slow ways. She liked to hitch up to him on the bench and watch while he cleaned and oiled the harnesses. No one hugged or kissed him anymore, but young Mary often held his hand and climbed onto his knee. He found comfort in her presence, and she loved his smell of leather and linseed oil.

George Gurwood was concerned about the old foreman and made regular visits to the stable. He did his best to help Dickon come to terms with his loss.

'Your grief is a testament to the deep love you had for Isabel,' he said. 'We all understand what you're going through, and we'll help in any way we can but – the more you love, the more you grieve. I'm afraid, Dickon, there's no short cut.'

The vicar often felt useless when faced with grief. As he returned to the vicarage he knew he was also unequal to the task of rearing eight daughters. Of late, his girls had become obsessed with fashion. It was his fault. He'd left out his newspapers and some old copies of *The Spectator*, and they'd read of the women's fashions in London. Now they were excited by the coming of the fan hoop and were eager to have gowns made up from the new, printed linens which were more colourful than ever before. George Gurwood sighed as he entered his home; the glebe land was well-managed and profitable, and he had some tithes, but he was by no means a wealthy man.

Before the vicar had even sat down, he had to deal with something else his daughters had found – an old pamphlet from London. It was all about the scandals of a group of well-born young men who had caused mayhem at night. He was horrified to hear Cecilia relating the escapades of the Mohocks to her younger sisters.

'They put an old woman in a barrel and pushed her down the street,' Cecilia told them. She didn't stint on the gory details. 'They put fish hooks through your cheeks.' She gave them time to imagine it. 'Yes, and drag you along with fishing lines.'

'Ugh. That's horrible,' Jane interrupted. 'I don't think I want to know anymore.'

'No,' said her father. 'That's quite enough, Cecilia. You'll frighten your sisters and they won't sleep.' Cecilia stopped and apologised.

That night, when they were all in bed, Cecilia continued with the details she'd omitted, whispering in the dark.

'Do you know what they do to men's faces?' She paused for effect and then went on. 'They slit their noses and bore out their eyes – with a finger!' Her sisters squirmed with a mixture of fear and delight. 'Or they might cut your hand off – or slit your throat with a razor,' Cecilia added as she warmed to her theme.

The girls gasped and clung to each other. The youngest two, Priscilla and Mary, started to whimper. They thought the Mohocks might get them in their beds. Cecilia, full of mischief, grinned in the dark.

'And if they catch a woman, they might tie her feet together with rope and hang her upside down.' Her sisters could visualise this only too well, haunted by the idea of a woman's bottom on show in public. They believed whatever they saw in print, and fear of the Mohocks preyed on their minds.

Their father sat them all down one day and endeavoured to knock some sense into them. 'No one's actually been killed by these gangs,' he said. 'It's all exaggerated. They're just young men with too much time on their hands and too much money. They're merely out to be a nuisance – like tipping coaches into rubbish heaps, or breaking a few windows and beating up the nightwatchmen.'

The girls looked more disappointed than relieved, especially Cecilia who challenged her father. 'But they do carry razors, don't they? And knives? And clubs with lead weights in them?'

'Well, yes, I suppose some of them get violent, perhaps, when they're drunk. They're more cowardly than you think though. They simply pick on the weak, on old men, children and women.' He wished he hadn't mentioned women.

'Don't give me those wide eyes! The gangs are not coming here,' he hastened to add. 'It was last year they were in London, and London's miles away. I give up!'

As he went to the door, his son John entered. George pointed with his thumb over his shoulder at the girls. 'I'll leave you to your sisters. Maybe you can make them see sense. I can't.' He closed the door with a bang.

Cecilia grabbed John's arm. 'Listen,' she began, 'I bet you know all about the Mohocks. Tell us what *you* think.'

'Well, I know London was in a panic. Women were warned not to venture out at night.'

'What else?' she demanded.

'I hear men took armed bodyguards when they went to the theatre.'

'And what else? What about the swords the Mohocks had?'

'Oh yes, they were supposed to have stuck their swords up through sedan chairs.'

Cecilia rubbed her hands. 'I knew there was more,' she gloated. 'Don't tell father what you've told us. He thinks a lot of it's made up.'

'Father's probably right.' The girls ignored that remark and chose to believe all the reports.

George Gurwood despaired of his daughters. They continued to chatter about the gangs, now thinking that the Mohocks were something to do with the savage, uncivilised Mohawk Indians of America. He guessed why they were confused; a few years ago, he'd sat them down and read a report of four 'kings' of the Mohawk tribe who had come to England and been granted an audience with Queen Anne.

'Listen to me,' he said as he stood all his daughters in front of him. 'Queen Anne found the Indians very polite and humble when they came. They were not savages.' The girls glanced at each other. They were not convinced. 'Look, I'm rather tired of all this senseless talk,' he added. 'I forbid you to mention the Mohocks again.'

His daughters made sure their father didn't catch them at it and had great fun spreading Mohock rumours round the village. Young Mary and her brother Francis heard the stories. Instantly, Mary wanted to be a Mohock. She wanted to charge up and down in the dark, at night. Francis, however, was scared by the thought of a gang of men breaking into the house and cutting off his nose. Like the vicar, their mother forbade any further talk of Mohocks, but with little success. It was going to be a very long winter.

Part Three

Young Mary

Chapter 20

1712-13

The long winter months indoors were difficult for the children. Young Mary felt the strain most. Her brother was content to help mother and Jane while Mary hated being cooped up in the kitchen. She drove her mother mad with endless questions and gave no one any peace. In the end, her mother had the brilliant idea of making a den. Jane brought a couple of old blankets and they laid them over the kitchen table so that they draped to the floor. Young Mary could crawl underneath and make a home for herself there – out of everyone's way. It kept her out of mischief except for when she smuggled away their kitchen utensils. Whenever something was missing, they'd only have to look under the table and they'd find Mary talking away to herself surrounded by spoons, ladles and pans.

Aunt Elizabeth helped to occupy young Mary by teaching her how to plait. From under the table, young Mary grabbed handfuls of reeds from the floor and set them out in threes. Then she spent ages plaiting each group of reeds before placing them in family groups. She dressed them up with leftover bits of wool and cloth to show which ones were mothers or fathers. If Francis crawled under the table to join her, he was not allowed to touch anything, least of all the reed people.

Eventually, these pretend families grew so numerous that they spread into the parlour and even into the milkhouse. No one was allowed to move them. She'd arranged them how she wanted and knew exactly where each 'family' lived. The reed people soon became a problem.

'It's getting ridiculous,' Mary complained to William. 'We can't clean up for fear of disturbing her precious reeds.'

When he just shrugged in his usual manner, she grew angry. 'You don't have to live with it day in day out. You never see any wrong in her. I'd like to see you try and work with young Mary under your feet.'

He knew it was true; he never did see any wrong in the girl. When he came home in the early evening he encouraged his daughter. He sat on the floor with her and chatted about the reed folk.

William's behaviour annoyed Mary. Part of the trouble was that, by the end of winter, she was feeling run down. The lack of fresh food and a diet high in salt made her more irritable. It didn't help that her clothes were full of lice. Too many hours spent in the dark, smoky kitchen made her long for spring to come.

Spring arrived at last only to give young Mary new energy. She couldn't keep still. Her mother released her from the stiff bodice that she'd worn for months, and the little girl could move and breathe properly again. From dawn to dusk she rushed about full of things to do. She never walked anywhere – she always ran.

The whole village grew accustomed to seeing her charge up and down the lane or up past the church to Uphall, and then back down again to see old Ben. As she ran, chestnut curls escaped from her bonnet, and her chunky legs pounded up and down beneath her gown.

Ben and Dickon looked forward to her visits. Her face was full of expression and her eyes were either wide with wonder or screwed up in laughter. Whenever she was unsure what to say or stood deep in thought, her nose twitched to one side and she'd frown.

One warm morning, the children were to have their first big wash of the year. Mary and Jane stripped Francis and his sister of all their clothes. They led them out into the garden to the wooden tub. It was half full of lukewarm water. Francis climbed in first and then Mary. The children huddled up, one at each end, resting their lily-white backs gingerly against the sloping ends of the tub. Neither of them relished the experience. Their bodies had not been exposed to the air for months and they shivered and complained bitterly.

Their mother was quite brutal in her efficiency. She chafed them all over with a lump of rock-hard soap, and the more they yelled, the harder she worked. They begged her to stop and, when she finished, at last, she rubbed them down with a rough, wet cloth and then rinsed them. It was all over in minutes, but it left the children shocked and breathless. They were told to run about in the garden to get dry.

Young Mary jumped up and down on the tiny plot of grass and then ran backwards and forwards. Francis followed her example with less enthusiasm. As usual, it was Mary who had an idea. She waited until her mother and Jane had gone indoors.

'Let's climb the apple tree,' she said. 'Look, the sun's up there. It'll be warm.'

He squinted into the sunlight. 'But we haven't any clothes on.'

'So?' she challenged, wide-eyed, her hands on her hips.

He gazed up at the tree. There weren't many leaves out yet and he could see the branches clearly. 'Very well.' He always gave in.

She made him stand on the log at the base of the trunk to get his first foothold. Being taller than Mary, and two years older, he managed to climb to the third branch before he felt unsafe. He leant down and hauled Mary up to join him. It was not such a good idea as she'd first thought. Their tender bottoms and thighs were scrubbed by the rough bark, and they couldn't find anywhere comfortable to sit. Both had scraped their shins on the way up and they were bloody and dirty. In their scramble to get up, they'd also knocked off quite a few apple blossoms.

'I think we should go back down,' suggested Francis. The muscles in his legs were beginning to tremble with the effort of holding his bottom off the branch. 'You'll have to go first,' he said. 'I can't climb past you.'

Mary began to edge her way down. It was so much harder to go down than to go up. She couldn't see where to put her toes and kept grazing them. Almost in tears, she slid the last few feet and landed with a jolt. Just then her mother appeared in the doorway.

'What on earth!' she cried. Young Mary shrugged and then turned to glance up at Francis still stuck in the tree.

'Jane!' her mother yelled. 'Come quick and help.' Jane ran out, wondering what young Mary had been doing now. 'That little rascal's been up the tree, and look – Francis is still there.'

'That lass is always up to something,' Jane grumbled as she hurried over to the tree. 'I don't know who she takes after. Come on, Francis, don't worry – I'll help you. Come on, put your foot here, and here.'

With Jane's help, he climbed down and looked relieved to be back on firm ground. She took him inside to dress him. Shaken by the morning's experiences, he was content to do as he was told. His mother, meanwhile, ranted on at Mary in the garden, guessing that she'd be at the bottom of it.

'What possesses you? Just tell me.' She shook her daughter. 'Where do you get all your ideas from? It's not from me or your father.' The girl gave a blank stare. '*I* don't know,' her mother went on, exasperated. 'Look at you! I've only just washed you and you're filthy again.' Young Mary shivered. 'Come on then, get inside and I'll wipe you clean and put your clothes on.' She pulled her into the kitchen. 'And you'd best sit still and behave yourself for once.'

Young Mary had never been dressed so quickly or so roughly. All the time, her mother muttered under her breath. As soon as she was released, she crawled under the kitchen table to take comfort from her reed families. Luckily, her mother had not noticed the damage to the apple blossom.

Throughout spring and the early summer, young Mary grew ever more boisterous. She'd always been competitive with her brother, but now she bossed and bullied him almost daily. She'd never liked his delicate ways and wanted him to be more like other boys. All winter he'd been unable to play out in the snow for long; he'd cry that his hands were too cold, or his ears ached, and would leave her in the garden to play alone. Now that they were outside more, she forever challenged him to throw a stone further, run faster or hold his breath longer. She teased him when he couldn't spit as far as she could.

Francis didn't see the point in such competitions and had no ambition to spit great distances. He was rather put out though when she learned to whistle before he did. When her mother first heard her doing it, she was appalled.

'It's beyond belief,' she complained to William once the children were in bed. 'Girls don't whistle. It'll bring nothing but bad luck. And they don't spit either. I don't know what folk'll say.'

A frown hid William's amusement. 'Leave her be.'

'Oh yes – that's what you say. It's all very well for you, but she's forever up to something. I can't keep up with her. And poor Francis gets the worst of it. Poor lad – he doesn't know whether he's coming or going.'

'He's a lad and ought to behave like one. You and Jane and Elizabeth – you've spoilt him. Mary's more of a lad than he is.'

'You said it! That's exactly it. She acts like one. I do believe she wants to be a lad. There's no stopping her. I don't know what to do anymore.' She sat down heavily at the table, her head in her hands, and then decided to tell him what was upsetting her the most. She looked him full in the eye.

'And your mother – she had the nerve to find fault yesterday, and she even used the Bible to back her up. 'Foolishness is bound i' the heart of a child,' she said, 'but the rod of correction shall drive it far from 'im.' Does she really expect me to beat young Mary? William – are you listening?'

'I know that quotation,' he murmured after some thought. 'I think it's from Proverbs somewhere. 'Train up a child in the way he should go: and when he is old, he will not depart from it. There's something in that – don't go beating her though. Young Mary's special. Leave her be. You'll see – she'll turn out all right in the end.'

'So, leave her be. It's what you always say. Leave her be. Leave her be. Very well, then, I will leave her be, and then we'll see how she turns out.'

Chapter 21

1713

The Gurwood girls grew excited when their sister, Jane, began to be courted formally by Robert Read, a yeoman from Speeton. It was not unexpected; she was the eldest daughter and by far the most striking. The young couple had seen each other at various village events over the past two years, and Jane's parents encouraged the match. If and when she married, they wanted her to live close by. Speeton, just a short walk away, was perfect.

Robert Read's parents were more than satisfied; one generation ago they were tenant farmers, and it would be another step up to have links with the Gurwoods. They suggested that Robert visit Jane once a month on a Sunday afternoon. Time and effort were spent in preparing for these visits. His mother made him a new linen shirt, and a blue cravat was bought to match his eyes.

Jane's sister, Cecilia, was also keen to improve Robert's chances; the sooner Jane was married, the sooner she'd have a bed to herself. Unbeknown to everyone, she stole a copy of her father's paper, *The Spectator*, and walked over the hill to Speeton. She handed it to Robert.

'This will be useful,' she informed him. 'In there, you'll find all sorts of advice on how a gentleman should conduct a courtship.'

He read the relevant page and practised what to say to Jane. He even procured a small bottle of cologne which he sprinkled on his shirt and handkerchief. The following Sunday, his black riding boots were polished to perfection, and his bay horse was groomed till it shone. On reaching the vicarage, he rode behind the house as usual and tied his horse to one of the plum trees in the garden. Then he walked round to the front door, knocked three times and waited. As soon as the door was opened he gave a sweeping bow which he'd practised many times at home. Once inside the house, he was less sure of himself. *The Spectator* hadn't told him everything, and he didn't know if it was good manners or not to remove your hat indoors. The uncertainty made him ill at ease.

The next month he arrived in a long-sleeved, fitted waistcoat embroidered by his mother with peacocks. It was edged with lace. The Gurwood girls nudged each other; they admired how it fitted closely and then curved over his hips. Robert was taller than most and, with his buckskin breeches, he cut a dashing figure.

When Robert was led to the parlour and seated in one of the best chairs, he was very attentive. He rushed to be the first to pass Jane anything she needed and stood whenever she rose from her chair. He asked politely about her health and the family's welfare, and paid Jane outrageous compliments in a clumsy attempt to display his social graces. Jane's sisters stifled their giggles though they were impressed; one day, they hoped to have such a suitor themselves.

After a few months, when the couple showed signs of relaxing with each other, Jane's father took her into the parlour for a quiet word. It was late on a Sunday afternoon. Robert had gone home and the rest of the family had taken a walk.

'Sit down please, Jane, and listen. As a vicar's daughter, your conduct must be exemplary. Robert's visits are purely to give you time to be better acquainted. They're to help you become more comfortable in each other's company. But, listen, Jane – you must remain above reproach at all times.' He wagged his finger. 'There are to be no outward signs of intimacy. None at all. I don't need to remind you – you've been brought up in godliness, virtue and sobriety. Now is the time to show it.'

She blushed and looked at her feet. It was so unfair. Robert was never left alone with her. How on earth would they ever get the chance to be close enough for intimacy? She frowned, bit her lip and glanced up at her father.

He knew that look in her face. 'Alright then, you may kiss briefly on the cheek … and perhaps have a fleeting embrace, fleeting mind you, but only so long as both are conducted in a mannerly fashion. On no account must you be lustful.'

Jane nodded, pleased with the compromise. Since her father was in such a generous mood, she dared to speak about something else.

'You know how Robert dresses so well?' she ventured. 'Well, I know he does it just to woo me, but folk do judge you by your clothes.'

He raised his eyebrows, wondering what she was getting at.

'Father, I can't help it – I'm ashamed of my gowns.'

'Oh, are you now! Your mother will be most upset to hear it. How many times do I have to tell you girls – a person's outward appearance says nothing about their inner qualities. I do believe though, that an excess in dress speaks of luxury and pride.' He got up from his chair and paced up and down. His daughters never ceased to amaze him. Neither spoke for a while.

Jane was lost for words. How could she be proud when she and her sisters possessed just one best home-made gown each? Only the youngest girls were allowed to alter and mend their passed down clothes to suit the latest fashion. Jane, being the eldest, did make the most of her gown by wearing leather stays underneath, and she thought the boned bodice defined her shape to perfection.

Her father stopped abruptly in his pacing and stared at his daughter. He could see nothing that was lacking in her appearance. Her lavender gown was beautiful. The sleeves came just below her elbow, revealing enough of her arms to be pleasing without being common. He knew she'd stitched the small, white apron herself. Underneath the gown, he could see she had a dark blue petticoat, embroidered with red roses. Her hair was shiny, almost black, and drawn up into a high bun. Ringlets fell onto her neck and tiny curls escaped at her temples. Her pure white cap, pinned to the top of her head, contrasted so well with her dark hair. He smiled at her. She looked the picture of a healthy, young lady ready for marriage.

'You look good enough to me. Anyone would want you for a wife.'

She was not going to be put off. She picked up the edges of her gown. 'Father, this material is not in fashion. What I need is some printed Irish linen or some Indian chintz.'

'Too expensive,' he snorted. 'You and your sisters must be content with worsted. Maybe, once you're married, your husband will let you follow the latest fashion.'

'Would you let us wear a hoop then?'

'Definitely not. What is the point of wearing something that makes it almost impossible to get through a doorway?'

'But it's summer now,' she argued. 'I'll feel cooler with a hoop under my gown.'

'Maybe, maybe, but I'm not having you show your ankles every time you step out.'

Their discussion ended, though neither appeared happy.

After nagging her mother for days, Jane was permitted to wear a small 'pocket' hoop or 'false hips' as her father called them. Her sisters were more devious – they stitched withies into their petticoats to give the same effect.

Jane and Robert need not have worried about their appearances. She could see that he was honest and quite straightforward beneath his fancy clothes and compliments, and loved him for trying so hard to court her. In turn, he thought her very attractive, and was relieved to find her not too fashionable or over-dressed. Each month, Jane received a small token from him. A ring, some money and a pair of gloves were stored away in a chest. As the months progressed, he grew more confident of Jane's affections. He attached a miniature handkerchief to his hat that she'd decorated with tiny tassels and buttons. Now everyone would know of their courtship.

All Jane's sisters liked and appreciated Robert Read though their approval did not stop their teasing.

When they'd gone to bed for the night, Cecilia was always the first to lower the tone of the conversation. She loved to embarrass her sister and whispered across to the other beds where three girls were crowded into each.

'I reckon there's more behind Robert's breeches than we can see. Did anyone see *any* kind of bulge? Perhaps it's colder weather in Speeton.' The girls old enough to understand began to giggle while Jane put her hands over her ears.

'What about his hat, then?' Susanna asked.

'What about his hat? What are you implying?' Cecilia asked, puzzled.

'Well, I mean to say, isn't a hat with three equal angles known as ...?' She waited for the light to dawn.

Suddenly, Cecilia got the joke. 'A Mathematical Cock!' The girls shrieked with pleasure. 'Now what does *that* say about Robert? *I* wonder.'

Cecilia left them to ponder the possible meanings. They all had their own ideas – did his parts work like clockwork? Or were his three organs a perfect triangle? Or could his cock add up, divide, or multiply? There was no stopping them. They became so noisy that their mother came in. The girls held their breath.

'What are you girls up to? Get to sleep, all of you. I don't know what's got into you. On a Sunday, of all days!'

As soon as their mother had closed the door, they breathed out again. Their sides ached and their eyes watered from laughing.

Jane was not amused. She made a solemn announcement. 'The hat, because it has equal angles, and because he wears it squarely on his head, shows that he's serious in his intentions. That's all. Now go to sleep, the lot of you. You're only jealous.' They calmed down somewhat, though the crude monthly conversations were too enjoyable to give up.

Cecilia was in the habit of taking books from her father's shelves without asking, books such as 'Aristotle's Masterpiece'.[1] In it, she read of the relationship in size

[1] First published in 1684, this popular sex manual and book on midwifery is by an unknown author but was attributed, wrongly, to Aristotle.

between a nose and the male member. One Sunday evening, she read this out to them by candlelight.

'He who hath a long and great nose is an admirer of the fair sex, and well-accomplished for the wars of Venus.'

The sisters thought about the noses of the men they knew. Secretly, Jane was rather pleased; Robert Read did have quite a prominent nose.

'And,' continued Cecilia, 'just listen to this. Aristotle says, he whose nostrils are great and wide, is usually well-hung and lustful.'

Jane was rather relieved that Robert had normal nostrils; she wasn't sure if she could cope with too much lust.

Cecilia thought aloud. 'I wonder if that applies to women as well. You know Matthew Smith's wife has *huge* nostrils.' They gasped. It was true. Straight away, they fingered their own nostrils and breathed in and out to see how wide they could flare them. Sundays had never been so interesting.

Chapter 22

That summer, Matthew Smith announced that another baby was on the way. Being with child suited Ellen. Her skin glowed and she reckoned she'd been put on this earth just to marry Matthew and have lots of children. The Gurwood girls put it down to her flared nostrils. She had no morning sickness or illness of any kind, and carried on both fetching water from the well and working hard with her mother-in-law, even late into her pregnancy. Folk often complimented Matthew on his good fortune.

William's wife, Mary, also worked hard, but she was still apt to find fault with him and lose her temper with the children. When William's mother asked him to go on an errand, he wanted to take his daughter with him. He knew his wife would object. As Jane and the children were out in the garden, he took the chance of mentioning the proposed trip.

'Mother's made a bed cover for my brother, Francis, and his wife over at Argam,' he explained. 'She wants me to take it. They lost their baby in February, and mother rarely sees him these days. Also, I want to see the bull they keep there. I want to check it out, see if it's worth using to improve our herd. I thought young Mary might go with me.'

'What? I don't see why you need to take *her.*'

'I want to take her. She'll enjoy the change.'

'Take your son instead. You hardly ever do things with him.'

When William ignored her and walked to the back door, she shouted after him. 'Be it on your head then.'

It was an easy journey to Argam. With young Mary once more strapped tightly in front of him, William followed the line of the ancient earthworks stretching south-west all the way from the back of St Helen's Lane. It was sunny and, from the high, open ground, they could see for miles. Large fields lay in strips of pale yellow or green, depending on the crop, and everywhere else was dotted with sheep. Any trees were few and far between; there was little to break up the landscape.

As they neared Argam, they both felt the change in atmosphere. They had to travel down a dark and narrow lane. Tall and twisted ancient hawthorns formed a canopy over one side; a noisy rookery loomed over the other. Dappled light filtered through the branches. Each time their horse edged forward, unknown creatures scurried away in the undergrowth. Lying at the very bottom of this lane was Argam.

It was a desolate place. Nothing much was left of the deserted hamlet except a few bumps in the field where buildings had once stood. A large flock of sheep now grazed there. William's brother lived in one of the remaining small cottages at the end of the lane. William felt sorry for the Jordans living there. They led a solitary, meagre existence. Argam didn't even have a church. To fulfil his obligations, the rector responsible for the place preached a sermon once a year out in the fields. His brother did have two young sons and his wife, Dottie, was with child again, despite not having recovered yet from the death of her baby in the winter. William guessed the next child would be a mixed blessing – another mouth to feed.

William's visit was a welcome surprise though it emphasised the difference between the brothers. While William was healthy and well-dressed, his brother was very thin and in patched clothes. It was an embarrassment for him to invite William and his daughter into the two-roomed cottage.

Young Mary was ushered in through the low door and confronted by two small boys standing by a smoky fire.

Her uncle led her forward. 'Here are your cousins, Mary. I'd like you to meet John and Francis.' The boys eyed Mary with suspicion; they'd not met any other children yet.

Mary strode forward. 'Good morning. How do you do?'

The adults laughed, but the boys didn't move. They had no idea what was expected of them.

'Well,' remarked Dottie, intrigued by the little girl. 'Leave Mary 'ere wi' me while tha goes an' does whatever it is tha's come about.'

'I've brought you this coverlet,' William said, handing over the parcel. 'Mother made it especially for you. She thought, since … well … Anyway, here it is.'

Dottie took it from him and began to open it. She found a large piece of worked linen, embroidered in bright colours.

'Oh, William, it's lovely.' She didn't know what else to say. She was overcome by Dorothy Jordan's unexpected generosity and the beauty of the thing.

'I'll let mother know how much you like it.'

Dottie laid the cover gently on the table and gave William a hug. 'It's so kind o' tha mother. Make sure thoo thanks 'er prop'ly.'

'You can depend on it. I'll tell her. I've also come to have a look at the great Argam bull.' He turned to his brother. 'I've heard so much about it. Can I see it?'

'Why, aye. We'll have a walk up to yon shed.'

'Can I come?' asked Mary, tugging at her father's sleeve.

'Is it all right if she comes?' William asked.

'Aye, I suppose so – if she'd rather be with us than inside.'

The three of them left the cottage, glad to be out again in the fresh air and sunshine. It was quite a walk to the shed where the famous bull was kept, but Mary skipped along and managed always to keep just ahead of them. When they reached the shed, her father lifted her up to peep through the narrow window in the wall. A warm smell of straw wafted through the opening. The bull stood quite still watching her. She gazed into its eyes. It didn't move a muscle. It was so huge, so powerful and yet so still. No part of it moved, not even an eyelash. It just stared at her.

Her father looked on with quiet respect for the dumb animal. He knew its worth for breeding, yet, with such size and strength, it was a force for destruction as well as creation. It stood there unflinching, hidden away in the dark shed, a mighty beast confined, waiting for its turn in the sun.

William put Mary down and began discussing the bull's merits, asking whether the bull could be loaned. Mary sat down on the grass by the wall. She'd never seen an animal like that before. When she followed them back to the cottage for their dinner, she was thinking about the bull. While they spooned in the thin, non-descript broth and tore chunks of bread from the loaf, Mary still thought about the bull. She was subdued, which was very unusual. At last, she spoke.

'I think the bull wants to be let out.'

'Now then,' said her uncle, 'I'm sure he does, but he has to stay there and behave himself.'

'Why?' asked Mary.

'Why? Because it's not time for him to be out.' He saw she was not to be fobbed off. 'Don't worry, lass, he'll be in the field with the cows again next year.'

'Bulls can be very dangerous,' warned William. 'You can't go feeling sorry for them just because they have those big, sad eyes. I've seen bulls go berserk and trample folk, even try to gore them. They're not like cows.'

Mary sighed. 'Mother said I was like a bull in the milkhouse.'

'Ah, well,' her father mumbled with a smile, 'there may be some truth in that. Your mother knows what strength and energy you have – you just need to be more careful, and then you won't be so clumsy.'

Mary sighed again and finished her broth in silence. She did not stop thinking about the bull. She had a plan in mind.

Chapter 23

1713

Young Mary forgot about the bull at Argam for the time being. It was summer, and Aunt Elizabeth promised to take her and Francis for their first experience of the sea. She walked them to the cliff top where they stood for a while shielding their eyes from the sun. They gazed down at the calm, bright blue water that glittered in the sun's path like silver paper. On the horizon, a mist merged the sea with the sky. The weather had been dry, and it was safe for Elizabeth to lead the way down the ravine, past the tangles of wild white roses and briars all the way to the beach. The tide was halfway out.

As soon as young Mary stepped onto the sand, she let go of Elizabeth and charged as fast as she could to the water's edge. Elizabeth yelled for her to stop and hitched up her skirt to race after her. When Mary reached the sea she kept on running. The waves splashed over her shoes, ruining them. She paused only when the water was waist-high and she felt the cold through her wet clothes.

Elizabeth reached her at last, ruining her shoes as well in the process. She yanked Mary out of the sea and carried her back under one arm. Francis, still at the foot of the cliff where he was left, saw his sister dumped like a sack on the beach and scolded for disobedience.

'Our clothes are wet through. Look!' Elizabeth began to wring out the bottom of her skirt. 'And our shoes will never be the same. God knows what your mother will say. We'll have to dry our things out before we dare go home. Come on. Strip off.'

Francis watched with interest as Mary took off all her clothes, and Elizabeth untied her own top skirt. The wet clothes were draped across various boulders. He stood apart, thinking the seashore a very strange place. The sand was unpredictable – firm in some places and soft in others. There were deep pools of water around the larger stones and no grass anywhere – he didn't know what to make of it. The air was different too; a cool freshness smacked his face and filled his lungs.

Mary urged him to leave the safety of the cliffs. 'Come on, Francis. Don't be a baby. Come and play.'

They had the whole beach to themselves. She danced round the boulders and ran up and down the hard, flat sand until out of breath. Suddenly, she paused for a moment to look for Francis. He was sitting cross-legged on a large stone with Elizabeth, watching the seabirds glide overhead. Elizabeth was pointing out the sailing ships near the horizon and the cobles in the bay. Mary thought that Francis might as well be an old man for all the good he was to play with. No – that wasn't true. Old Ben was more fun. She stood naked in front of him, arms akimbo, and challenged him.

'Come in the sea,' she said. 'It's nice, Francis. Come on. Take *your* clothes off.' He shook his head and looked to Elizabeth for support.

'Your brother doesn't want to. You go, but be careful, and don't go further in than this.' She pointed to Mary's stomach.

Mary turned and ran straight into the sea. She leapt through the waves, flopped down on her bottom in them, and then lay by the water's edge on her stomach to let the waves wash over her. Tiring of this she found that, if she stood very still, her feet sank into the wet sand and made holes which filled with water.

When it was noon, and time to eat their hard-boiled eggs, Elizabeth had to drag Mary from the sea. As soon as the girl had eaten, she wanted to play again.

'No, Mary!' Elizabeth was firm. 'You mustn't go back in the sea. You must rest now and get dry.'

Confined to the beach and forbidden to step foot into any of the pools, Mary ran about collecting white pebbles and shells to decorate the boulders. Francis joined in and they kept busy for over an hour. Elizabeth smiled to see them play happily together, though she fretted about the clothes and the state of young Mary's shoes.

It was late in the afternoon when they arrived home. Elizabeth contrived to sneak the children in unnoticed. As Jane and Mary were busy in the milkhouse, Elizabeth hid the girl's shoes. It wasn't until after supper time that Mary found them. They were dry by then but stiff and white with salty tide marks. The children were already in bed so it was William who bore the brunt of her anger.

'Just look at these shoes! It'll take me ages to get them right again. William, pass me that goose grease.' When he handed her the pot, she gave him one of the shoes. 'Here, take this and see if *you* can make anything of it. I'll do my best with this one.' Chuntering under her breath, she rubbed the fat into the leather. 'I don't know. Is it worth the effort, letting Elizabeth have the children for the day? I wonder!'

William had a suggestion. 'Why don't you let the children go barefoot like others do – just for the summer?'

Mary put down the shoe. What was he thinking of! She didn't like to think of her offspring as being the same as 'others'. His idea was sensible though, she had to admit. She sighed and chewed her lip.

'Alright,' she agreed. 'I'll keep the shoes for winter. Young Mary can have Francis's old shoes if hers don't fit anymore.'

Young Mary continued to test her mother's patience. The same week as the day on the beach, Francis was persuaded to accompany his sister to the top of Reighton hill and roll down. Not content with a straightforward roll, she showed him how to pull his arms out of his sleeves and roll with his arms tucked inside his clothes. It was more fun that way, but also more dangerous. There were clumps of gorse to bypass and it wasn't long before she'd ripped her clothes.

They returned home for dinner looking, as Jane said, 'as if they'd been pulled through a hedge backwards'.

Not only that but the children found, when they undressed for bed, their clothes were full of tiny gorse thorns, some of which had fallen on the floor and got mixed up with the reeds. Their mother had to remove the prickles from little William's feet. Being only just over a year old, his feet were still tender.

The next day, their mother was determined to keep the children indoors. Francis helped his mother and Jane make bread. Young Mary asked if she could play with her plaited reed families, now kept in a wooden box. She did not know, as yet, how babies were made. She understood from the Bible that people had children after they'd 'known' each other. 'And he knew her' was often repeated in the Bible. Applying this meagre information to her reed people, she turned all the wives over so that they were face down on the floor; their usually unseen sides were then visible to their husbands. This meant that the husbands 'knew' their wives and could have children. No one in the family suspected what she was doing as she turned over various reed people and then plaited some more reed children. It wasn't long before her box was full to the brim with the reed families, and her mother forbade her making anymore.

'Listen, you can leave them out for a short while in the evening, and then they'll have to be tidied away. I can't have little William finding them and putting them in his mouth. I've only just got rid of all the thorns.'

Young Mary was not happy. As soon as she'd organised and placed her families where she wanted them, there was hardly any time left for play and she had to clear them away.

In the daytime, without her reeds to play with, she was bored. Forbidden to play out, she fidgeted and wandered about the kitchen, pushing things about with her toes in an aimless fashion. This soon got on her mother's nerves.

'Can't you find something better to do? Get your knitting out.' The girl screwed up her nose in disgust. 'Then get your sewing out. You could certainly do with the practice.' The girl hated sewing even more than knitting.

'Can I go out and see Ben?' Seeing her mother waver, she added, 'He might want me to help him.'

This was a good ploy. Everyone was happy. With young Mary out of the way, Francis was left in peace and the women could get on with their jobs. One problem occurred to them – they could never know what she might get up to at Ben's.

Chapter 24

Young Mary ran to Ben's and found him at the back of the cottage. He was sitting on his bench enjoying the sunshine while whittling with his knife. He was shaping a piece of wood into a bird. She shunted up next to him and watched as he pared off thin shavings. The shape of a dove emerged.

'How do you do that?' she asked with wide eyes.

'It's easy, lass. It's there already – all I does is shave off bits that i'n't like a dove.' He winked at her. ''Ere, take it. It's for thee.'

She took it from his calloused hands and laid it in her lap, turning it around and viewing it from all angles.

'It's still a bit rough,' he added. 'Get tha father to smooth it when 'e 'as time.'

'I love this bird,' she murmured, not taking her eyes from it. After stroking it for a while, she remembered why she'd come. 'Mother sent me to help you.'

'Did she now? I bet she'll be wantin' a pot o' me beeswax or some 'oney. Well, we'll 'ave to see, won't we?'

They sat listening to the hum of bees in the lavender. After a while, he put his grizzled head to her ear and whispered. 'We must keep our eyes peeled for swarms this time o' year.'

'Why?' she whispered back as if they were sharing some grave secret.

'Next lot o' bees'll be wantin' to start a new 'ome.' He pointed to the branches of the nearby trees. ''Appen that's where they'll gather. See over yon?' He waved towards a pile of skeps by the hedge. 'Them's ready for any new swarms. I've 'ad 'em licked clean by tha gran'father's pigs, an' I've wiped 'em an' – guess what I've put inside to entice bees?' Mary shrugged and pulled a face. 'Balm mint. If we see a swarm, tha can run an' get 'elp.'

Mary wasn't sure she wanted to see a swarm. He saw the look on her face and changed the subject.

'Well, lass, what shall we do today? I know what I was plannin' to do – make a new skep. Thoo can 'elp for a bit if tha'd like.' She cheered up, but he felt obliged to add, 'It's not a quick job. It'll take most o' day. Tha can stay for as long as tha wants though.'

She put her arm through his and held onto him. 'I don't want to go back home yet.'

'Well then, let me go an' fetch all stuff we'll be needin'.' He got up stiffly.

She put the carving on the bench and followed him to the lean-to shed. There was a trough of water nearby loaded with straw.

'See i' there,' he said. 'There's straw I've left to soak. It's been there all night, an' some bramble stems. We'll use them stems for bindin'.' He disappeared into the shed and came out with an enormous piece of sackcloth which he spread open on the ground.

'Come on, lass, 'elp me pile all this straw onto sack.'

She enjoyed lifting out the straws, carrying armfuls of it until she was wet through. Ben folded the sack over to keep the straw moist and carried it to the garden. He went back to the shed, followed by Mary, and he passed her various tools – a special wooden block and mallet, a bone bodkin and part of a cow horn open at both ends. She was intrigued and eager to see what they were all for.

'I'll just nip into 'ouse to fetch a stool to sit on. Thoo can sit o' grass. Now, I'll need me tarred apron an' some water. Fetch yon pail, Mary, an' see if tha can carry it to trough.'

She struggled and half dragged, half carried the heavy wooden pail. It banged against her legs but she managed to reach the trough and even lift it in. He helped her pull the pail back out, full of water, and then carried it on his own to the garden.

'Now then, let's see. I've just the job for thee. See all straws laid o' sack? Well, take some straws out an' put 'em o' this wood block, like this. Then, pick up mallet an' just bruise 'em gently like this. It's just to flatten 'em a bit. An' look 'ere – this side o' block is smooth an' round. If tha bends straws over this end, it'll 'elp give 'em a curve. I'll do a few to get us started.'

She watched as he grabbed a handful of straws and began to pound them. Once they were flat and curved, he told her to fetch the wooden tray from the kitchen to put them in. She set it down on the grass by his side.

'Now I can get goin',' he said. 'Take over wi' mallet, an' keep yon straws comin'. Once I start, I'll be needin' lots an' lots.'

Young Mary settled herself on the grass with the block between her legs. She felt very important as she flattened and curved the straws and then placed them in the tray. Ben sat on the stool with his apron over his knees. He selected the most pliable of the straws and stuffed them into the wide end of the cow horn. Then he pushed the straws out through the narrow end. Mary was fascinated as the straw came out of the horn like a thick rope. She watched as he took some bramble twine and bound the straw. At the same time, he bent the straw into a tight spiral.

'This is first spiral for top o' skep,' he explained. 'Now I just 'ave to keep feedin' straw through this cow 'orn to keep all coils same thickness. Then I'll stitch 'em all together to make one big coil.'

It was slow work, but Ben had strong hands and no end of patience. Mary, however, soon tired. Once the novelty of beating the straw had worn off, she began to fidget and yawn. After a while, Ben stopped.

'I think thoo's 'ad enough. I didn't think thoo'd last.' Mary felt she'd let him down though she knew she couldn't sit still any longer. He smiled at her. 'Why not go back 'ome wi' some 'oney for tha mother? Tell 'er tha's been 'elpin' me make a skep. She'll be proud o' thee. Tha can come back an' 'elp me finish later.'

Mary needed no further excuse. She grabbed her carving from the bench, took a pot of honey from his table in the kitchen, and carried them home carefully. She found her mother busy with Jane in the milkhouse. Francis was keeping an eye on little William in the garden. She hovered by the door, hiding the carving behind her back, and showed the pot of honey to her mother.

'You haven't been pestering Ben, have you? I hope he hasn't sent you home for misbehaving.'

This remark didn't curb the girl's enthusiasm. 'No, mother, I've been helping him make a new skep for the bees. I've been squashing straws. He said I can go back after and do some more.'

Her mother stared at her. She wondered why her daughter never wanted to help at home or learn anything with her.

'Well, alright,' she agreed, 'as long as you're not a nuisance. If you want a job here you can weed the garden. Francis is out there – help him watch William.'

Mary put her carving behind the apple tree and then spent the next hour crawling around the potatoes, cabbages and leeks, more interested in butterflies and bugs than the task of weeding. Her brother was sawing small logs and making a neat pile by the back wall. It annoyed her that she was not allowed anywhere near the saw; she'd be better at sawing than Francis. She got up from weeding, filthy from the soil that had stuck to her damp clothes. Francis took one look at her, clicked his tongue and sighed. He was just like their mother.

'Mother will be angry if she sees you like that.'

'I don't care. I'm going back to Ben's. See you at supper time.' As an afterthought, she shouted over her shoulder as she left, 'Those logs – I bet they'll topple down.' She knew how Francis liked to stack them perfectly. Now he'd have to start again and rearrange them.

When young Mary arrived, Ben was still in his garden binding the coils. He looked tired, but the skep was almost finished. A beautiful yellow dome lay on his knees with an intricate pattern of stitches holding it all together. She couldn't see any openings in it.

'How do the bees get in?' she asked.

'Thoo'll see when it's finished. I'm goin' to rest it on a piece o' wood that 'as a groove cut in it. Bees can get in through gap at bottom. Thoo'll see.'

As he added more stitching to the bottom of the dome, he explained how extra binding would protect it from wear. He handed her the finished skep. She put it over her head and was amazed how dark it was inside.

'You could make a straw hat,' she suggested as he lifted it off.

'Nay, I don't mind doin' it for bees.' He stroked it. 'This skep'll see me out. Feel 'ow strong it is.' She knocked on it with her knuckles and then sat on it. He winked at her. 'There is another job to do. I'm not sure tha'll like it.'

'Tidy up?' she asked, wrinkling her nose. It's what her mother always said.

'Nay, lass. Cloomin'.' Mary was puzzled. 'We 'ave to cloom skep to keep rain out.'

She was none the wiser when he explained they were going to walk to the cow pasture with a pail, and collect some fresh cow muck. But that was what was so good about being with Ben – there was always something interesting to do. It was much better than being at home.

Ben carried the pail and a shovel while Mary carried an old ladle. It was a smelly job. It was also fun to scoop up the fresh green cow-clap. On one occasion, Ben had been lucky enough to be in the right place at the right time; he put the pail under a cow's tail and caught the sloppy load as it squirted out. They soon had enough and set off back to Ben's, Mary skipping along in front as usual.

At the back of the cottage, Ben mixed some sand with the cow dung, and stirred it in well. Then he got the skep and began to work the stinking mixture into the straw with his bare hands. Mary didn't fancy helping this time. He didn't mind the smell at all, absorbed as he was with plastering the skep. She stood admiring it from a distance. When it was done he soaked his hands in the water trough and scrubbed them as best he could. He grinned at her as she still wrinkled up her nose.

'All done! I reckon we've 'ad a good day's work. I'll tell tha father 'ow good tha's been.'

Mary grinned and then realised it was time to go home. If she was late for supper there'd be trouble.

Chapter 25

1713

That night young Mary needn't have worried about being late. Her mother and father ignored her, for some reason deep in conversation about rabbits. She didn't even get to tell her father about Ben and the skep, or show her carving. While not listening attentively, she got the impression that Hunmanby was being overrun with herds of rabbits, and that folk were very angry. She had visions of rabbits hurtling along the streets, diving under women's gowns and tripping people up.

'Father – will the rabbits come here?' she asked, showing a sudden interest.

'No, lass, they belong in a warren up on the moor there. They'll not come here.' He grinned. 'If they do, we'll have them in a pie.' At this, she frowned. 'Come on, Mary,' he prompted, 'eat up your supper. Don't go getting any ideas about rabbits.' He hadn't forgotten his daughter's reaction to seeing the Argam bull.

'There's going to be a special bonfire here soon,' he announced to change the subject. 'And a feast as well.'

The children glanced up from their bowls, eager to hear more.

'Yes,' he informed them, 'the vicar says we're to hold a day of thanksgiving. He said Queen Anne has appointed July 7th as the day. That's Francis's birthday as well. It's to celebrate England's victories and the peace, so *there's* something for us all to look forward to.'

As the feast and bonfire were prepared, young Mary was too excited to sleep. She lay awake till late each night with her eyes wide open. Though jealous that it was all going to happen on the same day as Francis's sixth birthday, she kept him awake with her chatter and endless questions.

Tom and Dickon were given time off work to go round the village with a horse and cart and ask for things for the bonfire. Young Mary, eager to escape the bustle of the kitchen where her brother was helping meekly, as usual, ran out to join the two men as they toured the village. Dickon's face lit up as he swung her round and lifted her into the cart.

From her higher vantage point, she felt rather important. She expected everyone to be pleased to see her and the cart, but this was far from the truth. Many avoided them. They'd already had their own midsummer fire and had no waste to donate for another one. Anything that would burn was now to be used for cottage fires and, besides, folk were long accustomed to reusing any old pieces of wood and cloth.

'It's nowt but a waste o' time an' fuel,' was the general answer to Tom's request for rubbish. Even old Ben complained, and he loved to see a good fire.

'Why should we 'ave to celebrate?' he grumbled. 'Them foreign wars 'ave never benefitted us.'

By midday, the cart was only half full. Tom suggested they take a sled and go down to the beach to search for driftwood. Young Mary was thrilled with the idea. She exhausted herself running backwards and forwards carrying small dead branches and the odd bleached length of pine. When her hands got splinters, Dickon sat her on a rock and tried to get them out.

'Don't worry lass. If I can't get 'em all out, tell tha mother to put some o' Sarah Ezard's ointment on 'em. That stuff'll soon draw 'em out.' His face crinkled up as he smiled.

Tom watched and thought it was almost like the old days before Isabel had died. He and Dickon had been happy then, spending all day together on their outdoor jobs.

'I've some cold meats wrapped up,' he said, 'an' some cheese. Let's stay o' beach an' 'ave a rest.'

They made a space to sit on the sled. Tom cut the meat and cheese with his knife and shared out the slices. As they ate, Mary entertained them. She pretended to be old Ben and walked stiffly along the beach, eyeing up the weather.

'By lass!' shouted Dickon. 'Thoo's got 'im off right enough. Look, Tom – see 'ow she's got 'im.' They both started to laugh which encouraged Mary even more. She then imitated her grandmother telling them off for wasting time and finished by striding along the beach like Robert Storey.

'I don't know 'ow she does it,' croaked Dickon between bursts of laughter. 'By lass – don't let tha mother catch thee at it. She'll fetch thee such a crack.'

'Aye, Mary,' added Tom. 'Save it for us. We'll not tell. We'd best be gettin' on though. We can't sit 'ere all day enjoyin' ourselves. Come on, we'll 'ead back up cliffs an' sort out bonfire.'

On the way up the ravine, Dickon plucked some wild roses to put in Mary's hair. When they'd loaded the cart, he positioned her on top. She rode into Reighton like a queen.

The bonfire was situated on top of the hill and was shared with Speeton village. Despite Tom and Dickon's efforts, it was a modest heap of bits and pieces filled out with brushwood. Old Ben thought they might have trouble getting it alight and so had made some torches from branches dipped in tar. On the appointed day, the whole village turned out – even those who had complained the most. Francis Jordan thought the celebrations particularly ill-timed as they were right in the middle of haymaking. He grumbled to his wife.

'We've always reckoned on 'avin' four good days to mow an' dry. We've 'ad just two of 'em an' we're wastin' a good day. It's sinful.'

'Aye,' his wife replied. She folded her arms and scanned the people milling about on the hill. Eyeing the kegs of ale, she shook her head. 'An' they'll be none too fit tomorrow, not if they get all that lot drunk.'

As food was laid out on the grass for all to share, the families from both villages mingled. The Gurwoods sat with Robert Read's family; the courting of Jane and Robert was progressing well. William and Mary arrived with their children, bringing Jane along to help with little William who was walking on his own now and needed constant watching. Matthew Smith and Ellen joined them with their daughter Ann, the same age as William.

Jane blushed as Ellen rushed forward to kiss her on the cheek. No matter how much she thought she'd got over her love for Ellen, her heart told her otherwise; it was like a trapped bird under her bodice. She was sure people would notice, but all eyes were on the two small children who had dropped to the grass together and were now squaring up and trying to grab each other's hair.

Jane stood awkwardly and watched as Matthew put his arm around Ellen's waist and gave her a squeeze. Though she was seven months gone, Ellen was as healthy and as attractive as ever. No wonder Matthew was so happy. Jane envied them. She couldn't imagine such happiness for herself; all she had to look forward to was more caring for others – unless, of course, John Dawson showed some interest.

She gazed round the hill seeking him out. He was with Tom and Dickon, helping with the bonfire. To her annoyance, she saw her sister, Dorothy, walk over to him. Dorothy would always have a better chance. She saw him every day, spent mealtimes with him, mended his clothes and even helped to tend him if he was ill. All Jane got to do was see him in church or spot him working in a distant field. She never had an opportunity to speak to him or let him know she liked him. It was most unfair.

Young Mary had been watching Jane, and noted her change of mood without knowing the reason. She knew that Jane often daydreamed and looked sad, yet Jane's lack of attention allowed her more freedom. Everyone was either busy with the bonfire or busy sorting food and drink. There was a lot of chattering and laughing going on. No one was watching her. She sidled up to her brother, Francis.

'Want to do something exciting?'

'What?'

'Come with me to Argam. There's a bull there. He's so unhappy. We can let him out.'

'We can't do that. It's too far.'

'I know the way. Father took me.'

Francis sighed. He was in two minds. He ought not to go, yet he didn't enjoy the large public gathering round the bonfire. Though it was his birthday, he felt shy and inadequate. It would be good to escape for a while.

'Alright,' he agreed. I'll come.'

Mary took his hand and, with a last glance around to check that no one was looking, they walked quickly from the hill, down past the church and through the quiet, deserted village. It was strange and thrilling to be unseen as they took the short cut behind their house to the Argam dike.

Once at the top of the rise, and about to start the real journey, Francis had misgivings. He hadn't seen the bull, but imagined a very large and dangerous beast. They could get hurt, even killed. It was a bad idea whichever way he looked at it. He stopped and turned his head, pretending to admire the view of Filey.

'Come on,' Mary insisted. 'It's this way.' She pulled on his hand. He wouldn't budge.

'No,' he said firmly. 'I'm not going any further. It's wrong what you're doing. I'm going back.' He pulled his hand free and stepped away from her.

'Oh, Francis!' she cried, and stamped her foot in frustration.

'I don't care what you say – I'm not going.' He began to walk back. He thought she'd follow, but she shouted after him.

'Go on then, go to mother and Jane. Be a baby. I'll let the bull out by myself.'

Chapter 26

Francis thought his sister was bluffing, thought she'd eventually run after him. By the time he reached the main street he knew she meant it, and he'd be the one to explain where she was.

Mary marched on in the direction of Argam, angry that Francis had let her down yet again. He was such a spoiler. She quickened her pace, determined to make up for her brother's lack of adventure, but hadn't reckoned on the distance. The last time she'd travelled there was on horseback. Now she was alone and with nothing to eat or drink. It was hot and she was stifled in her best clothes. If she thought to stop and turn back, she only had to recall the sad eyes of the captive bull.

Francis rejoined his parents. He dreaded their questions, yet they hadn't noticed his absence. They'd assumed that he and Mary had been playing with the children from Speeton or that they were with the young Gurwood girls. It was some time before William asked him where his sister was. Francis stared sheepishly at his feet. William took hold of his shoulders and shook him.

'I asked you a question. Where's Mary?' The boy shrugged and gazed across the field, looking anywhere except at his father's face.

'Where is Mary?' William repeated. By then, his mother and Jane were paying more attention and gathered round. Francis couldn't escape.

'She's gone to Argam,' he mumbled, his head down.

'What?' William asked, unsure he'd heard him correctly. '*Where* did you say she was?'

'Argam,' he mumbled again. Then he lifted his head. 'She wants to let the bull out.'

'Oh my God!' whispered William. 'When was this? When did she go?' He began to panic. He might be too late. Francis just shrugged again – he had no idea of the time.

'Was it before Ben and Sarah Ezard arrived?' Francis nodded. 'Right then.' William glanced at Mary. 'I'll get one of the horses and get off quick.'

He strode off cursing everyone and everything in his way. Once clear of the crowd on the hill, he sprinted to Uphall, grabbed a bridle and saddle from the stable and then ran to the pasture. His horse ambled towards him when called, but became jittery when William fumbled to get the bit in its mouth. The horse sensed fear and, when William put the saddle on and mounted, the horse wouldn't respond. Stubborn and alarmed at being treated so roughly, it danced sideways. He swore at it and gave its rear an enormous slap with the flat of his hand. The horse got the message and trotted in the right direction.

William cursed the slow horse, the fierce midday sun and, most of all, the day he'd taken Mary to see the bull. And he wished he'd never taken her the Argam dike route. He should have taken her on the roads. Not knowing how far she'd walked, he shielded his eyes against the sun, trying desperately to see her tiny figure. If she was still wearing her white bonnet, it should stand out.

He'd travelled for a few more minutes before he spotted the white bonnet bobbing along ahead. He called out to her as he narrowed the distance between them. At last, she heard him and turned her head.

As soon as she saw it was her father, she stood still and waited. She was worn out and regretted her plan to free the bull. All she wanted now was to be picked up and hugged, and have a ride home.

William leapt off the horse and gripped her by the shoulders. He shouted into her face. 'What in God's name were you thinking? Are you mad? I've been worried sick. You could've been killed – or got lost. What possessed you?'

143

His hands were hurting her. She burst into tears and tried to twist herself from his grip. 'I don't know,' was all she could sob.

He realised how tightly he was holding her and let go. Seeing her tear-stained face, he took a deep breath to calm himself.

'I'm sorry. I was just so worried, Mary. I thought I might've lost you.' He dropped to his knees and held open his arms. 'Come here, lass.'

She wrapped her arms around him and wiped her face against his chest. He kissed the top of her head and held her close, whispering into her ear.

'You know I'll always love you, no matter what idiotic things you get up to. You're my own little Mary.' He held her out at arm's length and peered deep into her hazel eyes. 'We'll ride home now, eh, get us both washed, have a drink and something to eat, and then we'll join the bonfire, all right?' She nodded, wiped more tears away with her hand and smiled at last.

He grinned back at her. 'And I'll try to stop your mother going on too much.' He winced at the thought of that, and what his own mother would say. Mary kissed his cheek and he knew there was no doubt – she was the most difficult of his three children, yet he loved her the most.

They set off for home with Mary seated in front and grasping the horse's mane with her sweaty hands. As they neared Reighton, William tried to think up excuses for her behaviour. She'd have to be watched more closely in future. He bent his head over her warm bonnet, damp with perspiration, and kissed it, knowing how she'd hate to lose any freedom. Although relieved at finding her, he was tired from the worry, and sighed every now and again at the thought of facing his wife. Instead of taking himself and Mary home, he realised he ought to go straight to the hill and let everyone know she was safe.

Word had soon gone round of the girl's disappearance. The village was divided between those who were genuinely concerned for her safety, and those who hoped she might have had some minor mishap to curtail her behaviour. When William and his daughter arrived, everyone went quiet. The crowd watched, curious to see how the girl would be received.

His wife was so furious or embarrassed her face had gone dark red. William dismounted but dared not lift young Mary down – she might be beaten.

'I'm sorry,' he said. He didn't know why he was apologising for the girl, but she was so vulnerable at that moment with all eyes on them. He waited for his wife to calm down. She wouldn't want to have a row in full view of everyone. When he deemed it safe, he lifted young Mary from the horse. Fearing her mother's wrath, she hid behind his legs.

'Come on,' he coaxed, 'let go of me – don't be frightened. Your mother's been worried. Like me, she's just glad you're safe.'

Some folk began to move away and return to the food and drink. They thought the drama was over. William's mother had something to say though. She pushed her daughter-in-law aside.

'Thoo's spoilin' that bairn. What she needs is a good thrashin'. Bairns is born wi' devil in 'em, an' thoo must beat 'im out.'

There was a murmur of agreement around them. William sensed the general displeasure and hated to see people taking sides against him and his daughter. He used the excuse of taking her home for a wash to avoid hearing any more advice.

His wife was left at a disadvantage, being seen as an ineffectual mother in public. No doubt they'd all be saying her daughter had too much of her own way, and needed a stronger hand to raise her. She knelt down and busied herself with young William to hide her shame.

The bonfire was set alight later in the afternoon. It was a very smoky affair due partly to Ben's tarred branches, but the south-westerly breeze took the worst of the smoke out to sea. Ben gave the young Jordan boys from Uphall a tarred stick each to wave as torches, and they whooped and danced round the fire like pagans. Their mother clicked her tongue in disapproval and their father sighed, still thinking of the hay lying in rows waiting to be turned. Everyone else smiled to see the younger generation having fun. Young Mary returned to the hill, more subdued, and had to watch without complaint when her brother, and not her, was given his own torch to carry.

The day's celebrations gave the Gurwoods an excellent opportunity to become better acquainted with Robert Read's family. The vicar and his wife enjoyed their company and thought their daughter would be in good hands. As yet, no date was fixed – in fact, Robert hadn't even asked George Gurwood for his daughter's hand. George watched the couple together and was convinced that the two were well-matched.

'Just look at them,' he whispered to his wife. 'You can tell by their eyes how much they care for each other. And aren't they handsome together!'

Robert was wearing a white linen shirt and blue neckerchief. His sunburnt face accentuated the blue of his eyes. Jane looked most attractive in her best summer gown embroidered with wild roses. It was rare for them to spend a whole day together. Neither could stop smiling and everyone saw they were a beautiful couple.

When John Gurwood began to play his fiddle, Jane and Robert were the first to dance, soon joined by all of Jane's sisters. The youngest one even managed to drag out the reluctant young Francis Jordan. Matthew Smith would have loved to dance with his wife but, with her being so pregnant, he chose to stand and watch. Unable to keep still, he danced in a fashion with his one-year-old daughter instead.

Both the Jordan sisters had their eyes on Ellen's brother, John Dawson. It was unlikely that he'd ask anyone to dance. As usual, he kept close to Dickon and Tom, hoping to avoid attention. Ellen saw that Dorothy Jordan was plucking up the courage to ask him to dance. She thought of putting an obstacle in her way – maybe by getting John to dance with Jane instead. It was one way of paying Dorothy back for never making her welcome at Uphall. Ellen had a plan and walked over to her brother.

'John – thoo must join in more. Go an' 'ave a chat wi' William an' Mary. Thoo can talk about 'arvest.' She knew that he'd rather talk about crops than dance and, while he was with William, he'd be obliged to acknowledge Jane in some way.

John was only too glad of the opportunity to avoid dancing. He strode over to where William was sitting with his family.

Jane saw him approach and gulped. It was a shock to have John Dawson thrust before her without warning. She glanced across at Ellen, her eyes pleading for help. Ellen's response was a smile and a wink.

Dorothy watched from a distance, furious at losing her opportunity to get John to dance. She needn't have worried that he was paying any attention to Jane. He nodded just once in recognition, and then ignored her. All he talked about was his regret over the missed day of the hay harvest, and then discussed at length the weather prospects for the coming week.

As he left them, the wind suddenly changed direction. The tide had turned and a cold wind now came in from the sea. Those who were dancing on the western side of the bonfire were engulfed in smoke. They ran hastily to the other side, their eyes stinging and their hair and clothes reeking of bonfire. Robert Read wrapped his arms around Jane Gurwood, lifted her off her feet and rushed her out of the smoke.

When he set her down again she could hardly breathe. She'd never been so close to his body before and was rather dizzy and overcome. Good God, she thought, my mother never prepared me for this. A whole new world had opened up for her. All she wanted now was for Robert to stay close and hold her again. She couldn't wait to be married.

Robert felt the same but, after this one lapse, kept her at a respectable distance. He remembered the rules of courtship.

By evening, the fire had died down to a pile of glowing embers. It was still giving off plenty of heat, and the dancers sat around it to rest and drink. Many of the older folk had already gone home, knowing that they had to be up early for work in the morning.

Young Mary, exhausted by her day's exertions, had fallen asleep with her brothers and her cousin Ann. They lay in a warm muddle like a litter of puppies. William and Mary sat together, though not as intimately as they might have done considering the summer evening, the ale consumed and the wistful music now being played. Their daughter's latest escapade had caused another rift between them. They could not agree on how to handle her and neither of them wished to discuss it. Instead, they sat lost in their own thoughts, and stared sullenly into the ashes of the fire.

George Gurwood and his wife took their girls home and allowed Robert Read to walk Jane home on his own. With great reluctance, the young couple left the warmth of the fire where they'd been sitting eating baked potatoes. It was the best evening of their lives, and Robert thought he'd never get a better chance to find out how much Jane liked him. As they left the fire, he slipped an arm around her waist and turned her to look at him. Her hair had come loose. Her eyes were wide and soft, and her face was flushed.

'Jane,' he murmured, and then cleared his throat. 'You look beautiful. Do you think you could be my wife?'

'Oh Robert – that's all I want. I thought you'd never ask. Please, let's get married soon.'

He couldn't believe his luck. As they strolled very slowly back to the vicarage, they hoped for a wedding before Christmas.

Chapter 27

Ellen gave birth to a healthy boy on the first day of September. Like his sister, the boy had a full head of black hair and huge eyes – 'exact image of 'is mother', as Sarah Ezard announced on seeing his head appear. He was to be christened Thomas. Mary Jordan was convinced that Ellen did this on purpose; it was the second time that she'd named her child after one of her lost babies. William refused to be drawn into any discussion, and he and Mary drifted further apart. Instead of bringing them closer, the arrival of their children had driven a wedge between them. Apart from disagreements on the upbringing of their daughter, Mary had become so tired that she no longer had the energy to try and be a good wife. Their problems did not go unnoticed.

William's mother had a remedy for Mary's short temper and moodiness, and didn't hesitate to tell him. 'Get 'er wi' child again. That'll sort 'er out. Shake 'er up, it will. Sarah Ezard thinks same. Another bairn might do trick.'

The obedient son had Mary pregnant by the end of September. Strange, he thought, how often she'd conceived at harvest time; maybe they were more relaxed.

Mary was not happy to find there'd be another child the next summer. Two out of three of her summer births had resulted in early deaths. Also, she hated to be heavy with child in the hot weather when there was so much work to do. She kept all this to herself and couldn't even confide in her sister, Elizabeth, who was going through another difficult time with her husband.

Elizabeth, still without child, always put on a brave face but, faced with her brother's new son and her sister's latest news, she found this more difficult. At thirty-five years of age, she was getting desperate. To help her conceive, she'd already tried a few old methods – all without success. Now she decided to see Sarah Ezard for a different potion.

The village healer raised her eyebrows on hearing what Elizabeth had come for. 'I thought tha problem was Robert.'

'No, Sarah, I think it might be me as well.' Not wanting to discuss Robert or his lack of attention, she carried on. 'Listen, I've come for some medicine that *I* can take to help *me* – something Robert needn't know about.'

Sarah pursed her lips, inhaled noisily through her nose and then held her breath while she thought. At last, she breathed out again and began rummaging at the back of a wall-cupboard. She soon found what she was looking for.

''Aven't 'ad to use this for some time,' she said as she lifted out a wooden box and placed it on the table. 'It might still be potent though.' She opened the lid. The box was full of dried mistletoe leaves. 'I'll make thee a drink – it'd be better if leaves were a bit fresher.' She put a few leaves in a skillet and added water. 'They'll need to soak. Come back tomorrow an' tha can take a bottle 'ome, but don't start drinkin' it o' Friday whatever tha does. It won't bring any luck to start summat on a Friday.'

'If it doesn't work, have you anything else?'

'Tha can always try mugwort. I'll give thee some dried leaves – then tha can make some tea whenever tha likes. Tha can always give Robert more garlic an' onions an' make 'im drink mead.'

'No, he doesn't usually drink mead, and he might get suspicious if I suggest it.'

'Thoo won't want to tie dock seeds onto tha left arm then? Or carry an acorn, or 'azel nuts?'

'No, he's bound to ask questions.'

Sarah smiled. 'What about a dried horse's bollock under tha pillow?'

'Certainly not!'

'Well, Elizabeth, thoo's not got much choice.' Sarah shrugged her shoulders and sniffed. Elizabeth ought to have consulted her much earlier, she thought, and not left it till she was in her mid-thirties. As a last resort, Sarah added, 'Tha can try wearin' green more – green's always been good for fertility an' luck.'

Elizabeth knew that already. She nodded and thanked Sarah for her help.

As Elizabeth left, Sarah wondered if there was some way of treating Robert Storey without him noticing. With this in mind, she decided to pay a visit to old Ben.

When she arrived at his cottage he was out in the garden picking up windfall apples. She watched him for a while as he bent down painfully and rubbed his knees. She made a mental note to mix more horseradish and grease for his joints.

'Now then, Ben,' she shouted across the garden, 'does tha need any 'elp?'

He raised his hand and smiled, pleased to see her. 'Nay, I've about done for today. Young Mary'll be along soon no doubt. She can pick rest up.'

'Is tha goin' to make some mead this year?'

'Why, does tha want some?'

'Aye – tha knows I can always use it. 'Ow about if I give thee some ointment for tha joints in exchange for some mead?' She waited until he'd walked back to the cottage and put down his basket before adding, 'I wonder if tha could give Elizabeth some mead? I think it might 'elp 'er an' Robert.' She winked, knowing he'd understand.

'Aye, I'll get young Mary to 'elp me. She can take it round to their 'ouse. It'll seem more innocent like, comin' from 'er.'

Young Mary was delighted when she turned up at Ben's to find they were to make some mead. She was not so pleased when he told her their first job was to scrub their hands and the table and all the things they'd be using. Ben had the water already heated over the fire. He poured some into a bowl and carried it to the table. Then he handed her a hard chunk of soap and a brush. Her heart sank. He laughed and tried to cheer her up.

'Look, I'll 'elp. Thoo's only got little 'ands. We'll do it together an' sing while we scrub, eh?'

They scrubbed away and sang, their ill-matched, off-key voices making quite a racket. Once the table was clean and rinsed well, they scrubbed each other's hands, and Ben cleaned the dirt from under his nails with a knife. Then he winked and fetched the pail of honeycombs. Most of the honey had already been taken out though plenty was left – enough for his purpose. He filled a large tub with warm water and showed her how to crush the combs into it. They took turns to prod and stir the bits around, making sure all the honey dissolved. Then he strained it into earthenware bowls.

'That's it,' he announced. 'We'll leave it for a few weeks, or months, or years.'

Mary could not believe what she'd heard. Making mead was not as much fun as she'd thought. She sighed and stifled a yawn.

'If tha likes,' he added, 'tha could 'elp me chop up some o' them apples over yon. We can make a diff'rent drink.'

Her face brightened as she looked forward to using a knife – something she wasn't allowed to do at home. He sat her up to the table on the bench and then put a block of wood under her so that she could reach up better. They spent a happy half hour chopping the apples into tiny pieces, which they then put into yet another bowl of warm water. Ben took a jar of honey from his shelf and poured it all in, letting Mary clean out the jar afterwards with her fingers. Then there was nothing to do again but wait for the mixture to ferment.

The smoke from the fire was beginning to sting Mary's eyes. She yawned and started to fidget. Ben realised he couldn't keep her entertained any longer. Reluctantly, he lifted her off the bench. She almost ran out of the door, eager to be back in the fresh air. He shouted after her though she was already halfway down the garden.

'Don't forget to come back an' taste our mead.'

Not wanting to go home yet, young Mary ran all the way to her aunt and uncle's house, to Elizabeth and Robert. She knew that Robert might show her his Bible and teach her to read, and Aunt Lizzie was bound to give her something to eat. Today was no exception. She entered their house at top speed to find them sitting in silence at opposite ends of the kitchen table. Their faces lifted on seeing her. On asking the reason for the visit, they heard all about her morning with Ben. Mary showed off her clean hands and nails which so impressed Robert that he sat her on his knee for a closer inspection. A sweet aroma of apples and honey rose from her hair while her clothes had the more familiar odour of wood smoke.

'Would you like me to read to you?' he asked, sure of her answer.

She leapt from his lap and went to the window where he always sat to read in the daytime. His enormous family Bible lay open on a table. He joined her on the window seat and Mary gazed at the columns of print. She tried to guess which story he'd been reading.

'Is it David and Goliath?' she hazarded.

'No.'

'Is it Joseph in the pit?' He shook his head. 'Is it Jonah and the whale?'

'No, no. It's none of those. You wouldn't like this story much. It's very long and ... I'll read it to you when you're older.'

She moved her fingers along the letters. 'The man's name begins with a J, like Jonah and Joseph. I can read it. His name's Job.' She mispronounced it, but he was pleased.

'Very good, Mary. I still think we'll leave him till you're older. How about I read you the story of the men in the fiery furnace? You'll like that.'

She snuggled up close, eager for him to start. Elizabeth watched them and smiled. Robert had grown very fond of Mary. It hurt to think how different their life might be if only they had a child of their own. She took up her knitting and listened to Robert's deep voice and Mary's constant interruptions.

When the story was over, Mary ran in circles round the kitchen table. She repeated the strange names of the young Hebrews – Shadrach, Meshach and Abednego – and showed off by saying the name of the king, Nebuchadnezzar. Elizabeth gave her a slice of apple dumpling as a reward.

'Don't forget to tell your mother and father about the story,' she said. 'Then they'll know you haven't wasted your day.' She glanced at the window. 'It's getting late now – I'd better walk you home.'

They strolled hand in hand down the hill and along St Helen's Lane. As they neared the house, young Mary gripped her aunt's hand tightly and hung back.

'What's the matter?' Elizabeth asked. 'Are you all right?'

Mary could not say; she could not put into words her feelings about her family, about her mother.

Elizabeth tried to lift her spirits. 'Remember the story Robert read to you? You're going to tell them all about it.'

Mary's face was blank. She shrugged as her earlier excitement drained away, like water spilt onto sand.

In the house, everyone was preoccupied. Mary was mending clothes while keeping an eye on little William in case he wandered too near the fire. Jane was sitting with Francis, helping him with his knitting. They hardly looked up when young Mary walked in. Elizabeth sensed the unwelcome atmosphere and tried to lighten things by telling them about the Bible reading. She remembered too late her sister's thoughts on teaching a girl to read. 'It'll spoil the child and lead to trouble when she has to find a husband.' Mary had said this more than once, but Elizabeth had already pushed her niece forward.

'There were three Hebrews,' the girl began, 'Shadrach, Meshach and To Bed You Go and …' She was interrupted by the giggles coming from her mother and Jane. Her brother Francis joined in, though he had no idea what was so funny. Elizabeth was embarrassed for the girl who now stuttered and, with tears welling in her eyes, shouted, 'The, the king was Nebuchadnezzar!'

'That's right,' said Elizabeth, putting an arm around her. 'You pronounced his name perfectly. Well done.'

Young Mary almost smiled, but then all at once she scowled, shrugged off her aunt and marched straight out of the door and into the garden. The back door slammed shut behind her.

'Leave her there,' growled her mother. 'She'll come back when she's calmed down. She needs to learn some manners. You know she spends most of her time with Ben, or with Dickon and Tom. She's even started to talk like them. I've warned William about it. He's blind. He doesn't see any problem – doesn't see beyond his own daft love for the lass. He'll ruin her.'

'Would you like me to take young Mary more often to *my* house?' Elizabeth offered.

'No, don't bother.' Mary feared that she'd lost control of her daughter, and didn't want Elizabeth and Robert to succeed where she'd failed.

Elizabeth wondered if her sister was grumpy because she was with child again. 'Are you keeping well in yourself?' she asked. 'Is there nothing I can do to help?'

With callous disregard for Elizabeth's lack of children, Mary told her sister exactly how she felt.

'It's autumn. I'm with child. There'll be another mouth to feed next summer. What's new? You plant in autumn, you reap in summer. The rams tup in November. I'm just another stock animal here – only fit for breeding. They castrate the young bullocks in autumn, before the frosts come, don't they? Maybe they should do it to some men as well.'

Elizabeth was shocked. To hide her feelings, she turned her back and walked out of the door without another word. She vowed to take her niece away whenever she could. As she took the shortcut behind the house, she noticed young Mary sitting on the log by the back door. She was facing the apple tree. Though it was a chilly autumn afternoon, the air was still. The birds were singing and the girl was watching them flit through the gaps in the hedge. Elizabeth saw that the weeds had died down; they were brown and wilting. The logs were all chopped and stacked nearby. Winter was coming. She shivered at the thought of the long months ahead for the little girl, all to be spent indoors with her family. She wiped a tear from her eye and carried on up the hill.

Chapter 28

In the evening, Mary had words with William about where her daughter spent most of her time, and who with.

'It's no secret I can't get on with her,' she admitted. 'We rub each other up the wrong way. When I make her stay at home there's no end of trouble. She knocks things over, drops them or breaks them. I don't know what to do for the best.'

'She could spend more time at Uphall, not with Dickon and Tom, but with my mother and Dorothy.'

Mary was aghast. 'The two dreaded Dorothies, you mean?'

'Oh, they're not that bad.'

'I can't see her getting on with either of *them* for long.'

'We can give it a try. I can start by taking her on Sundays to visit – get her used to the place more.'

Mary agreed to this. At least her daughter would be out of her hair for a few hours each Sunday and allow her some peace and quiet.

Depending on the time of the church service, William took his daughter to Uphall either for the morning or the afternoon. He could tell his mother was smug about being given a say in the rearing of her granddaughter. She couldn't wait to use her influence. However, she'd never dealt with a child quite like young Mary before and, after each Sunday visit, she was exhausted. The girl had a boy's appetite and boundless energy.

Dorothy attempted to get the girl sewing, but she squirmed and fidgeted and the once white linen soon turned grubby in her sweaty hands. Then Dorothy tried knitting, but the girl stared about her too much and kept dropping stitches. Young Mary was always more interested in what the men were doing to ever pay full attention to her grandmother. Thinking the girl would enjoy more robust activities, Dorothy asked William to bring her to Uphall when they were ready to cure the meat for winter.

Young Mary was excited to be let into the curing chamber to help her grandmother and Aunt Dorothy but, on entering the room, she was chilled to the bone. Neither women minded the cold and had rolled up their sleeves ready for work. They washed their hands in a pail and made Mary do the same. Her grandfather and Dickon had already carried in the butchered meat and hoisted it up onto the hooks. They'd also filled the two troughs with salt. Her grandmother counted out spoonfuls of large sugar crystals and mixed them in with the salt.

'That's to give a better flavour,' she explained. 'Look – I'll add some peppercorns as well.'

The women lowered a leg into the trough. Mary patted it with her hand; it was clammy, clean and lifeless, so unlike the hog she'd seen rooting among the straw.

'Come on,' urged her grandmother, 'don't just stroke it an' gawp.' Mary saw them grab handfuls of the salty mixture, sprinkle it over the pork and then rub it in.

'Get tha fingers in an' rub 'ard, like this. Fetch yon stool so tha can reach.'

She got the stool to stand on and joined them at the trough. She watched how they used their fingers to probe inside the meat, and how they used the heel of their hands and all their weight to press the mixture well in. After delving her hands into the cold crystals, she began to rub the salt in as best she could. When they'd finished, the women stood the leg on edge and banged it to shake off the loose salt. Then they laid it on the wooden draining board and lowered the other leg.

Young Mary's fingers began to ache and some salt had found its way into a cut on her wrist. Pleased to be useful and doing a proper job, she bit her lip and carried on. Soon they were all washing their hands and admiring the glistening white hams laid out on the board.

'We'll leave 'em to drain for a week,' Dorothy announced. 'I'll come each day an' turn 'em over an' rub more salt in. Then we'll rinse 'em an' leave 'em to dry, an' then we can 'ang 'em up to smoke. If tha wants, tha can come back later an' 'elp salt loins an' bellies.'

Mary nodded. She thanked her grandmother politely and skipped all the way home. She was happy because her father would want to hear about the work she'd done. As soon as she sat at the table next to him, she began to chatter.

Her mother frowned. 'Be quiet for once. We haven't said grace yet.'

As soon as that was done, young Mary began talking again, hardly stopping to chew before swallowing. Francis ignored her and fed his young brother with bread dipped in gravy while the adults ate in silence and waited for the girl to finish.

William spoke at last. 'I hear George Gurwood is against his daughter getting married this winter. He wants a spring wedding so everyone can enjoy being outdoors. Robert Read won't like it. He was all set for Christmas – so was Jane, I imagine. I do think it's always best to wed in winter. We've all got more time on our hands then.'

Mary sighed. 'Well, George is both vicar and father so it's up to him. I hope he knows what's best.'

Young Mary also sighed. She didn't see what was so interesting about a wedding. Having seen her mother and all the other wives worked off their feet, she decided she'd never marry.

When the time for the November hirings came round, John Dawson accompanied the Uphall lads to Hunmanby. Though he had no intention of leaving Reighton himself, he wanted to meet up with old friends and have a drink or two. He found them lounging in the market place and they hailed each other like long-lost brothers.

'Now then, John,' they shouted. 'Where is thoo workin', eh? Is tha farm a good un?'

Josh grabbed him in an arm lock. 'Is thoo i' charge o' ploughin' yet? Is thoo still a virgin?'

John refused to answer though he felt his face colouring up. They teased him some more and wrestled him to the ground. There were too many of them and he gave in. Josh yawned, tired of the game, and brushed the dirt off his jacket.

'Come on,' he shouted, 'let's get in yon ale'ouse. I'm thirsty.'

John was plied with far too many tankards of ale. He soon became light-headed, happy and carefree, even talkative. His friends laughed to see the change in him. Usually, John never spoke unless it was about oxen and ploughing.

Josh had an idea. He winked at the others. 'I saw me cousin i' market square earlier,' he said. 'She lost 'er 'usband last year. I bet she'll be ready for tuppin'. I tell you what, John, I'll buy 'er a few drinks an' then she'll be keen enough.' He gave John a hefty nudge and, before John knew what was happening, they'd planned a way for him to meet this young widow.

'She's perfect for thee,' Josh added with a grin. 'She's a bit older – thoo'll be glad of 'er experience.'

An hour later John found himself bustled outside. He was glad to get away from the noise and the fog of pipe smoke, but didn't know where they were pushing him. They aimed him towards an outhouse at the back. Once shoved inside the tarred, wooden shed, they closed the door and leant against it to stop his escape.

At first, he saw nothing. There was only a small window and it was covered up. As his eyes grew used to the dark, he saw sacks of potatoes and strings of onions hanging up. He thought it must be the storehouse of the nearby inn. All at once, he heard movement behind him, and a small pair of hands came over his eyes. A soft, yielding body pressed against his back.

'No need to be shy,' a woman's voice murmured. 'Turn round an' I'll give thee a kiss.'

He turned to see a woman in a white bonnet and a light-coloured shawl about her shoulders. She took each of his hands and placed them on her hips. Then she reached up on tiptoe to kiss him.

He'd never been this close to a woman before. Her soft, wet lips set his heart beating so fast he thought he'd faint. As he gasped for breath, she whispered something in his ear and stuck her tongue inside. She undid his belt and put a hand down his breeches. He was on fire. Before he knew it, she had him on top of her. She guided him in with one hand while her other hand clutched the curls at the back of his head.

It was all over so quickly. She was soon up and straightening her petticoat while he was left to see to his breeches. It was only then that he got a good look at her face. Her nose was the most prominent feature, large and yet not unattractive, and the hair beneath her bonnet was fair. He never did know her name. She rushed out of the shed before he could ask her.

He rejoined his friends in the alehouse and the memory of the encounter in the shed faded as more ale was drunk. Later in the afternoon, he stumbled back to Reighton and forgot about her.

As the days grew shorter and colder, young Mary was forced to spend more time indoors at home. She fretted, however, if she went for more than a few days without seeing Ben or Dickon. In the end, William decided to invite Dickon to his home once a week. Dickon could eat with them and stay and amuse the children. He'd enjoy being part of the family, and his daughter would have a captive audience.

William and Mary had not seen much of Dickon lately and, when he entered the kitchen, they were shocked to see how much he'd aged. When he spooned in his food, they saw young Mary rest her hand on his until the trembling stopped. Then she let go and carried on eating as if everything was normal.

William noticed how Dickon's nails had grown thick and horny; they were dirty and he obviously never cut them. He thought that if Dickon had an itch and scratched himself with those nails, he'd likely get an infection. His bristly beard irritated him and, where he'd scratched, there were dry red patches. Whenever young Mary caught him having a sly scratch, she grabbed his hand and told him off like a naughty child. He pretended to obey and then, also like a child, as soon as she wasn't looking, he'd have another go.

One day after their dinner, Dickon got a basket and took Mary and her brother for a walk – to go 'sticking'. She loved any excuse to be outside and knew where all the ash trees grew. Ben had already taught her which wood was best for fires. She showed off her knowledge of trees, imitating the way Ben spoke.

'Birch'll burn fast an' so will 'olly an' 'awthorn, but ash'll give out most warmth. Ash'll even burn when green.'

Her brother rolled his eyes. His sister thought she knew everything. She annoyed him further by being the quickest to spot the thin, bendy ash twigs that lay half-hidden under the wet leaves.

'Look, Francis,' she cried, waving a stick in his face, 'this looks just like a chicken's foot.'

He backed away disconcerted and busied himself with Dickon. They snapped the twigs across their thighs into smaller lengths for kindling, and dropped them into the basket. Francis was relieved when the basket was full and they could go back home. He was sick of hearing his sister and wanted to be back in the kitchen where it was warm.

Hard as they tried, Jane and Mary could not amuse or keep young Mary occupied for long. Mary often looked tired and Jane knew the children were too much for her.

'Perhaps I could take all three children to Uphall on Sundays,' she suggested to William. 'Mary would benefit from some time without the children.'

William saw the sense in this. His wife did need more rest now that she was pregnant again. So he agreed, unaware that Jane had an ulterior motive.

Jane hardly saw Ellen anymore; staring at the back of her head in church once a week didn't count. She knew that Ellen always visited her brother at Uphall on Sundays. Now she had the perfect excuse to be there. To see John Dawson too was an added incentive.

Each Sunday, as Christmas approached, Jane took the children and spent a few hours at Uphall. Young Mary pranced around as if she owned the place. Her brothers followed in her wake, and Francis was shy when his sister introduced him to the various farmhands. As soon as Ellen arrived with her daughter and new baby, the two toddlers, Ann and William, sat down together to play. Francis and his sister were left safely with the Jordan boys, and Jane and Ellen had time to sit down and chat. They were not alone though. Jane's mother never left the room, and neither did her sister Dorothy who didn't trust her younger sister one bit.

Jane and Ellen made themselves comfortable on the settle, their feet stretched towards the great fire. Jane couldn't help noticing how matronly Ellen was becoming, how different she was from the girl she'd been besotted with. Yet there'd always be some moment when Ellen moved in a certain way or gave Jane an intimate look, and then Jane's stomach would lurch, and her heart thud as if nothing had changed between them.

Jane wondered if she'd ever be free of Ellen's hold on her. She tried to transfer her affections onto Ellen's brother, John, partly to spite Dorothy who blushed whenever he was near. Jane watched how he strode across the room and noted how broad his shoulders had become. His eyes were the same bright, penetrating blue as his sister's, and he arched his eyebrows at times just like Ellen. Jane asked herself over and over again whether she could love him as a woman should feel for a man, but she always baulked at the dark, curly hair sprouting from the top of his shirt. He would be rough and hard while Ellen was so smooth and soft. She sighed.

Dorothy watched her from across the kitchen. She thought her sister's longing gaze was for John. From that moment, she concentrated all her efforts each Sunday on making sure that John and Jane were never left alone together.

Chapter 29

Young Mary and Francis looked forward to Sundays. He enjoyed the quiet routine of walking up the hill to church, seeing the same faces in the same pews, wearing the same Sunday best clothes and seeing the same view of Filey as they left for Uphall. It always took him a few weeks to settle whenever the seasons changed; if he had his way, nothing would ever alter. His sister, on the other hand, relished the unpredictable. She found Uphall perfect with its larger rooms and numerous family members and farmhands. The meal times were the best. As soon as she entered the kitchen her nose was filled with the smell of meat cooking over the fire. The gravies at Uphall were so much richer than at home, and her eyes grew wide at the enormous pies and stews set out on the long table.

There were always more than a dozen to feed at any time. The men in the family served themselves first, in descending order, and the women took what was left. Young Mary found there was always still plenty left for her. She chose to sit near the Jordan boys. They talked of ploughing and the fun they'd had at the hiring fair. They chatted as they gobbled up their food. They belched and farted, unlike the women. Mary eyed her brother sitting quietly beside Jane. She thought, not for the first time, that he wasn't like the other boys.

One day, before Christmas, young Mary sneaked off to Ben's thinking that the mead would be ready. She was disappointed to learn that the new mead might not be fit to drink until next year or even later.

'Don't worry,' said Ben. 'I've some for thee to taste from other years.' He lifted down a dusty bottle and uncorked it. 'I can only give thee a tiny sip, mind. It's a bit strong for young lasses.' He took a small mug and poured out a little

163

of his best vintage, a pale, golden liquid that smelled like old cider. He took a deep breath to inhale the aroma before tasting it.

'Mmm, it smells right enough. It should taste smooth an' mellow.' He took a mouthful and swirled it round his tongue. 'Aye, it's perfect.'

When Mary tried a sip, she screwed up her nose. She couldn't believe how he could ever think it was perfect.

'If tha didn't like this,' he laughed, 'thoo'll not be wantin' to taste anymore.'

'No – I do, I do,' she cried, jumping up and down and pulling on his sleeve.

'Alright then, I've two more we can try.'

One of them was so bitter and acidic that she gagged and was desperate to wash out her mouth. Even then, her teeth felt so on edge that she couldn't stop gnashing them. Finally, they tasted the mead they'd made together in October. It was not so bad.

'It's a bit rough still,' Ben pronounced after a few sips. 'It 'as an unpleasant aftertaste, but it's gettin' there.' He decided to send Mary to her Uncle Robert with a bottle of his very best.

'Thoo must walk all way,' he warned, 'an' I mean walk! Look 'ere – I'll put it i' this basket, then tha can carry it better.' To be on the safe side, he packed the bottle with an old shirt. 'Tell 'im it's a present for Yuletide, a present from our bees, a most natural an' 'ealth-givin' drink.'

The mead did reach its destination in one piece and Robert accepted the gift. Elizabeth pretended to be surprised by the present and was very thankful to Ben and Sarah Ezard. Perhaps she might be with child one day soon; it was the right time of year – long, dark nights with the need to cuddle up in bed and keep warm. She could always hope.

Robert was not one to change his habits. He continued his 'no meat' fasting throughout Advent and shunned all intoxicating drink. Elizabeth knew that, by the time he did begin to eat and drink properly again, she'd have started her monthly bleeding. Another chance for a child would be wasted.

Elizabeth's sister, Mary, was still unhappy in her pregnancy. She thought she'd grown out of the sickness of the first few months and yet, one morning towards the middle of December, the nausea returned. Jane usually milked their cow but she was laid up with a bad cough. William had already left for Uphall so the milking was left to Mary. She got up while it was still dark though she'd have preferred to stay snuggled up in bed. She was wearing all her clothes from the day before as it had been too cold to even think of undressing. After draping two thick shawls over her shoulders, she also wrapped a woollen cloth about her head to cover her ears.

Tired and queasy with an empty stomach, Mary prepared the lantern and took a clean pail from the milkhouse. She shuffled to the tiny cow shed next to the kitchen and pulled open the door. She hit a wall of stench – the hot reek of pittled straw. It made her retch over and over again. She leant her head weakly against the door, breathing in the icy December air. The cold revived her enough to have a second go at entering the shed.

She grabbed a handful of hay to feed the cow and didn't like the look in its eyes; the cow was used to Jane's voice and hands and it kept backing away. She decided to hobble its hind legs before even trying to milk it.

The cow did not object too much and, once Mary sat on the stool and rested her cheek against the cow's warm belly, she felt a little better. She hummed a Christmas carol and began to pull and squeeze the udders, almost falling asleep with the rhythm. The cow seemed content and turned its head to watch her as the milk squirted into the pail. She got more than a few pints that morning and, seeing as it was her daughter's birthday, decided to use the cream, as well as the milk, for the morning's porridge.

Young Mary had not forgotten that she was now four years old. She leapt out of bed despite the cold weather, raking the covers off Francis as she went. They went into the kitchen to find their mother making breakfast.

'There's cream in it today,' she announced. 'Happy birthday, Mary.'

How Francis hated his sister at times. Fancy having cream in the porridge just because it was your birthday! No fuss was ever made on his birthdays; it was a coincidence there'd been a bonfire and a feast when he was six. He guessed his mother wouldn't spoil his sister much, but his father ... yes, he'd probably want to treat her.

In secret, William, Dickon and Ben had spent time carving things out of wood for young Mary – a small bowl, and a spoon and cup. On each item was carved an M. William had not told his wife.

He presented them to his daughter at dinner time. Everyone round the table went silent. Not since William had given his future wife a carved knitting sheath had he given such a thoughtful gift.

'I carved that bowl from hazel,' he said, 'and Dickon and Ben carved those from applewood.' The girl's eyes sparkled. She held the bowl in both hands, feeling the smooth wood, and then sniffed the cup to see if it smelled of apples.

Her brother glowered as he watched her trace the M with her finger; his father had always favoured Mary. He glanced sideways at his mother. She was frowning.

'Put the things over there,' she said. 'They're too good to be using every day.'

Young Mary looked up at her father. She pulled the bowl closer.

'It's all right,' he whispered. 'You can use them on Sundays and special days – like today.'

In bed that night, Mary turned her back on William. He lay still for a while. He couldn't understand why she resented their daughter's presents so much. Angry that she'd taken away some of the pleasure in giving them, he reproached her.

'What harm can a few wooden things do?' he demanded.

'If you don't know ...,' Mary chuntered.

166

'There's nothing wrong with the gifts. Young Mary *is* my only daughter and if I want to treat her, then I will.'

They kept their backs turned on each other in spite of the cold night. Christmas was coming and both wondered how they'd get through it without further disagreements.

The week before Christmas, William and John made a trip to Bridlington to buy presents and various extra spices and dried fruits. They returned with a surprise gift. Hoping to find something special for his daughter, William saw a man with a basket on his arm. On inspection, William found four puppies inside. They were mostly black and, despite what the man said, they were not of any particular breed. They were smooth-haired and had small paws, so William guessed they'd never be large dogs. The man insisted they were ready to leave their mother. William doubted this very much as the puppies mewed with their eyes closed like kittens, and huddled together for warmth and comfort.

John knew what William was thinking and didn't want any part of it. A puppy in the house would cause trouble.

'What do you want the dog for?' he asked. 'It's got to have some use.'

William hadn't reckoned on any purpose other than pleasing his daughter. He shrugged.

'Well,' John added, 'I bet Mary won't be happy with having another mouth to feed, and it'll get under her feet.'

William ignored him and picked up one of the puppies by the scruff of its neck. He turned it over to determine its sex and decided that, if there was a bitch to his liking, he'd buy it. Of the two bitches he found, he went against John's better judgement and chose the smallest one.

'You've forgotten the old saying about buying a horse,' he prompted. 'One white foot, buy him. Two white feet, try him. Three white feet deny him. Four white feet – throw him to the crows.' He thought it might apply to dogs too.

The puppy he chose had also a white chest, and the white on her paw extended half-way up her leg so that it looked as if she wore a bandage. She was perfect for young Mary.

He paid the man half a shilling and tucked the puppy inside his coat so that just her nose poked out. She cried constantly for her companions.

'What are you going to do with it once we get home?' John asked as they set off back to Reighton.

'I don't know. I can't leave it at Uphall – the other dogs might get it. Perhaps old Ben could take it in – keep it till Christmas Eve. He's soft on all kinds of animals.'

When they arrived back home, William left John to give out the various food packages while he went straight to Ben's cottage. Ben was in the kitchen and had a good fire going. William stood in front of him, grinning broadly and wondering when Ben would notice the strange little bulge at the top of his coat. It was a while before Ben realised there was a dog's nose sticking out.

'It's for young Mary,' William explained. 'I want it kept secret until Christmas Eve. Can you look after it?'

Ben didn't hesitate. He was only too pleased to have some company but, on holding the dog in his hands, he was afraid it might not live that long.

'Why, poor thing should be with its mother. See? It's nudgin' for a teat. It's not weaned yet. I'll 'ave to feed it milk an' keep it warm.' He shook his head. 'I'll do me best.'

'I know you will. I'm trusting you, Ben. Remember, don't tell a soul about it.'

Chapter 30

Ben spent the whole week caring for the puppy. He let her share his bed for warmth and fed her every few hours. He hadn't been so happy since he'd trained the mule, and grew sad as Christmas Eve approached. There was no fear that young Mary would come and find out – there was so much preparation going on in her house for Christmas.

Young Mary went out with Jane and Francis to fetch holly, ivy and mistletoe to decorate the rooms, and she helped Jane and her mother make Yule cakes. Using the currants and lemons brought from Bridlington, her mother made enough mixture for the family to have a small cake each on Christmas Eve. There was also the Hackin Pudding to make for Christmas morning. For once, young Mary was allowed to help measure out the suet, and mix it with the dried fruit and brandy. Her mother, in a good mood, even passed her the nutmeg and cinnamon to spice it up. Young Mary was then told to knead the mixture but, when her hands got too sticky, her mother complained and took over. The pudding was made into a ball and put in a sheep's stomach to boil.

'It's going to take six hours to cook,' Mary explained, 'so I want you and Francis to keep the fire fed with sticks.' The job kept the children busy.

On Christmas Eve, William and John lifted in the chosen Yule log and let young Mary sit on top.

'It's seasoned ash,' William explained as it was set down in front of the fire. 'It should keep burning for a day or two. Come on Francis, fetch young William. You can all take turns to sit on it now and make your three wishes.' He pointed a finger at them. 'Don't forget to keep them a secret, or they won't come true.'

When they'd all finished, Jane brought in the remnants of last year's log, kept safe all year for good luck. William got the old piece of log alight first and then he and John put the Yule log on top to catch fire.

Satisfied that all the Christmas rites were being carried out and in the correct order, Mary's next job was to make the frumenty drink. William had already fetched the wheat ears from Uphall the day before and had soaked them in water. Mary put the mush into a bag.

'Come on,' she shouted to the children, 'you can all take turns to bash it on the floor and knock the husks off.'

Young Mary was determined to bash harder than Francis. As she raised the bag way above her head, her mother gasped and thrust out an arm.

'Stop! You'll break the bag, and then we'll have a mess. Go more gently, like Francis.'

The girl's face reddened and she glowered at her brother. She saw him smirk as she brought the bag down with a half-hearted wallop.

When they'd all had a turn, Mary emptied the bag into a large bowl of water. The children were invited to gather round and pick out the floating husks as fast as they could. That was more fun. Competitive as ever, young Mary flicked her fingers in and out faster than her brothers could. What remained was put in a pan by the fire.

'That's it for now,' said Mary. 'The grains have to soften for a few hours.'

The children jiggled about, not knowing what to do with themselves while they waited. No one wanted to knit. William did his best to make the time pass. He tried bouncing them on his knee, recited nursery rhymes and even sang carols.

At long last, they heard the church bells ringing, and Mary poured milk into the pan of wheat. She brought it to the boil and added sugar and nutmeg. The instant the frumenty drink was ready, Jane brought out their individual Yule cakes and they gathered round the kitchen table. This was the real start of Christmas.

While Mary poured out the drinks, William picked up his youngest son and helped him light a special candle from the Yule log. He put it in the holder and placed it carefully in the middle of the table. Then he glared at his children and warned them.

'You can sit up at the table now, but listen, all of you – none of you must touch the Yule candle. If it goes out, even by accident, there'll be bad luck for all of us.'

Young Mary and Francis stared in awe at the small flickering flame and hardly dare breathe as they nibbled their cakes. As soon as they'd finished and drunk the frumenty, it was time for the gifts. The children waited while their parents exchanged presents.

Mary went into the parlour and returned with a waistcoat for William that she'd embroidered herself. He gave her a package containing a lace cap and a piece of cobweb lawn.

'It's the finest, the most transparent linen I could find. I got it at Bridlington.'

They thanked each other formally and then Mary brought out a gift for Jane – a red cape with a hood that she'd made in secret. It suited the young girl well and she blushed at the generosity shown; in return, she could only give her brother some tobacco, and Mary a new, blue earthenware bowl to replace the one she and young Mary had dropped that summer.

The children leapt from the table and rushed forward to receive their presents. Francis, being the eldest, was first.

'Close your eyes, Francis,' William ordered, 'and hold out your hands.'

The boy felt a knife of some kind being placed on his palms. On opening his eyes, he saw a brand new blade with a hart's horn handle. He was so pleased he stammered his thanks.

Young Mary stepped forward, her eyes glistening in anticipation, only to be told, with a wink, to wait till last. William had not told his wife about the puppy, intending to keep her in the dark until it was too late. He could tell she was anxious and wondering what on earth he might have bought. He ignored her suspicious gaze and knelt down to give his young son a tiny pair of boots. The boy took them and put them down again. He was tired and rubbed his eyes, more interested in the crumbs on his chest left from the Yule cake. Young Mary again pushed forward eager for her present.

'Put your cloak on and your boots,' said William. 'We're off to see Ben. Your present is there, waiting for you.'

His wife rolled her eyes and sighed. 'I suppose I'll stay here with Jane and the boys then. At least we'll be warm. Go on then – off you go. But make sure you wrap her up well.'

Young Mary fumbled in her excitement to get her boots on, and William had to hold her back until she was properly dressed. Soon they were standing alone in St Helen's Lane in the pitch dark. The thin crescent moon did nothing to light their way, so William went back for a lantern.

Young Mary waited on the frozen road and shivered with anticipation. As soon as he returned, she held his free hand and they set off, their breath steaming into the night air. It was cold enough for snow and, as they trod eastwards, the icy air made their cheeks raw. In the distance, they saw a dim light hovering in Ben's garden. The light stayed in one place for a while and then moved on. William was intrigued and shouted out as they approached.

'Hoy there! Ben! Is it you?'

Ben stopped immediately and held up his lantern to see who was coming. He called out to explain.

'I'm waitin' till midnight wi' me bees. We must welcome in Kesmas Day together.' As William and his daughter came closer, Ben dropped his voice. 'Thoo never knows – I might even 'ear 'em 'ummin' a carol.'

Young Mary's eyes widened. 'I've come for my Christmas gift, Ben,' she whispered. 'Father says it's here, waiting for me.'

'That's right,' Ben replied, trying to hide a huge grin. 'Come wi' me an' see summat thoo'd never guess at.'

William and Ben each took one of the girl's hands and they half swung, half walked her through the frosty grass to the cottage. Once inside, Mary was disappointed. It was dim and smoky and, as she looked round, she couldn't see anything like a gift. William noticed a basket by the fire with a rough blanket draped over it. He glanced at Ben and raised his eyebrows. When Ben nodded, William went to stand by the fire and warm his hands. He beckoned to his daughter to do the same.

'Mary,' he said with as much innocence as he could muster, 'I wonder if there might be a little something for you in this basket.' He poked it with his toe. She walked up to it but did not dare look inside. 'Go on,' William urged. 'Take a peep.' Then he whispered, 'Be careful though. It might bite.' Intrigued, she bent down for a closer look.

'Go on, lass,' encouraged Ben. 'Tha father's teasin'. There's nothin' to be scared of.'

She lifted a corner of the blanket and saw the puppy's black nose, its eyelashes and floppy ears. It was fast asleep and twitched as if dreaming. She couldn't believe that it could be hers.

'Lift 'er out then,' said Ben. 'She'll be wantin' feedin' again soon. Look, I've some milk warmin' over yon.'

Very gingerly, Mary slid her hands underneath the sleeping puppy and lifted her out. She held her close and kissed the head; it smelled of yeast and biscuits. Then all of a sudden the puppy woke up and yawned. When Mary saw the little tongue and black lips, she fell in love. The puppy, in return, gazed at her with bluish eyes, licked her chin and tried to take hold of it.

''Ere,' said Ben. 'Take this 'orn. I've filled it wi' milk an' it 'as a teat on end. See if she'll drink. Sit down 'ere o' this stool by fire an' get comfy.'

She settled herself down with the puppy cradled in her lap and smiled at her father. Her eyes shone in the firelight. William wiped away a tear. He'd never seen his daughter so happy.

Chapter 31

Young Mary woke up first on Christmas morning. She'd taken the flea-ridden puppy to bed with her, much against Francis's wishes and her mother's advice. She persuaded Jane to lift the cover off the fire, poke it into life and warm up some milk. As the puppy was being fed, the rest of the family got up for breakfast. The Hackin pudding had cooled enough for Mary to cut into the sheepskin stomach and dish it onto the plate. The aroma of Christmas drifted out – a mixture of raisins, nutmeg and brandy. No matter what uncharitable feelings had been shared last night over the puppy, there were smiles all round as everyone tucked into their pudding.

Before they left for church, William gave the cow and chickens a double feed so he wouldn't have to do it again later. He'd made sure that extra threshing had been done at Uphall the previous week so they could all have time off work, and he looked forward to spending the entire day with his family. As he put a small sheaf of corn on the roof for the birds, he heard the gun being fired at Uphall.

William walked back into the kitchen and saw that his youngest son was about to cry.

'That's only your grandfather,' he explained, 'he's shooting in the Christmas.' He lifted the boy up and comforted him. 'Everything's all right. It's Christmas Day and we're going to church, and then we're going to Uphall for the *whole* day. Won't that be good!' He kissed the boy's head and put him down. It was then that he noticed his wife standing with her hands on her hips. She and Jane were staring at young Mary sitting with the puppy.

'She won't leave it,' Mary complained. 'We're not taking it to church.'

'But the puppy's still very young,' ventured William. 'We can take her in the basket. She'll sleep – there'll be no problem.'

'Well, you make sure she doesn't play with it!'

In church, the basket with the puppy was placed between William and his daughter. Mary leant forward and warned the girl not to touch it, but young Mary was distracted by the decorations. She thought she'd entered a fairy forest. Cobwebs had been swept away and greenery was everywhere. The candlelight made the holly leaves glisten, and there were starry-leaved yew branches dangling from the pillars. Dark green garlands hung wherever possible and the rush floor was strewn with lavender and rosemary.

She hardly noticed the service at all and craned her neck to see all the different hangings. Then she bent down to the floor and picked up bits of herbs to rub them between her fingers. Bored after a few minutes of smelling them, she sneaked one hand into the basket and stroked the puppy. The dog woke up and began to squirm. Young Mary couldn't wait to show people what she'd got for Christmas. When her Uncle Robert stood to read one of the lessons, she tried to get his attention.

Her mother was horrified to see the girl hold the puppy up in her hands. 'Stop her,' she hissed at William. 'She's waving it about. Everyone will see.'

Robert was far too engrossed to notice. He was in a private, solemn world of his own. For him, Christmas Day was the culmination of days of fasting and self-examination. If he had his way, he wouldn't even celebrate Christmas in December since the Bible didn't give it a date.

When young Mary's parents took Holy Communion with the others, she became bored again. It was freezing cold in the church and, despite the novel beauty of the place, she was glad when they could leave and go to Uphall for dinner.

The family was welcomed in with a lot of fuss, particularly from the younger Jordan boys who were excited to have other children's company. The youngest boy, Richard, could not leave the puppy alone. He sat beside the basket and took turns to hold her.

'What are you going to call her?' he asked.

'Don't know.'

'You should give her a Christmassy name.' She didn't know what he meant. 'Call her Holly or Ivy.'

'No – I don't like those names.'

'Well, how about Christie?' She thought about it and whispered the name into the puppy's ear. It wasn't quite right.

'I like Christina better,' she said. The name proved to be too long and, within hours, the dog was called by an abbreviated version – 'Stina'. They only called her by the full name if she pissed on them.

All morning, Francis kept away from the puppy. Though resentful of his sister's gift, he was happy enough showing off the new knife to his uncles. As noon approached though, he grew shier; the farmhands were getting noisy and were shoving each other about. He heard his grandmother say she'd serve up ale so long as the Yule log stayed alight. He glanced at the fire. The log was massive.

By the time the plum porridge was served up as the first course, Francis could see that everyone was more than merry. It was going to be a long day. Before he could even eat, his father made him join in and sing 'I Saw Three Ships.' When the lads kept time by banging their spoons on the table, he put his hands over his ears.

Young Mary enjoyed the singing, but the porridge was too rich for her taste; she pushed the currants and raisins around in her bowl, and didn't fancy the ragged pieces of beef either. She was glad to be sitting away from the main table with the other children. There she could watch what was going on and still fondle the puppy.

When all the bowls were empty, a huge, roasted goose was carried in. Everyone cheered and more ale was poured out. Toasts were drunk to Uphall and the fields, to the cattle and the sheep. They drank toasts to the fruit trees, to the chickens, to the geese – to anything they could think of.

They ate until they were stuffed and could hardly move, yet still found the energy to sing all the carols they knew. Young Mary and the other children joined in the choruses.

In the afternoon, the farmhands persuaded Tom to dress up in green and act the fool as Father Christmas. Normally, he would have refused, but he'd drunk so much ale that he didn't care. They danced round him and pushed and pulled him while he tried to catch the women. When everyone began to fall over, Dorothy called a halt and suggested they all rest for a while. Tom, still in his ridiculous outfit, slumped into a corner and gazed around with bleary eyes. The others calmed down and, within a minute, it became very quiet and peaceful.

Young Mary lay drowsing by the fire with her head on the puppy's basket, half-listening to the murmured conversations. She got the impression that her grandmother did not approve of what went on.

'When we was young,' she heard her grandmother muttering, 'our fathers was strict. We spent a sober Christmas Day. I bet Robert Storey will be doin' it proper. 'E'll be at 'ome readin' 'is Bible like as not.'

Young Mary sighed and raised her head. Her grandmother was always cross about something, just like her mother. She watched her grandmother get up stiffly and put some apples by the fire to roast.

While they waited for the apples to be cooked, Dickon offered to tell a ghost story. Despite hearing it often before, everyone gathered near the fire to listen. The flames flickered on the walls and the rushlights sputtered in the draught. Young Mary held tightly onto the puppy, her eyes pricking with fear before the story had even started. Her cousin, Richard, though ten years old, moved closer for comfort.

Some of the farmhands grew bold and snuggled up next to the maids. Jane noticed her sister, Dorothy, edge up to John Dawson. Annoyed, she sat next to Tom, who she knew would be no trouble and certainly looked in need of propping up. Young Francis sat as close to his mother as possible.

Dickon peered round at the eager audience, scratched the stubble on his chin and began. 'Long, long ago, i' time o' good Queen Bess, there were a young lass sittin' one night in 'er cottage. It were Kesmas time an' all 'ad gone out wassailin'. She were left alone – just firelight for company.' He stretched his hands out to warm them at the fire, and shifted on the settle to be more comfortable.

'An' then she 'eard a strange, unearthly 'owlin' noise.' He imitated the sound, and young Mary flinched.

'Aye, it were a sound to freeze blood i' tha veins. Lass didn't know what to do when, all at once ...' He rapped his knuckles on the settle and made them all jump.

'There were a knock on door. Should she go an' see? 'Er parents 'ad warned 'er never to open it to anyone.' Dickon paused. He peered round at their faces.

'Then there were a kind o' scratchin' noise outside, an' a whimperin'. Poor lass thought it might be a dog i' pain – wounded or summat. She put 'er ear against door an' listened.' He put one hand to his ear.

'All she 'eard were a deep breathin' – it might 'ave been wind 'owlin' i' trees. It were a cold, dark night an' she pitied any animal out there. Forgettin' what 'er parents 'ad said ... she opened door. In rushed largest wolf thoo ever clapped eyes on.'

Young Mary held her breath.

'Aye ... an' it lay down beside 'er an' rested its great, soft 'ead against 'er. She fondled its ears an' felt sorry for it – an' then she noticed its eyes.' Dickon stared at them, opening his own eyes very wide.

'They wasn't a wolf's eyes. They was same eyes as 'er bewitched lost lover. Before she could speak, wolf leaps up an' gives 'er a great bite on 'er arm. She fell in a faint an', as she lay there, still as death, wolf licked a drop o' blood that were oozin' from 'er arm. At that very moment, she began to change. 'Er body swelled up an' turned grey. Then bristly 'air grew all over. 'Er 'ands an' feet changed into great big pads, an' last of all, 'er mouth grew great sharp fangs. Only

178

'er eyes remained same. She sprang up an' looked at wolf an' knew 'im at last.'

He bent down to pick up his beer and take a sip. 'When 'er parents returned 'ome, their cottage were empty. All they saw were 'er bloodstained gown an' marks o' scratches all way down door. They was grief-stricken. Next mornin' a party set out to track an' kill wolf that 'ad taken an' maybe eaten their daughter. It weren't long before they found a pair o' tracks i' snow, an' followed 'em onto moors. Soon they spotted a couple o' wolves. Lass's father took aim an' ... shot one of 'em dead. The other wolf ran off wi' such a piteous cry. They thought they'd killed wolf that 'ad eaten their daughter ... but they'd shot 'er instead.' He gazed into the fire.

'From that day, they saw a lone wolf's tracks on fields an' moors around their farm. They 'eard a whimperin' an' 'owlin' as ghost o' poor lass tried to return 'ome. Ev'ry Kesmas they'd 'ear a scratchin' noise outside, an' 'owlin' sounds, but they never dared to open door. Even now, if thoo 'ears such sounds, tha must turn away an' ignore 'em, or *thoo* might be taken off by wolf.'

Suddenly, one of the farm lads cupped his hands and made a howling noise. Everyone laughed except young Mary. Instead, she stared deep into the eyes of the puppy and wondered.

Chapter 32

1713-14

On New Year's Eve, the family returned to Uphall and met up with everyone in the kitchen. Dorothy put the wassail bowl on the table, and William and Mary gathered their children round. William pointed to the bowl.

'That's been in our family for a long time,' he explained. It was made of wood and his mother had been busy decorating it with green and red ribbons. He lifted young Mary up so she could see.

'Look in there,' he said. 'See the lambs' wool?' She gazed into the bowl. There was a liquid inside. It looked frothy and soft, but it wasn't wool.

'Careful – it's 'ot,' warned her grandmother. 'Thoo might not like it – it's ale wi' ginger an' nutmeg an' cloves.' All the children wrinkled their noses. 'I've whisked in egg yolks,' she added. 'An' I baked some apples an' made 'em into a pulp wi' brown sugar. They've just been put in.' Young Mary could see there were tiny pieces of roasted crab apples floating on the top. Her grandmother waved a hand towards the fire.

''We've some bread toastin' over yon. Thoo can all dip it in.'

The bowl was passed round and everyone sang the wassail as they awaited their turn. Once they'd finished, the young Jordans and the farmhands put on their coats and grabbed sprigs of holly hanging by the door. Young Mary pulled on her father's sleeve. She wanted to join them.

'Nay,' her grandmother warned. 'Wassailin' is not for young lasses like thee. Thoo must stay indoors wi' tha father an' mother an' tha brothers.' The only consolation was that Francis was not allowed out either.

The wassailers put the lid on the bowl and carried it outside. They'd been drinking all day and it was a shock to leave the steamy warmth of Uphall. They staggered from place to place, taking turns to carry the bowl. At each dwelling, they sang as loud as they could and rapped on the door. In return for their good cheer, they were given money or food or ale. Most were happy to greet them and drink their wassail, though some of the older folk shunned them. Sarah Ezard and Ben were left in peace as their homes were in darkness. When they reached Robert Storey's home, they were in two minds.

'Elizabeth will welcome us,' coaxed Dorothy Jordan.

'Maybe, but what about Robert?' was the general response.

Dorothy was undeterred. 'Let's sing quietly first,' she suggested, 'and see if a light appears.'

Most did their best to sing gently and in tune. Tom forgot and then was nudged so roughly that he fell over and brought down two more with him. They couldn't get up again for laughing. The sight of the group helpless on the ground set everyone off. The more they tried to stifle their laughter in case Robert came out, the more they giggled. Luckily, it was Elizabeth who came to the door.

'Hush, hush,' she repeated though she couldn't help smiling at them lying collapsed on the ground. Whenever Tom tried to get up, someone would push him back down and they'd start laughing again.

'Sorry, Elizabeth,' they managed to say. 'We wish thoo well. God bless.' They sang the wassail chorus once more, but they were exhausted and the singing was ragged. Elizabeth held up a hand.

'Stop, for pity's sake,' she cried. 'You all look as if you've had enough. You should be home in bed. Thank you for coming though. Wait while I fetch you some gingerbread, and then you *must* go before Robert wakes up.' They stood quietly enough and then, after she'd handed round the dark cake, shuffled off.

Tom was half carried to the next house. He'd drunk far more than he was used to and was growing morose.

When he began to talk about Anna Jordan and how life had been when she was alive, they ignored him. He would have gone to Dorothy for sympathy, since she knew Anna the best, yet Dorothy was strolling arm in arm with John Dawson. Instead, he almost threw himself onto Jane.

Tom was well aware of the past goings-on between Jane and Ellen. He also knew of the rivalry between Jane and Dorothy over John Dawson. He was drunk though, and nothing could prevent him from thinking he had a chance of courting Jane himself. She reminded him of Anna now that she was older. It was true that he was a servant and nine years her senior; it was also New Year's Eve and anything was possible. As the wassailing reached its end at the Smiths' house, he put his arm around Jane and stole a kiss.

She'd also drunk far more than usual and found it pleasant to be close to Tom's warm body. Her desire for Ellen now seemed childish. Perhaps she didn't care so much about John Dawson either. Tom liked her and it was good to feel wanted.

By the time the wassailers returned to Uphall, the group had disbanded somewhat. Many were paired off, holding each other up against the occasional flurries of snow now flying in from the north. John Dawson and Dorothy led the way with a lantern and the now empty wassail bowl. The drunken farmhands straggled far behind.

Jane and Tom stumbled along, keeping an eye on the lantern ahead. Tonight they were carefree; tomorrow was another day. They each wondered how different it might be in the cold, clear light of morning.

Tom was one of the first up on New Year's Day. He went outside and sobered himself up by sticking his head through the ice in the pail. He held his head under the water for as long as he could bear it, and then shook the freezing cold water off his hair like a dog. Putting his head round the kitchen door, he announced that he was going first-footing after breakfast.

'Dickon'll see to animals if I'm not 'ere,' he explained to his master and mistress. They didn't know why he was suddenly so keen to be out visiting. John Dawson had been the usual choice of first footer since he had such black hair.

As Tom ate his porridge, John Dawson came down for breakfast all prepared to go out first-footing. The two grunted by way of a greeting. Dorothy Jordan stared at the pair of them as they glowered at each other across the table.

'Tha can't both go first-footin',' she said. 'On second thoughts, maybe Tom could start one way, an' John – thoo can go t'other. Thoo'll meet up i' middle o' village.'

They mulled this over. Tom was only intent on visiting William and Mary's house so he could see Jane. John shrugged. It meant nothing to him either way. Tom finished eating first and grabbed a piece of bread and some coal; he already had some money in his pocket and his coat was still decorated with holly. Being the first one ready, he told John which way he was going and set off.

Dorothy was puzzled and looked at John. He couldn't enlighten her. Just then, Dickon wandered in asking for an oatcake. Having got what he wanted, he went to the cowshed and balanced the oatcake on one of the cow's horns. Then he danced round the cow and sang until the cake fell off. This year it fell off sideways and he cursed. Ah well, he sighed as he ambled back to the kitchen. He was also put out that Tom had gone off and left him to see to the stock.

Tom rushed down the hill in the gloom of the late dawn. He went straight to William's house. As he stood at the door, his courage failed. He removed his hat and smoothed down his hair. Then he cleared his throat and tapped on the door.

Jane was alone in the kitchen stoking the fire up for breakfast. No one else was up. When she opened the door she was surprised, and didn't know what to say. He waved the bread and coal and wished her a Happy New Year.

'You'd better step in then,' she said. 'Bring us some luck. Come on,' she beckoned, 'step over the threshold.'

He felt clumsy as he stooped to go through the doorway and squeeze past her.

'Go on into the kitchen and have a drink', she added. 'They're all still in bed.'

Once he'd sat by the fire with a beaker of small beer, it seemed more natural for them to be alone together. Jane was friendly and chatted about the children and about William and Mary. He was happy to just sit and listen and look at her face. He watched her pour boiling milk onto the oatmeal and would have liked to stay longer, but he heard movements in the parlour. William and Mary were getting up.

'I'd best be off,' he mumbled. 'I've other folk to visit.' He bent over to kiss her cheek. She dodged out of the way.

'Don't forget the pan of ashes to take outside!' she said to cover her embarrassment. She passed him the ashes from the fire. 'We must get rid of the old year, eh?' she added as she opened the door for him. 'Goodbye, Tom,' she shouted as he walked away. He turned and smiled, waved once and was gone.

She was sad as she closed the door behind him. Why did he have to rush things and try to kiss her? She wasn't ready for any of that. Why couldn't he be just a friend for now? She put thoughts of Tom behind her as she set the table. She needn't see much of him.

Tom was confused as he moved on through the village. Part of him wished he'd never had the idea of meeting Jane so soon, and yet he'd enjoyed being alone with her. Most of all he wanted to know how she felt about him. He went over their time together in his mind, alternating between hope and despair. It was a relief to meet up with John Dawson in the middle of the street. Tom was desperate to talk to someone yet couldn't confide in John. The two young men walked back in silence.

At Uphall, Tom searched for Dickon and found him sitting oiling harnesses in the stable. Dickon was looking glum.

'Me oatcake fell off wrong way,' he complained. 'I'm wonderin' what bad luck'll come.'

Tom sat beside him and thought it unfair to burden him with more worries. At least he had one more excuse to see Jane before the farm work began in earnest once more. Twelfth Night was just days away.

Chapter 33

1714

On Twelfth Night Dorothy Jordan made preparations for the final feast. The traditional cake was ready with the usual dried bean hidden in one half for the men, and a pea in the other half for the women. She put it in the middle of the table and wondered who'd be the lucky finders. One thing was sure – as king and queen for the night, they'd boss the others about.

William and his family arrived and went straight into the kitchen. Young Mary saw the large cake and climbed onto the bench.

'Nay, nay!' her grandmother said, 'thoo must sit over yon for now. Tha can join us later. Thoo's not brought tha dog?'

'No,' Mary mumbled, glowering. 'Not allowed.' She frowned and pushed out her bottom lip. With a longing look at the cake, she slid slowly off the bench to join her brothers at the little table.

At the main table, the others stared at the slice of cake put before each of them.

'Now, go steady,' Dorothy warned the farmhands. 'Mind tha doesn't swallow the bean.'

They picked at their cake, wary of swallowing the bean or pea by mistake. All of a sudden, Tom announced that he had the bean. This came as no surprise; he was at the heart of the fun this year. Soon afterwards, Jane's sister, Dorothy, found the pea. They all cheered as Tom, king for the night, ordered more drink to be brought and then demanded they sing his favourite song, 'Old Tup'.

When that long song was finally over, he carried the garland of mistletoe around the room and held it above each girl.

They had no choice but to do his bidding and take a kiss. The farmhands whistled and roared as each kiss was taken. When it came to Jane's turn, she blushed. Tom stood beside her and paused. He'd saved her till last. He did not want to give a quick peck on the cheek as he'd given the other girls. The lads were banging their fists on the table. They started at a slow tempo and then built up speed and made more noise as the kiss was about to be taken. All at once, Tom leant forward and aimed for her mouth. He caught the side of her lips as she turned her cheek. To hide his embarrassment, he shouted to Dorothy.

''Ere – catch!' He threw her the mistletoe. 'What shall we play next?'

'Hot cockles!' she yelled in reply. 'I'll go first, I'm Queen.'

As the table was moved aside, Jane wondered why her sister was so keen to play that particular game; she suspected it had something to do with John Dawson. She watched her sister fetch a cloth. Then she was asked to blindfold her. Dorothy then knelt in the middle of the room. She put one hand behind her back with her palm open. Everyone seated themselves around wherever they could.

'Hot cockles, hot!' Dorothy shouted and waited for someone to strike her hand. Those closest to her made signals as to who should go first. William put his finger to his lips, crept up in stocking feet and gave her hand a hard slap. Jane grinned – it must have stung quite a bit. Dorothy swung her arm round quickly and managed to grab his sleeve. She felt his large, rough hand and the material of his shirt.

'It's William!' she cried. They all cheered and then went very quiet as they waited for the next person to step up.

'Hot cockles, hot!' she repeated. Two of the farmhands shoved John Dawson forward. He was most reluctant. With no way out, he gave her hand such a gentle tap that she thought it must be a woman. She swung round to grab whoever it was, but he was too quick and she missed him altogether.

'I think it's Mary!' she shouted.

'Nay!' they all replied and laughed. 'It were John Dawson!' Dorothy was mortified. Worse was to come. 'Forfeit! Forfeit!

Forfeit!' They chanted and stamped their feet and clapped. Jane had an idea and whispered in Tom's ear.

He yelled above the noise. 'She must kiss whoever's nearest on 'er left.'

Everyone laughed because it was Dickon. Dorothy stood up and walked to her left with her arms held out in front. She hoped it might be John Dawson. She bumped into the settle and felt a rough, gnarled face and a balding head. Her heart sank. They were making a fool of her, but she had no choice. She stooped down and gave Dickon the briefest kiss on the cheek amid cheering. She ripped the blindfold off.

'I've had enough,' she mumbled. 'I have a headache.'

They groaned in disappointment yet used the opportunity to replenish their drinks.

So far, young Mary and the other children had not joined in any of the fun. She was getting bored. Francis was already half asleep, lying on one side of the fire with his head in his mother's lap. When she heard Tom demand they play Snap Apple next, she saw the look of worry on her grandmother's face. Immediately, young Mary was interested.

The idea, she understood, was to try and take a bite from one of the apples stuck on each end of a piece of wood hanging from the ceiling. That was easy she thought, but then Tom put another piece of wood across it and fixed a stubby candle on each end. He lit them, let them settle to a good flame and then spun the wood gently round.

'Who's goin' first?' he shouted. 'Who dares bite an apple – an' risk bein' burnt?'

The lads began to tuck their hair behind their ears, frightened of it catching fire, though there was just as much danger of burning their eyelashes or their lips. John Dawson had downy hair growing on his chin and the beginnings of a moustache. When his turn came, his hair was singed. Everyone laughed.

Dorothy was sorry for him. She ran and fetched a slice of raw potato and rubbed it on his burnt face. As she was queen for the night he could not turn away.

Tom announced the next game – Shoeing the Wild Mare. William and Mary glanced at each other; the games were getting more boisterous. This one always ended with some injury or other. Tom dragged out the old wooden beam to hang from the rafters. Young Mary, eager to find out what it was for, nudged her father.

He sighed. 'The lads will take turns to sit astride it,' he told her in spite of his wife shaking her head and signalling to the door. 'They've got to try and stay on the beam while they hit it underneath with a hammer. It's supposed to be like shoeing a horse, but the beam sways about. They always fall off.'

Mary coughed to get his attention. 'We have to go now,' she hinted. 'It's getting late.' Young Mary ran to Jane and clutched her gown. She did not want to go home.

Jane prised off the girl's fingers. Though disappointed at missing further games, she'd be leaving with them. The Christmas festivities were over. When they got home they'd have to burn the decorations of holly and ivy and extinguish the Yule log. At least, Jane thought, there was one more thing to look forward to – Plough Monday.

At Uphall, on the Monday after Twelfth Night, everyone was up early. The men ate a huge breakfast of fatty bacon with hunks of barley bread. Dickon and Tom had already gone out to disable one of the ploughs. They removed the sharp metal share, fitted the mouldboard the wrong way round and decorated the plough with ribbons. It was now ready to be carried through the village.

For Tom and the other lads, the procession with the plough was the last chance for mayhem. For Dickon and his master, it marked the end of the laziness and the start of proper work. They were beginning to chafe at being idle and indoors for so long and wanted to get back to work again, back into some routine.

It had been an old Jordan tradition for their eldest boy to act as Blether Dick, master of the ploughmen, while the Smith family had provided his consort. This year was different. Tom begged to be Blether Dick. He wanted to dance about and shout, lead the band of ploughboys and wear the fancy coloured hat. Francis Jordan had a brief discussion with his wife.

'I don't know why 'e's so keen to dress up an' act the fool,' he murmured, scratching his head.

'Aye, all 'oliday season 'e's been full of 'imself,' his wife agreed. 'It's maybe summat to do wi' some lass 'e's after. Let 'im 'ave 'is way, poor lad.'

'An' what about Matthew Smith?' Francis asked. 'As a rule, 'e's taken part o' Besom Bet. 'Appen, now 'e's a settled married man wi' bairns, 'e'll be glad to give it up.'

'Thoo's right. Let's ask John Dawson to take it on.'

John did not relish the idea of accompanying Tom in women's clothes. At least his face would be blackened and he'd be in disguise. To get in the mood, he and the other lads drank ale with their breakfast. Then they rubbed soot into their faces and Tom and John donned their outfits. Before long, John Gurwood called round with his fiddle and asked if they were ready.

'Not yet,' Tom complained. 'I 'aven't got me stick.' Dickon brought it in. There was a blown-up bladder tied on the end and he gave Tom a wallop as he passed it over. The dried peas inside rattled against his ears. When they laughed, Tom went round and hit them all on the head.

'Come on,' he shouted, 'let's get started. Plough lads ho!'

They rushed out into the yard where the decorated 'fond' plough stood. The lads lifted it up and set off, making as much noise as possible. They sang and shouted as they paraded through the lanes. Tom urged them on with the bladder on a stick while John Dawson hopped and skipped about in front with a broom. He pretended to sweep the way clean, and made a play of brushing away the bystanders.

When the procession reached William and Mary's house, the family were already gathered outside. Young Mary begged to join the lads. They had such black faces and made such a racket. Her brother was not so keen; he peered from behind his mother's gown as Tom danced about in front of them, threatening to plough up the lane if they didn't pay up. William handed them some money and told Jane to bring out beer and cheese.

It was soon obvious to all why Tom had been so keen to be their commander-in-chief. He bobbed up and down to the sound of the fiddle, showing off to Jane the fancy feathers on his hat. She was obliged to play with his ribbons and admire his fantastic clothes full of coloured patches. A few lads whistled. When Tom played out the traditional role of killing the 'old woman' or Besom Bet, he threw himself into the part.

John Dawson took it all in good faith; he duly sank down onto his knees, as if dying. The plough lads danced round and leapt as high as they could, and then the 'dead' John Dawson came back to life and sprang up again.

'God speed our plough,' they all shouted. The lads were in high spirits and wanted more fun. They took hold of John and thrust him in front of Jane. Though he looked ridiculous in a gown and petticoat, Jane didn't disappoint them. She took one of John's arms in hers and began to dance a jig. John Gurwood took this as a signal to strike up a tune for all to join in.

Tom didn't dance. His plans for the day were in tatters like his outfit. Only young Mary noticed his sad face. She tugged at his breeches to get his attention. He glanced down and managed a smile as she asked him to dance.

Jane saw him dancing with the girl and realised, with a twinge of guilt, how disappointed he must be. She was not being fair to him. She would have to make up for it.

Chapter 34

1714

Jane was soon to have plenty of opportunity to make it up to Tom. Her mother was beginning to suffer from swollen joints in her hands. Working in the cold curing chamber had brought on rheumatism and, by the middle of January, Dorothy Jordan had no option but to give in and accept her limitations. This was not done without tears. She'd always prided herself on being able to cope, and had been hiding her pain and clumsiness for some time. It was with reluctance that she asked William to send Jane back to Uphall to help out.

At first, Jane managed to work at both houses. She arose at dawn, stoked up the fire and prepared breakfast at William's house before walking to Uphall. She often took young Mary with her. Each day, Jane and the girl saw Tom at dinner. He made them laugh and they enjoyed his company. Often he'd do quite ridiculous things just to make them smile – like making a ladle stick on his forehead. He adored Jane and would do anything to please her.

Life at Uphall was not all fun for young Mary. She was always in trouble. She didn't *feel* clumsy, but pots got knocked over sometimes or fell from her hands. Dickon began to call her Little Miss Upskell.

'She's always upsettin' summat, that lass,' he said. 'She's forever in a rush.'

She couldn't bear to walk if there was a clear space to run, and her desire for speed came at the expense of bowls, jugs and pails. Her grandfather threatened her.

'Be'ave thassen or tha'll end up i' Kidcote cell. Constable'll 'ave thee.'

The girl's behaviour was too much for her grandmother. Dorothy found it hard enough to direct her two daughters in their work without having to clear up young Mary's mess, or worry what the girl might be up to when out of sight. It wasn't long before Jane was told not to bring her anymore.

In order to help his wife, William took young Mary out ploughing with him on fine days. He looked forward to their time together. Sometimes they were out all day and ate their dinner in the field. Workers on the adjacent strips grew accustomed to the sight of young Mary running up and down the grassy balk shouting to her father. Sometimes her brother, Francis, was not needed at home and he came along as well to help break up bigger clods with a stick.

William had always liked ploughing and took pleasure in seeing the dark earth turn over. The leather traces felt familiar as they pulled against his back, and the worn plough handles fitted his hands as if they were made especially for him. When his daughter tired of following him, she waited at the end of each furrow and passed him his drink. As he rested, he pointed out the men ploughing nearby.

'There's Richard Maltby, and look – there's William Jefferson and his son, Stephen. You'll have seen them in church.'

'And there's Uncle Robert,' she said, and waved to catch his eye.

'That's right – he's making sure the glebe land is ploughed properly.' He explained to her the different parts of the upfield and showed her the direction of various places.

'In Rudston over there you can see a very strange stone. It stands in the churchyard and, you'll not believe this, it's nearly as tall as the church.' Her eyes widened further as he added, 'Some folk say it's a spear the devil threw because he was angry about the church being built. Maybe I'll take you there one day.'

At home, in the evening, young Mary related all she'd learnt, much to her mother's annoyance.

'Eat your supper then get to bed,' was all she could say. She was tired and fed up. She couldn't be outdoors even if she wanted to and so complained to William.

'I have so much more housework and childminding to do now that Jane spends most of her time at Uphall. You've no idea what it's like trying to work with a small boy under your feet.'

William thought it best not to answer. Instead, he sought consolation in his daughter. Even when they came home exhausted, he often took young Mary outside in the evening to see the stars. One night she sat astride his shoulders and he pointed out her favourite – the Plough. He moved her finger up to the Pole Star. Turning to face a different way, he pointed again.

'See that giant W across the sky there? That's my own set of stars – a W for William.' She believed him and searched for the letter M.

William took pride in his daughter's learning, but his wife grew wary. It was tempting fate to love the girl so much. He should keep his love within normal bounds. She realised she might as well ask the grass to stop growing.

One evening, the girl began repeating what she'd heard her grandfather say about the plough coulter.

'Long, strong an' straight. Long, strong an' straight.' She kept repeating the same words until her mother suddenly threw down the shirt she was mending and leant over to swipe her.

'I'll give you 'long, strong an' straight' if you don't shut up. You're driving me mad.'

William put himself between them. He knew his daughter needed taking in hand. For the sake of peace in the family, he decided to visit George Gurwood. For some time, unbeknown to his wife, William had been wondering whether to let his daughter have lessons at the vicarage. George Gurwood gave his own daughters daily lessons in reading, writing and Bible study.

On hearing of William's problem, the vicar was only too pleased to allow Mary to join them free of charge. He knew how spirited she was and how quick to learn. He was also aware that many folk in the village thought it quite wrong to educate girls, that it was a waste of time and effort.

As soon as everyone heard about young Mary's lessons, they began to complain. It was the women who had the most to say. They grumbled together as they drew water from the well.

'Lasses should 'ave just enough learnin' to be useful at 'ome,' Martha Wrench asserted.

'Aye,' agreed Sarah Ezard. 'They need to know about kitchens an' milk'ouses an' a bit about Bible – owt else an' they'll get above thassens.'

The carpenter's wife had the last word. 'I don't think it's respectable to 'ave women bein' able to write. I can't understand why young Francis is not bein' taught instead.'

'Aye,' they all said, ''im an' not young Mary should be taught.'

It was apparent to both William and Mary that their son did not have the same quickness of mind or the same confidence as his sister. One day they did ask him if he wanted to accompany Mary. He shook his head, horrified at the idea of learning with so many girls. His mother understood and put a protective arm around him. She knew how he'd be teased. He'd be like a lamb to the slaughter.

When William and Mary took their children to church, they heard folk muttering behind them. They learnt they were fools who put all their eggs in one basket. There was no escape either when they visited Uphall. William's mother was furious about her granddaughter's lessons. She wagged her finger and pronounced that God would sort out William's pride.

'Never take too much pride an' pleasure in tha kith an' kin,' she warned in a prophetic voice. 'Our Lord gives an' our Lord takes away.'

This unnerved William; it was a quote from Job, his favourite book. The words came as shadows drifting across a sunlit hill. From that moment, at the back of his mind, was the fear that he could be punished at any time for his pride in the child. He did love her too much, and yet he also loved and respected God. For weeks he kept his thoughts to himself and read the Bible each night, seeking comfort.

George Gurwood was sensitive to the attitudes of his parishioners and began young Mary's education with Bible reading only. She was quick to learn passages by heart and could soon recite parts of the Psalms. One night in bed, she repeated her favourite bit of Psalm 148 to her brother. In the darkness, she whispered the words in a dramatic fashion and imagined what they portrayed.

'Praise ye him, sun and moon: praise him all ye stars of light ... Fire and hail, snow and stormy wind, mountains and hills, trees and beasts and all cattle, creeping things and flying fowl.'

Her brother was impressed and began to appreciate the Bible in a way that he'd never done in church.

One Monday afternoon in February, a storm gathered out at sea, and an easterly wind sent great wafts of smoke round Mary's kitchen. The children's eyes began to sting, and their mother grew upset to see everything covered with a fine coating of soot and ash. Every time she picked something up she dirtied her hands and her white apron.

William came home early. He feared a storm equal to the one of eleven years ago. As the wind increased, the family huddled together in the kitchen, choosing to be smoked like a kipper rather than frozen to death in the parlour. They felt the wind tug at the thatch and rock the house. William trusted that the ridging on the roof would hold, and reassured them that the house was safe – it was built from chalk blocks on solid cobblestone foundations. Young Mary picked up her dog and held her close. Needing more comfort, she hid her face in her father's jacket and murmured softly to herself.

'Cobblestones, cobblestones and chalk in our wall,
Cobblestones and cobblestones – God save us all.'

She repeated this over and over like a charm against the elements. Soon, Francis joined in. The wind was like a giant monster stalking them. There were quiet spells and then sudden pounces. William knew that the church and the houses on the high ground to the far south of the village would face the full force of the storm. St Helen's Lane was more sheltered. By evening, the wind had died down though the sea remained high. He shuddered to think of the ships foundering out there with broken masts and torn sails.

The next morning, as William left his daughter at the vicarage, he was told that the vicar was out at the church checking the damage. William found George Gurwood there with the churchwardens. Parts of the roof lay strewn across the graveyard, and some of the stones in the embattled part of the tower had worked loose. He commiserated with them for a minute or two, relieved not to be a churchwarden this year. As he walked on to Uphall to begin his day's work, he knew the last thing he wanted was to go round the village collecting extra funds or be responsible for the church repairs.

At the vicarage, his daughter settled down in the Gurwoods' parlour to hear the girls read from the Psalms. The two eldest, Jane and Cecilia, were excused from reading, being far too busy preparing items for Jane's bridal chest. As they sewed leaf and flower motifs onto bed linen, they only half-listened to their sisters. Since their father was out and their mother was occupied in the kitchen, Cecilia took the opportunity to discuss Jane's future wedding. She let her sewing fall into her lap and smiled as she glanced sideways at Jane.

'I wonder if it hurts, that first night you're with him.'

'Look,' Jane replied, 'you've wondered this before. Change your tune – none of us is interested. And besides, younger ears don't need to hear it.'

Young Mary's ears pricked up at that. The girls read a few more verses before Cecilia interrupted them again.

'According to father's book, your hymen *can* be broken accidentally.' The girls stopped reading again.

'What on earth is that?' they asked in unison. It sounded dangerous.

'Well,' said Cecilia, smoothing her gown and sitting more upright. 'According to the book, it's something inside you.' She stared at Jane. 'On your wedding night, when Robert goes inside you, it should break. If he finds it already broken, then you're not a virgin.'

Jane frowned. 'But you just said this hymen could be broken by accident. How?'

'Well,' whispered Cecilia, 'it can be destroyed when you're born – if the midwife's clumsy enough. Or it can break if you cough too hard, or have a sneezing fit.' Cecilia giggled as Jane was prone to sneezing fits.

'I don't believe you,' Jane snorted.

'Or if you have constipation,' Cecilia added. 'You know – if you strain too hard.'

Jane had had enough and was getting annoyed. 'This is too much. I can't believe it's that easy to break. You're just trying to scare me. Stop it now, or else I'll tell father.'

Cecilia couldn't resist having the last word. 'Well, I only hope your Robert's rod is long enough to break your hymen.' Jane raised her hand to her but Cecilia dodged. 'That's if your hymen is still intact anyway!' she sneered.

Just then their mother walked in to see if the fire needed mending. In a flash, the two sisters bent their heads to their sewing. The other girls were silent, having lost their place in the Bible. Young Mary sensed the unease and bent down to stroke her dog. She looked up and smiled innocently. The girls' mother ignored her and noted her daughters' flushed faces. Casting a suspicious eye, she turned to leave.

The girls stared at each other. If she'd overheard, there'd be trouble.

Chapter 35

When the days grew longer and the weather turned warmer, Mary put all the bedding out in the sunshine to kill off the various bugs. The very act of doing this lifted her spirits and she began to do the household chores with a lighter heart. She also took more interest again in her cooking. One week, William found his food flavoured with mint, and the next week she nearly blew their heads off with grated horseradish in one of the pies.

He smiled to see her back to her old self. The family functioned well now despite the absence of Jane. Little William was walking about, though with a slight list to one side; he was also talking a lot, and Francis was the perfect big brother, always looking out for him and ever ready to help his mother. William knew it was also more peaceful for everyone at home if young Mary was out. Even when she was not at the Gurwoods', she was in the fields with him or spending time at Ben's. And she took her dog wherever she went – another reason for the quiet at home.

George Gurwood believed in fresh air and exercise for a healthy, moral mind. He took his daughters for walks, pointing out to them the various spring flowers, and teaching them to identify birds from their songs. Young Mary accompanied them and loved the names cowslip and coltsfoot. Yellow was her favourite colour. When she came home she taught Francis the difference between a blue tit and a great tit and imitated their calls.

He was never sure whether to believe her as she was telling him so much these days. He grew so befuddled with new words that, when he closed his eyes to sleep, a particular word or phrase would reverberate in his mind. A verse from a psalm could keep him awake for hours – 'He giveth snow like wool: he scattereth the hoarfrost like ashes'. The names of wildflowers like pimpernel, eyebright and tormentil also echoed in his head and stopped him from sleeping.

The more new words Mary had, the happier she was and the more she wanted to learn. One day, she was sitting with the Gurwood girls learning to do daisy stitch when Robert Read called on Jane. All the girls began to rush about and fiddle with their clothes. They were ever so polite to the visitor, and even Cecilia behaved. Young Mary couldn't understand the change in them. Their talk was boring; it was not as interesting as birds and flowers. She decided there and then that she didn't want to grow up and be polite and silly like them.

Since Robert was to marry Jane in less than a month's time, the young couple were allowed to be alone together for an hour or two, either in the parlour or the garden. Once, as George Gurwood and the girls were returning from one of their walks, young Mary thought she saw Robert Read with his hand up Jane's petticoat. She wasn't sure, but wondered why he would do that. Perhaps Jane had lost something. When she mentioned it, Cecilia rubbed her hands in delight.

'I knew my sister wasn't as pure as snow.'

As the day of Jane and Robert's wedding approached, life became hectic at the vicarage. Young Mary wondered why she hardly saw John Gurwood anymore.

'Is it because of all the wedding fuss?' she asked the vicar.

'No, no,' he replied with a smile, 'though I can see why you thought that. No, he's working in Bridlington now – in a counting house. He's learning about money. He comes home every Saturday afternoon and spends Sundays here.'

They both thought John was lucky to be away as, throughout April, urgent preparations went on for the wedding and Jane's removal to Speeton.

Young Mary, like the vicar, often felt she was unwelcome and in the way. Wherever she took her dog that spring, everyone was busy and preoccupied. No one wanted her. The exceptionally dry weather meant that conversations at home and at Uphall were all about the poor growth of the crops, while conversations at the Gurwoods' were about the coming wedding. She was bored.

One morning, before dawn, young Mary woke up her brother. There was a hedgehog snuffling in the garden. She persuaded Francis to get up with her and see where it was going. They took the dog with them and watched as the hedgehog scuttled into the lane. Excited by the chase, the dog leapt past them barking. Just as Stina pounced, the hedgehog curled up into a ball. Ben, who had also risen early, heard the dog yelping in pain and came to see.

He found the two children in their nightclothes staring in shock at the dog. Stina was lying on her front with her paws folded over her bleeding nose. The hedgehog was still curled up.

'That'll teach thee to leave urchins alone,' he said as he rolled the hedgehog into the undergrowth with his foot. 'An' look what thoo's done to tha dog. She's 'urt, poor thing.'

'I'm sorry,' Mary mumbled and turned to lead the dog back home. Everything she did was wrong.

Two days later she was bored again. She dragged her feet as she walked into the garden looking for something to do. For a while, she watched the bees on the lavender. Then she saw that her father had happened to leave a bottle of linseed oil by the back step. George Gurwood had taught her that bees were a gift from God; he'd also said that you anointed a man with oil to make him a king. She wondered what would happen if she anointed a bee.

Sitting on the step, with the bottle held between her knees, she managed to prise out the cork. She walked back to the lavender. With great care, she held the bottle just above a bee and tilted it. Suddenly she realised that, if she spilt too much oil, her father would notice. She'd once seen her mother use a feather to put eye drops in, and so searched round for a suitable one. There was a dead crow hung on the fence. She plucked one of its feathers and stuck it into the bottle. With the tip of the feather steeped in oil, she went back to the bees.

She leant over a bee and was surprised when it ignored her completely and continued its task. She let one drop of oil fall on it. There was a dull, buzzing noise and then the bee fell to the ground. It was such an interesting reaction, and so easy to accomplish, that she did the same to another bee, and another. The power of anointing them went to her head.

Many more bees would have died if her mother had not gone into the garden to lay washing on the hedge. Young Mary was yanked aside and shouted at until she cried. When her mother found out the full story, worse was to follow.

'Right, young lady, you know how much Ben loves his bees – well, you can go straight to him now and explain what you've done and say you're sorry.'

With tears in her eyes, young Mary slouched towards Ben's cottage. Her dog leapt up at her all the way, puzzled why they weren't running as usual.

Ben was sitting outside on his bench, smoking a pipe. He had his back leant against the wall and was enjoying the warmth of the sun through his breeches. When he saw her coming he sighed to see her walking with her head down.

'What's up now, lass?'

She shook her head, not knowing how to explain. 'I've done something very bad,' she mumbled.

'Nowt can be so bad tha can't tell *me*.'

'I'm sorry Ben,' she said and burst into tears.

'Come 'ere, lass, an' sit down. Tell me what's up.'

Gradually, he coaxed out of her what she'd done. Although alarmed by the cruelty and ingenuity of her actions, he knew she hadn't meant any harm.

'No one likes me,' she sniffed. 'No one wants me. I get in the way. I break things.' She fondled the dog's ears. 'Only Stina likes me.'

Ben put an arm around her and pulled her towards him. She strained against him but was soon pressed into his rough jacket and was breathing in the familiar smell of tar and stale tobacco.

'Give a dog a bad name eh? I don't know Mary ... I just don't know what's to become o' thee.' He lifted her chin up. 'Why not, to make amends, why not 'elp me collect me next swarm o' bees? That'll put ev'rythin' right, won't it?'

She wiped her face with a grubby hand and peered up at him. Her cheeks were wet, and her eyes puffy.

'Alright,' she agreed, nodding her head. 'I'm really sorry.' She burst into tears again. They sat for a while in silence while he finished his pipe and she calmed down.

'Thoo'd best get back 'ome,' he said at last. 'Tell tha mother I forgive thee. Tell 'er worse things 'appen at sea.'

Young Mary didn't go home. She went to the Gurwoods' house instead, despite knowing there were to be no lessons that week. The girls were knitting and sewing in the parlour while their mother and Jane made the bridal cake. Mary chose to be in the kitchen, not wishing to be given any sewing to do. She left her dog in the garden and was soon set to work pounding sugar. Then she was told to sieve it.

Jane and her mother had already washed, dried and stoned the fruit and were now washing the butter in water. Mary watched as they rinsed it in rosewater, something she'd never seen before. Their way of making a cake was new to her. It still involved 'elbow grease' as her grandmother would say, because Jane spent ages just beating the eggs. Mary left before she saw the ingredients mixed together. As she walked home, she looked forward to having a slice of that cake. If only she didn't have to attend the wedding.

Chapter 36

On the day of the wedding, in the first week of May, young Mary was asked to join the Gurwood girls and help them pick flowers for the church and the bridal bouquet. She ran barefoot with Stina all the way to the vicarage, eager to spend the early morning wandering around Reighton. She pitied the other girls wearing shoes; they wouldn't feel the blades of grass tickling between their toes.

Cecilia took charge and had strict instructions from her mother. Among other flowers, they were to pick loads of celandines.

'This is a job for you, Mary,' Cecilia ordered when they reached the meadow. 'Just pick the flower heads – they're going to be thrown over Jane after the wedding.'

Young Mary was handed a basket. She sat down and began grabbing flowers by the fistful. Meanwhile, the other girls searched for cowslips.

'They're not hard to find,' Cecilia explained. 'They have short stalks – look out for them shaking in the breeze.'

When they'd gathered enough, Cecilia led her sisters to a sheltered dell to collect primroses. Then they headed down to the low-lying bottom meadow to gather buckbean. There they had to take off their shoes and stockings and hold up their petticoats before stepping into the boggier parts. By this time Mary had tired of picking celandines. She was now adding dandelion heads to the basket. They were larger and easier to pick. Proud of her efforts, she ran to join the others.

Cecilia took one look in the basket, then put her hands on her hips and scowled.

'Who told you to pick dandelions? I certainly didn't.'

'But they're yellow,' Mary insisted.

'I don't care. We're not having them. Don't you know if you pick those you'll wet the bed? That'll be fine for Jane and Robert on their wedding night!' Seeing the dismay on Mary's face, Cecilia added, 'It's only an old wives' tale – probably not true. Take them out of the basket though just in case. I don't want mother or Jane to see them.'

The other girls helped Mary to remove them and they threw them out of sight into the ditch.

'We're going to the cliff top now,' Cecilia told Mary. 'If you're coming with us, be careful. We don't want you toppling over the edge.' She remembered that Anna Jordan had fallen to her death somewhere along the same cliff. To be safe, she made the girls walk in single file as they searched for more flowers. Mary's dog bounced along in front.

'Watch your dog, Mary,' Cecilia shouted. 'She's daft enough to fall down the cliff.' Mary ran ahead to try and keep up with Stina but her foot slipped. Cecilia, horrified, rushed after her and yanked her back just in time.

'That dog'll be the death of you one day!'

Mary was shaken. She had been too near the edge. However, as Cecilia had pulled her back, she'd seen a large bunch of primroses growing a little way down the cliff. She explained what she'd seen and had an idea.

'I can get them if you dangle me down.' She thought it would make up for her mistake with the dandelions.

Cecilia chewed her bottom lip and shook her head. It was tempting. 'No, I'm not happy with it,' she said at last. She went to the edge and peered down. The primroses were beautiful. Against her better judgement, she agreed to hold onto Mary's legs.

'Don't wriggle,' she warned as she held Mary upside down over the cliff.

'You're tickling me.'

'Just get on with it. Can you reach yet?'

'Nearly. I'm nearly there …' She lunged forward and Cecilia lost hold of a leg. Mary managed to clutch the whole plant of primroses in one hand before she realised she was dangling by one ankle. Her free leg swung away from the cliff, twisting her body round.

'Help!'

'Let go of the flowers! Use your hands and hold on,' Cecilia shouted.

Mary would not let go. She was determined to bring the flowers back.

Cecilia panicked. 'Please, Mary – please leave the flowers,' she begged.

'No!'

The other girls held their breath as they peered over the edge. One of them clasped the dog in her arms, preventing Stina from jumping after her mistress. When Cecilia saw Mary's free leg swing back into the cliff, she leant out further and managed to grasp it. At last, Mary was hauled up onto the grass. The dog leapt forwards to lick her face.

'See – I still have the flowers,' she boasted.

Cecilia could have slapped her.

Mary then saw the state of her clothes. 'Don't tell my mother,' she pleaded. 'I just fell. That's all.'

There was no way any of them were going to admit to what they'd done.

On arriving back at the village, the girls were told to go and decorate the church. Cecilia was again left in charge. She ordered her sisters to scatter rosemary leaves on the floor.

'I'll put lavender sprigs in the porch to bring Jane a long and happy marriage. Then I'll hang up the ivy. You can set out the flowers. Not you, Mary, you'd better go home. We don't want your dog leaving any of her mess in the church.' Seeing Mary scowl, she added, 'You were very silly up on the cliff, but you were brave. Now, off you go. We have to get on as we'll be getting dressed for the service soon. We're all bridesmaids.'

Young Mary slouched off. She didn't want to go to the wedding. The best part was over – being out in the sunshine collecting flowers. Now there was just a boring church service and it was indoors. When she got home, her mother was angry with her for being late.

'I wanted to give you a good wash – and look at you. Where've you been to get so filthy?'

The excuse of falling in the road did not prevent a cuff round the ears.

'I've never seen a petticoat and bonnet get so mucky! And just look at your fingernails! And your feet! Right, young lady, get outside – you're going in the tub.'

As young Mary went out the back door, shoved from behind by her mother, she glowered at her brothers. They were already scrubbed clean and sitting quietly waiting for their father to arrive.

Everyone attended church that day. Half of Speeton was there too. They'd all come to see how George Gurwood would perform the marriage as both vicar and father of the bride. For one day they stopped worrying about the dry weather and took pleasure in the warm sunshine. On the south side of the church, sheltered from the wind, it was even hot.

Young Mary walked up the hill with her family, all in their Sunday clothes. She gazed into the blue sky. There was not a cloud in sight. She was glad to see Dickon standing by the church gate and puzzled to see him struggling to keep hold of a young lamb.

Her father explained. 'It's to bring Jane Gurwood good luck. She'd better turn up soon – he won't be able to hold it much longer.'

'Dickon doesn't like dressing for weddings,' she said in a monotone.

'No,' her father agreed. 'He's like you. He'd rather be in his working clothes out in the fields.' He suspected Dickon would prefer to miss the service altogether. Weddings would remind him of the wife he'd lost.

'Can I stay outside with Dickon?' young Mary asked. 'Or can I go home and stay with Stina?'

'No,' her mother intervened. 'Just be quiet. Get inside and don't stare at folk.'

Young Mary was almost pushed inside the porch. To her surprise, the church was like a garden. It smelled of rosemary, and green ivy had been interlaced with feathery, white buckbean. Once seated, she began to count the cowslips tied at the end of each pew.

Her mother was only glad that her daughter was sitting still. There were newts in the damp corners of the church and she was afraid the children would notice them. Like the rest of the congregation, she was admiring Jane Gurwood and her seven bridesmaids, all in blue gowns. The bridegroom was very handsome alongside them, dressed in dark brown with a white shirt and blue neckerchief.

The vicar read out one of his favourite Bible passages from 1 John, Chapter Four.

'Let us love one another; for love is of God; and everyone that loved is born of God, and knoweth God. He that loveth not knoweth not God; for God is love … If we love one another, God dwelleth in us, and his love is perfected in us.'

Jane Jordan thought of her sister, Anna, who would have been of marrying age had she lived. She wondered if Tom was also thinking of Anna, his former love. Her eyes wandered in his direction during the service. The more she stared at him, the more she thought that perhaps they could begin courting.

It would be a perfect match in many ways. They liked the same things and shared the same friends. They were even the same height and she'd noticed how, whenever they walked side by side, they remained in step. She knew how fond he was of her, and had an intuitive feeling that no one would ever want her more. He loved her just as she was, whatever she looked like or however she behaved.

As the service continued, Jane pondered Tom's appearance. His teeth were good and his eyes were a deep brown with amber lights, reminding her of a sheepdog they'd had at Uphall when she was a girl. Yet there was always something indefinable that held her back. She wasn't sure whether it was the colour of his skin, more red and freckly than she liked, or whether it was his smell – a mixture of male animal smells and coarse soap.

John Dawson, like Tom, was now included in the Jordan pews as if he was one of the family. It was a proud moment for him to be near the front of the church instead of on a bench at the back with the other farmhands. Although nothing had been said, it was a common assumption that Dorothy Jordan would soon get her way and marry him.

When he'd been out ploughing, he'd heard others singing her praises. He now saw her in a new light. He'd never been particularly attracted to Dorothy but, of late, he'd come to admire her. She'd taken on the extra work since her mother's bout of rheumatism, and she'd never complained. She might not be the prettiest of girls, yet her unselfish care of her family and Dickon was winning his affections. He no longer thought her haughty; she was really quite kind and thoughtful.

When the service ended, young Mary and the Jordan boys grabbed handfuls of celandines from the basket in the porch and threw them over Jane and Robert Read. Grains of wheat flew through the air from the pockets of Matthew Smith who wished them all the fertility in their marriage that he'd enjoyed.

Francis Jordan then fired his gun loaded with feathers. He aimed it high enough but the feathers fell back into their faces and stuck on their lips. John Gurwood took the gunshot as a signal to pick up his fiddle and start a tune. He danced a jig as he escorted the couple out of the churchyard and back to the vicarage.

When Robert Read neared the house, he was handed a piece of bridal cake on a plate. Jane ate a bit and then he flung it over his shoulder, plate and all. It shattered on the road behind him. Everyone cheered. Robert turned and saw the plate in pieces.

'Well done, Robert,' shouted John. 'Your future happiness is secured. Now you can relax. You can eat and drink and dance with us.'

Only the vicar's family and the new relations were allowed into the house; the rest of the village was entertained in the street. A barrel of rosemary-flavoured ale was set out at the front, and a table laden with pies and cured ham. A cheap posset made with ale and thickened with bread was provided for everyone to toast the couple.

While the adults filled their bellies, the children ran off, glad to be free. Young Mary raced up and down the street with the others and took on any challenges. The Jordan boys had not believed until then that girls could climb trees or throw an egg so far. Together, they terrorised the chickens in the Uphall yard until the geese charged at them and made them take refuge in the stable. There they found the mule and dared each other to sit on it. It was Dickon who heard the racket and dragged them back to the main street where the dancing had begun.

Dorothy was dancing with John Dawson, and her sister, Jane, was with Tom. The young Jordans soon paired off with the Gurwood girls of their own age. Young Mary, without a partner, joined in a large circle. As she twirled round and round she saw that her parents were just sitting watching. Her mother never had much fun; she looked uncomfortable and heavy. There was a baby inside her. Maybe that was why she was so crabby. She wondered if Jane Gurwood would end up like that. On the way out of church, she'd heard her grandmother chunter.

'Marry i' May an' thoo'll rue the day.'

Chapter 37

A week after the wedding, young Mary helped the Gurwood girls decorate the wain that was to take Jane's linen chest and some small items of furniture to the Reads' place in Speeton. Tom and Dickon tied ribbons onto the horns of the oxen and led the cart with much ceremony down the hill from Uphall to the vicarage. Mary hoped to travel with them and sit atop the furniture by the spinning wheel, but it was not to be. It was the new wife, Jane, who sat on top. As the loaded cart progressed back up the hill, Mary ran ahead with her dog, letting folk know the cart was on its way. Folk came out to wave goodbye and hand up small gifts. Various bowls, a ladle and a stool were added to the pile.

It was an easy ride due to the dry weather. On arrival, Jane was told exactly where to put everything. Robert's parents had agreed with the newly-wed couple as to which parts of the house they could count as theirs and even which parts of the garden and yard; Jane was told the agreement would be written up as a legal document.

At home in Reighton, Cecilia was missing her sister already. She had no one who was so easy to tease. Now, as the eldest daughter left at home, she'd have to take on more responsibility. Also, the onus would be on *her* now to find a suitor and to marry. Although she was twenty years old, she didn't want to leave home and become a wife. Her mother had given birth almost every year of her marriage. Cecilia couldn't think of anything worse.

Young Mary didn't think much to a woman's lot either. She saw how unhappy her mother looked. Every day she complained of not sleeping at night, and of getting heartburn after her meals. Despite the novel experience of feeling sorry for her mother, young Mary was relieved and excited when

Ben called round to say he had a swarm of bees in his garden. She leapt up straight away and called to her dog.

'Nay, nay,' he warned, 'Stina 'ad better stay at 'ome. We don't want to disturb bees more than we need.'

Before she left, she knelt by the dog and kissed her. 'You behave yourself, Stina. I won't be long.'

As they neared Ben's garden, she heard the droning of countless bees. All at once, she spotted the swarm. There was a dark shape moving on the branch of a tree – a mottled, heaving mass as if the branch itself had come to life. She faltered, unsure what was expected of her.

'Don't worry,' Ben cajoled. 'A swarm'll never sting a young maiden like thee. We can calm 'em down, make 'em fly more slowly, like. This is where thoo can 'elp. Stand 'ere while I fetch a kettle an' a pot.'

Mary stood absolutely still until he returned, keeping a wary eye on the cloud of bees. When he handed her a stick to go with the pot, he told her to bash it.

'Like this,' he said. 'Make a noise, but not too loud.' He demonstrated on the kettle, hitting it with a gentle rhythm. She joined in, hitting the pot, and they edged closer to the swarm.

'We won't frighten 'em off – they'll want to stay there. They've chosen that spot. They'll not fly off. They'll pitch themselves an' not flit elsewhere. Just keep on wi' tha gentle tappin' while I get some balm mint.'

He fetched a skep and rubbed a syrupy mess of sugar and balm into the bottom. Then he placed the skep under the tree. Mary wondered why he was peering into the tree and frowning and scratching his whiskers.

'I think I'd better trim off some o' yon branches before we knock swarm off into skep. Carry on beatin' wi' tha stick.'

Mary watched as he reached up into the tree. She beat the kettle as well as the pot alternately with the same rhythm. Without unsettling the swarm, he cut away some leaves and branches.

'A swarm o' bees i' May is worth a load of 'ay,' he whispered as a branch dropped to the ground. 'But a swarm o' bees i' June is worth a silver spoon.'

'What about July?' she asked.

'Not worth a fly.' He tossed a rope over the branch that held the swarm and pulled until both ends dangled down.

'Now Mary, stand o' this log, take 'old o' ropes an' shake branch a bit while I catch bees i' this skep.' He lifted her up and made sure that she could reach the rope ends. Then he stood beneath the branch and held the skep upside down.

'Now, when I count to three, give branch a shake. One, two, three!'

She gave a tentative pull. It was enough to jostle the branch and dislodge the swarm. The bees dropped into the skep. Ben turned it over and placed it on a thin stone slab in the shade of the tree. Mary sprang down from the log.

'I'll just put a stick under one side to make a gap for bees to come an' go. Thoo's done a good job, Mary. Well done.'

She hung back, afraid the bees would fly out and sting her.

'Come on, lass,' he coaxed, 'come an' watch.' When she came closer, he pointed out a few bees. 'See them bees stood o' their 'eads? See their wings workin'?' She knelt down to have a look. A lot of bees were just outside the skep and they were making a lot of fuss.

'Them bees there'll make sure all rest o' swarm'll come to this skep. It won't be long now before all bees'll be in. Let's 'ope we 'ave a queen bee or else we'll 'ave it all to do again.'

Mary rested her hands on her hips, shook her head and sighed. In an instant, Ben was reminded of her grandmother at Uphall.

'I'm sorry,' he said, 'there's nowt else to do but wait till evenin'. By then all bees'll be in. I'll move skep later on before it gets dark.'

Mary sighed again. She was disappointed. The excitement was over. To cheer her up he suggested they get some honey from one of the hives. He led her to the skeps at the bottom of the garden, all lined up on a high cobblestone bed.

'Which one, eh?' he asked. 'Thoo can choose.'

To Mary, they all looked the same. After a while, she decided to pick the seventh one since seven was a lucky number.

'That's a good choice, Mary. I reckon that skep'll 'ave plenty of 'oney, but we 'ave to be careful. Bees don't like to leave their comb. It's a good job tha's wearin' pale clothes today – it'll keep bees calm. Wait while I get a rag an' some brimstone.'

She waited patiently and didn't have a clue how he was going to get the honey out. When he returned he was carrying a cloth with yellow powder on it. He also carried a lighted taper. She followed him to a hole in the garden where he lit the rag and dropped it in.

'Stand well back,' he warned. 'Don't breathe it in.'

She'd already pinched her nose as the smell of rotten eggs rose from the hole. To her surprise, he then carried the chosen skep slowly across the garden and sat it over the reeking hole.

'Don't!' she cried. 'You'll kill the bees!'

'Aye, that I will, but it's only way to get 'oney out.'

She shied away shaking her head. 'But when *I* killed some bees, everyone was cross.'

'Listen, lass, I'll explain. This time, it's nowt to cry or worry about. We've just got a new swarm, 'aven't we? There'll be lots more swarms before spring is done. See, i' spring, all them skeps that are full of 'oney, well half o' bees'll leave an' swarm. They'll search an' find someplace else to settle an' make 'oney. An' so it goes on. It's way of it. Vicar'll be pleased – 'e gets a bit o' money for ev'ry first swarm.'

Mary remained unconvinced as they waited for the bees to cease buzzing.

'Listen, tha can 'elp me scrape off wax an' then tha can 'ave a bit o' comb to take 'ome wi' thee. Thoo'll like that I reckon.' Mary nodded. She had little option but to go along with whatever he said.

It wasn't long before he pulled the skep from the hole and led her to his cottage. She followed him into the dingy kitchen. There he warmed a knife by the fire and showed her how to scrape off the caps of wax. They had to keep dipping the knife in a jug of hot water or else the wax wouldn't scrape off properly. He broke off a bit of honeycomb and passed it to her, dripping with dark brown honey.

She licked it and curled her tongue into the holes. It was so sweet.

He sat back and smiled. 'It's that colour 'cos of all whin flowers around Reighton,' he explained. 'If I took me skeps up onto moors, then we'd 'ave 'eather 'oney an' a diff'rent taste an' colour. If bees 'ad been near dandelions, then we'd 'ave a bright, orange 'oney.'

'Thank you, Ben!' She stood up and was about to hug him.

'Whoa, lass, not wi' them sticky fingers. Lick 'em an' get off 'ome. Tha mother'll be wonderin' what's 'appened.'

In the middle of June, young Mary discovered that she had a new brother. It came as a shock to glimpse him only minutes after he was born. Never had she seen such a blotchy misshapen thing. She didn't believe what Sarah Ezard said, that his head wouldn't always be that shape. No one would want a brother with a head like a sausage. Mary cringed when she was handed the 'thing' and told to feed it with a comforter of butter and sugar.

'Come on, lass,' Sarah encouraged her, ''e's swaddled up tight an' can't wriggle. Tha won't drop 'im if tha sits down.'

Young Mary sat on the stool by the bed with the baby lying still in her lap. Her mother smiled at her though she looked very tired. Perhaps her mother would be kinder now that the baby was here.

While the women busied themselves soaking the linen to remove the bloodstains, they gossiped. Young Mary grasped snatches of their excited chatter. A young woman, a stranger, had been seen walking towards Uphall. She looked to be with child.

Part Four

An Unexpected Arrival

Chapter 38

1714

The young woman arrived on the Bridlington to Filey carrier. She asked the way to Uphall and, on arriving there, demanded to see John Dawson. She wore clothes of quite good quality though they'd seen better days, and she was expecting a child. Once she'd been allowed in and given a drink, John was sent for.

He entered the kitchen in all innocence and saw the woman at the table. At first, when she turned to face him, he didn't recognise her. Francis and Dorothy Jordan were standing to one side ill at ease. John listened as the woman spoke of their meeting at the Hunmanby hirings last November. The terrible truth hit him. He collapsed onto the bench opposite her and groaned with his head in his hands.

Francis stepped in. 'I'll deal wi' this,' he told his wife. 'Thoo'd best go an' keep Dorothy out o' way. She doesn't need to know details.'

With great reluctance, she left the kitchen. Maybe there was some mistake, but it was all most interesting.

John recalled that day at the hirings. He'd drunk far too much and his memory was hazy. There'd been a dark shed. It smelled of onions and sacking, and there was a woman in there. She must have found out where he was living and working. He remembered all too well the excitement, but it was over so quickly.

John could hardly speak. He was in shock. 'I'm sorry,' he gasped, 'I don't even know tha name.'

'Me name's Susannah 'Ovington. I'm from Burton Flemin'. I expect thoo to make an 'onest woman o' me.'

219

Francis intervened. 'This can't be right. Can it be true, John? I think not.'

John's face had lost its colour. 'I'm sorry, master,' he mumbled. 'I never meant anythin' by it. I never thought. I'm sorry.'

'Lord 'elp us!' cried Francis. 'I don't know what our Dorothy'll do. She's pinned all 'er 'opes o' thee.' He pushed a hand through his hair in desperation. 'Listen, lad – thoo doesn't know what trouble thoo's brought. All 'ell will break loose.' He stared at the young couple sitting opposite each other at the table; they seemed a most unlikely pair. Something had to be decided though, and soon by the look of her. He sighed.

'I'll leave both o' thee to talk. I'll find Dorothy an' see what she reckons. John – give lass another drink an' summat to eat. I'll try not to be too long.'

The couple had nothing to say to each other. John fetched her some bread and cheese and refilled her beaker with small beer. A few moments of pleasure and he'd have to pay for it. His hopes of a life at Uphall were slipping through his hands like water through a sieve. The Jordans would deem their trust in him misplaced, and he'd have to leave. His sister would be ashamed of him and Dorothy Jordan, who he'd thought perhaps to marry one day, was going to hate him.

Francis returned with his wife. He noticed John cringe like a dog about to be whipped. 'Listen,' he whispered to his wife as they walked towards the table. 'I'll do all talkin'. Thoo's too upset.'

Dorothy, more angry than upset, ignored him and spoke her piece. She pointed to the woman. 'That lass 'as brought nowt with 'er an' I don't see as I trust 'er. I'd send 'er straight back where she came from. Why, bairn might not even be John's.'

Francis eyed John up. The lad was so naive, anything was possible. 'What does thoo think, John?' he asked. 'If all lass says is true, thoo's not got much choice. Thoo must get wed, and soon, eh?'

Dorothy began to pace up and down the kitchen wringing her hands. Men were so gullible.

John glanced across at Susannah who kept her head down. 'Aye,' he mumbled with a nod. He swallowed hard. 'Aye, we'll wed.' His voice was low and hoarse as he asked, 'I'll 'ave to leave Up'all I suppose?'

Francis waved his hand in the air. 'I don't know – it's all much too soon to think about that.'

Dorothy had stopped pacing. She shook her head. 'I'm sayin' nowt else except I'm not 'avin' 'er stayin' 'ere.'

Francis wondered out loud. 'Well, maybe Sarah Ezard can take 'er in till ev'rythin's sorted.'

Rumours spread quickly round the village that a pregnant woman had been seen being escorted from Uphall. Susannah Hovington stayed with Sarah only until the carrier could take her back. Once the banns were read, she was to return on the carrier with her belongings and be married in Reighton.

George Gurwood agreed that the couple should be wed as soon as possible, before the haymaking. He'd have to read the banns for three weeks and, seeing as he was also the curate of Burton Fleming, he'd be able to read them in that parish too and write the certificate to prove it. He guessed that Matthew Smith would not object to the haste although his other churchwarden, Robert Storey, might have misgivings.

George Gurwood was right; Robert couldn't bring himself to condone the marriage. To him, Susannah was at best a common whore, and at worst, a temptress sent by the devil. While most folk were sorry for John Dawson, they couldn't side with him openly. He'd let the Jordans down, the family that had almost adopted him and given him a future. That could not be forgiven. They felt most sorry for young Dorothy who'd been making sheep's eyes at John ever since he'd arrived. Just as she was beginning to make some headway in his affections, this had to happen.

The young Dorothy Jordan was heartbroken. Her mother had great difficulty in making her eat and drink, and knew there'd be more problems in store if Francis decided to keep John at Uphall. Her fears were soon justified.

'Now listen to me,' Francis argued with his wife, 'we've never employed such a good ploughman an' I don't intend to lose 'im. Don't gi' me that look – I've already talked it over wi' William an' Dickon. We've decided to move John into Dickon's empty cottage.'

She had to agree that it made sense. John would not have to keep bumping into Dorothy; he'd be given a decent wage and could eat all his meals at the cottage.

George Gurwood was sick of hearing gossip about Susannah Hovington. On the Sunday before the wedding he delivered a harsh sermon, basing it on John Chapter 8. It was obvious that he included his parishioners among the scribes and Pharisees when he called them downright hypocrites. He didn't accuse anyone in particular, but told them that no one had the right to judge another unless they themselves were pure.

'He that is without sin among you, let him first cast a stone.'

Many of them stared down at their boots and shoes as if, all of a sudden, they needed adjusting. The vicar then looked straight at John Dawson, sitting once more at the rear of the church with the farmhands.

'Neither do I condemn thee,' George said. 'Go, and sin no more.'

John was grateful for the vicar's efforts and, for the next few days, people treated him with kindness. Sarah Ezard went out of her way to speak to him.

'I only knew Susannah for a few days, but I think she's a good lass. I like 'er. She's not first nor last woman to come a cropper.'

George Gurwood arranged for William and Mary's baby to be baptised the same morning as the wedding in the hope that more folk would attend. He still doubted that many would go. He knew that Dorothy Jordan, partly out of sympathy for her daughter's feelings, and partly from wounded pride, had forbidden anyone at Uphall to attend the service. Apart from the brief baptism of William and

Mary's new baby, the day was to be like any other – they were all to get up early and start work in the fields. The only ones certain to go were John's sister, Ellen, and her husband.

On the day of the wedding, Dorothy Jordan nudged her daughter at breakfast and whispered in her ear.

'It doesn't auger well for John. I'd never start owt new on a Friday.'

Her daughter was not consoled. That day, she avoided everyone as best she could. Her one comfort came from the thought that her sister, Jane, who'd also hankered after John Dawson, might be equally distressed by the marriage.

Jane pitied her sister, but was not overly distressed at all. She found the drama and the ensuing gossip both entertaining and exciting. There'd been nothing like it for years.

The marriage service was very brief. John and Susannah submitted without fuss to their mutual fate. Ellen gave her brother and his bride a quick kiss after the ceremony and wished them well. Matthew tried to raise John's spirits. He shook his hand and slapped him on the back.

'Look at me – marriage never did me any harm. And you're lucky to have a child coming.'

John grimaced, took his new wife on his arm and led her to Dickon's house to begin their new life.

Chapter 39

1714

Mary, confined indoors with her new baby, was kept abreast of the latest gossip. Jane told her that most of the men in the village were sorry for John Dawson; they thought he was most unfortunate to miss out on an Uphall wedding. The women blamed him. He had been either too stupid or too weak to get involved in the first place. They pitied Dorothy who deserved better. By the time Mary was able to go outside and resume normal life, folk had lost interest in John and his new wife. All were preoccupied with the hot, dry weather which, after an exceptionally dry spring, had resulted in a poor show of crops.

Things went from bad to worse. In July, rumours came from Bridlington of an outbreak of cattle plague in the south. Matthew Smith was worried for his large herd, and anyone with cattle sharing the common pasture grew fearful. On the other hand, Matthew surmised, if the Reighton herd kept clean of disease, there'd be higher prices paid for his cattle. Most folk remained disheartened. As if they hadn't heard enough, the blacksmith began spreading rumours about Queen Anne's ill health. He gleaned it all from the pedlars who called in on him.

Early one evening, towards the end of the month, the men returned from the fields and gathered in the forge. They lit their pipes and waited for the blacksmith to speak. Phineas had a new tale to tell and put down his hammer.

'Our queen 'ad a fit,' he said, 'an' they thought she were dead.' That got their attention. He paused and took up his hammer. 'Aye, but she revived again.'

The news unsettled them. No one wanted the queen's half-brother, James, to take the throne. He was a papist. Phineas knew what they were thinking.

'Aye, God forbid,' he grumbled, 'we don't want James for king. 'E'll get them Frenchies an' them Irish to come an' invade us.'

The men sucked deep on their pipes. It didn't bear thinking about.

Phineas had more to say. 'I 'eard that Tower o' London 'as a triple guard now.' He paused while they absorbed the information. He shook his head. 'Aye, it's a serious business what wi' Queen Anne so badly.' Then he began hammering again, the signal that his news had finished.

The men left the forge in a morbid frame of mind. It would soon be time to harvest the scant crops. The news of a possible Catholic invasion added to their despair.

George Gurwood, seated alone in the cool, quiet parlour, read the latest news. He worried that, although a Protestant succession had been agreed, Queen Anne had about fifty Catholic relatives with stronger claims to the throne. Moreover, George, the chosen successor, wasn't in England, didn't like the country and didn't speak English. The only positive was that he was Protestant.

William stood gazing across the fields, more concerned about the harvest than the future of England. There were bare patches in the fields and, in the areas where the crops *had* grown, the yield was half the size it should be. The wheat ears and barley awns were small and the bean and pea pods had not filled out. Though he trusted the vicar to be lenient with his portion of the tithes, worse was to come. Strong winds and heavy rain came right at the end of the month. What the sun and dry weather had almost succeeded in doing, the lashing rain and gales completed. The crops, meagre as they were, lay in ruins.

Queen Anne died on the first day of August. Folk began the harvest as usual on that day, ignorant of their monarch's death. They heard the news days later. William, depressed already, thought the day of her death appropriate to the bad harvest they were having.

George Gurwood praised the character of the deceased queen in his Sunday service. He referred to her great piety and affection for the people of England. In the congregation, his daughters remembered 'Good Queen Anne' more for her eighteen pregnancies. Cecilia covered her mouth with her hand and whispered to the sister sitting beside her.

'You know just five of her children were born alive. And not one of them lived to be full-grown.' When this message had been passed along the pew she added, 'I'm not surprised she loved her women servants. I'd prefer women after all those babies.'

At another opportune moment in the service, Cecilia whispered, 'You know the queen was small? Well, they're saying she was so swollen with dropsy that her coffin had to be square.' This information was also passed eagerly along the pew.

On 10th August, George of Hanover was proclaimed King and the vicar made the announcement in church. This alleviated the general unease though the king was still not in England and was not expected until mid-September.

It was the blacksmith who passed on the news of King George's arrival. He waited till he had a good audience standing around the forge.

'Our king's 'ere at long last,' he reported, 'but 'e picked a bad day to come. London 'ad thick fog an' 'e couldn't land. Aye, 'undreds 'ad turned out to greet 'im, lords an' ladies an' such, all i' their finery. They got so fed up waitin' they went back 'ome! Ha – just fancy our king steppin' out of 'is boat an' no one to meet 'im!'

Ben was leaning in a corner smoking his pipe. He shook his head in disbelief. 'Let's 'ope 'is reign is long an' prosperous, that's all I can say.'

'Aye,' they all murmured and sucked on their pipes. They had nothing to add. Tomorrow was yet another miserable day for them to harvest yet another poor crop.

There'd been too many changes for John Dawson. He could not get used to the quiet life in his cottage and missed the banter of the Uphall lads. Failing to make conversation with his wife, he was lonely in her company. One morning, Susannah spoke to him about the coming baby. She'd been anxious for a week already. The baby had been very still of late; she'd not felt it kick or squirm at all. She had an instinct that something was wrong and wanted to be at home with her mother. John couldn't persuade her to consult Sarah Ezard.

'I don't feel at 'ome i' Reighton,' she tried to explain. 'When thoo's ill or scared tha just wants tha mother.'

John borrowed the cart from Uphall and took her back to Burton Fleming. He promised to return for her in a month's time when she'd had the baby and could travel.

Susannah had only been home for a couple of days when she was violently sick and began to have labour pains. There was a very real possibility that the baby was dead. She had no choice but to deal with the pain and push the baby out. After an exhausting few hours, her mother managed to extract it – a little girl. She was dead as they'd both feared. Susannah asked to see, but her mother covered the baby up. She sliced through the cord with a knife and hurried with the baby into the kitchen.

The girl must have been dead for some time. Susannah's mother was alarmed to see her so bruised and mottled. As soon as she touched the body, the decomposing skin slid into ridges, some of it coming away in her hands. With her eyes full of tears, she rinsed the baby girl as best she could in a bowl of warm water. Then she wrapped her up in a piece of white cloth, walked back into the parlour and handed the small bundle to her daughter.

'That bruisin's all part o' bein' born,' she said, giving some excuse for the baby's colour. Quickly, she hid away some black, curly hair that had rubbed off the baby's head.

Susannah gazed at her child. The little girl would have been the image of her father. How could she ever go back to Reighton? And what would she say to John?

'Take it away,' she cried and burst into tears. She wanted to grieve, and yet resented the trouble the baby had brought.

Her mother buried the tiny girl in the garden.

John came to collect his wife at the end of the month as planned. He could hardly believe there was no child and suspected that she'd fooled him into marriage.

'Why didn't tha let me know?' he shouted at his wife sitting by the fire. 'Why couldn't tha send a message?' At the back of his mind was the thought that, if only she'd lost the baby earlier, they would not have married.

His mother-in-law soon set him straight. Before he knew what was happening she'd prodded him backwards into the wall.

'Thoo doesn't know 'alf o' what my daughter's been through. Why she's been at death's door for weeks with a fever. I've just 'ad time to see to 'er, not gad about sendin' messages.'

He looked again at his wife slumped by the fire. She was thinner than he remembered and pale and drawn. Her voice, when she managed to speak, sounded desolate.

'I'm so sorry,' she croaked. 'I'm sorry to spoil tha life. I'll make it up to thee. Thoo'll see – I'll be a good wife.'

He then realised how unfortunate she was, and how much worse off than him. She had to live in a village where she didn't belong, and among people that she didn't know. He apologised to his mother-in-law and promised to look after her daughter. As he took her back to Reighton, he was genuinely sorry and determined to make the best of a bad job.

The poor harvest was completed. As everyone took stock of the meagre supplies and dreaded the prospect of a harsh winter, Susannah found that she was with child again. She kept it a secret from her husband. She didn't want to tempt fate and decided to wait until Christmas before telling him. At least then, she hoped, the Jordans and the other villagers might be more charitable. She peered out of her cottage window at the steady rain and reflected on her lonely life. Folk talked *about* her but never *to* her. Just as she thought that no one would befriend her, the Scottish pedlar,

Speckledy Golightly, hurried past with her basket of ribbons and stockings.

Eager for any company, Susannah rapped on the window. When the woman turned her head, Susannah signalled for her to come in. So pleased to have a visitor in the cottage, she took the woman's cloak to dry by the fire and gave her some broth.

The pedlar was pleased to be out of the rain and was surprised by the sudden generosity. 'Ah'm no' welcome these days. It's a hard time ah've had,' she related. 'It's all 'cos o' death o' Queen Anne. Ah'm almost an outcast.'

'Thoo is from Scotland,' Susannah argued. The woman even looked Scottish with her red hair and freckles. 'Folk get suspicious. Thoo can't blame 'em.'

'Ah'm no Jacobite!' she hissed back. 'An' ah'm no spy neither. Ah don't deserve ti be chased oot fro' place ti place.'

'I'm sorry. I know what it's like to be an outcast.' She brought out some new barley bread to go with the broth. ''Ere, 'ave as much as tha wants.' Glad of someone to talk to, she told the woman all her misfortunes.

Speckledy Golightly listened as she finished her broth. She did not interrupt. When Susannah's tale had ended, she tipped her wares onto the table.

'Have anything you like,' she offered. 'Next time ah come, you'll be my first call. Ah'll save some o' my best stuff for thee.'

When the pedlar left, she promised to return at regular intervals. Susannah waved her goodbye. Though the Jordans and most of the village still rejected her, she had at least one friend now. The future was a little brighter. She closed the door with a smile on her face.

Chapter 40

1714

All through the autumn, Jane Jordan continued to help out both at Uphall and at William and Mary's house. It tired her to work in two places. The new baby, John, was small but he was feeding well and, luckily, Mary seemed to be coping. Francis was useful as he helped to look after his young brothers, and young Mary was out each morning having lessons at the vicarage; her absence enabled Jane and Mary to get more work done. Despite the help from Mary and her son, Jane fell exhausted into bed each night.

Tom was the only one at Uphall to notice that Jane was losing weight. He saw how she was rushing from one job to another in order to be back at William and Mary's house for supper. Whenever he could, he offered to carry water for her and kept nagging her to take a rest. The more he insisted, the more irritable she became. Frustrated, he asked Dickon to intervene on his behalf.

'Ask Dorothy to give Jane more indoor jobs,' he suggested. 'Jane gets a bad chest i' winter an' she's already started with a cough.'

Dickon mentioned this to Jane's mother, but she saw no reason to change or lighten Jane's duties.

''Ard work never killed no one,' she declared, though she had noticed Jane's face was often flushed. 'I'll tell 'er to wrap up more when she goes outside.'

When Dorothy heard Tom and Dickon fussing over Jane's little cough, she dosed her daughter with a tried and tested remedy. She scooped out an onion, filled it with brown sugar and left it overnight. In the morning it was full of liquid and she made Jane drink it.

The smell on Jane's breath kept even Tom away. She wished they'd all leave her alone and learnt to stifle her tickly cough when people were within earshot. She always took the opportunity to clear her chest when she walked between Uphall and William's house.

Early one morning, young Mary was out with Ben searching for mushrooms and caught Jane having a coughing spasm. Jane, bent double by the hedge, didn't see them and carried on coughing. Ben looked up in alarm.

'Sounds more like a sheep than a lass,' he said. 'I'll get summat from Sarah Ezard. We can't 'ave Jane badly, can we? She 'as over much work to do.'

The next day, Sarah Ezard brought a strange mutton broth to William's house.

'It's to be taken wi' bread an' salt,' she informed Jane. 'It's for tha chest. 'Ave it for both breakfast an' supper.'

Jane thanked her in good faith, not realising what was in it. Mary knew though – it was Sarah Ezard's infamous Snail Broth. It was a mutton chop boiled in water with a crust of bread and some mace, and then thirty grey snails added. At least Sarah hadn't asked Jane to swallow live snails. She'd made Ben do that once, making him believe the snails would eat the phlegm off his chest. At least, in the broth, the snails had been well-boiled. Mary watched as Jane had her first mouthful and chewed on the squidgy bits.

'How does it taste?' asked Mary.

'It's a bit earthy,' Jane decided, 'and it's rather bitter. Oh, well …' She took a few more spoonfuls. Mary never did tell her what it was.

Within days, Jane stopped coughing and began to feel fit again. Tom was delighted with her quick recovery, and spoiled her by giving her extra food saved from his own meals. Unfortunately, all the food was being rationed. Even the apples that year were smaller than usual, and there were ominous empty spaces in the barns that should have been full of sheaves and winter fodder.

At Michaelmas, Francis Jordan had the miserable task of assessing the stock with Dickon to decide which animals would have to be slaughtered. Due to the shortages, there was no way they could keep all their stock fed until spring. They were depressed as they made their choices, but at least they wouldn't be short of meat this coming winter.

William and Mary chose a day to kill their own pig, and invited relatives and neighbours round to help. Young Mary didn't want to miss the excitement and skipped her morning lessons. Her brother, Francis, dreaded the day. He remembered last year all too well – the terrible amount of blood and guts that came out of just one pig. It put him off bacon and sausages for months. With luck, he could stay in the house and look after his young brother and the baby.

When the women arrived wearing their old sack aprons, William went to fetch the pig. Francis stayed behind and hid under the table, miserable and fearful. He'd grown fond of the hog and had even given it a name – Chacky Pig.

Young Mary stood to watch with everyone else by the back door. Her father tied a rope through the pig's nose ring and proceeded to pull it from its sty into the open. On seeing so many people, the pig stood its ground and, when William tried to drag it out, it squealed. The pig sensed danger. Young Mary covered her ears with her hands. The high-pitched screams sent shivers through her whole body. She clamped her hands more tightly on her ears and prayed the pig would stop. Ben put an arm around her.

'Don't worry, lass. It'll all be over soon enough.'

Once the pig was in place on the prepared patch of straw, William tied up its jaw and pulled the rope taut. All went quiet. The pig tensed but did not move. Young Mary, still with her hands over her ears, watched and held her breath while her Uncle John held the punch between the pig's eyes. Then, on a nod from John, the blacksmith swung the wooden mell. It came down with such a sudden, accurate force. The pig's legs buckled and it dropped to the ground senseless. The men heaved it onto the wooden form and left its head lolling over the edge. Jane put a large pail underneath, and young Mary looked on as her father took a knife and cut its throat from ear to ear. The blood poured into the pail in torrents, and then it gushed in gentle spurts.

'Its heart's still beating,' Jane said.

Young Mary saw her mother plunge her arms into the blood. It was up to her elbows and she began to stir it round.

'Come on, Mary,' she shouted. 'Roll your sleeves up and join in. Keep stirring it so it doesn't set. Sarah Ezard's going to make black pudding with it.'

Young Mary peered into the bucket. It was dark and frothy. She thrust one arm in and began slowly pushing it around. The blood was warm and smelled of metal spoons. While she stirred, the other women poured scalding water onto the now dead pig and, as the skin softened, they began to scrape off the bristles.

'Fetch Francis out,' William called. 'I'm sure this is a job even *he* can do.'

Jane went in to get him. She found him watching from the window.

'Come on, Francis. Your father won't make you do anything you don't want to. Come on, there's a good lad.' She ruffled his hair and lifted up his chin. 'The baby's asleep and young William can come and watch us. We'll scrape the bristles off together, eh?'

When he came out into the garden, he glowered at his sister. She was smeared with blood and smiled at him as she stirred and played around in the pail. He avoided her gaze and concentrated on scraping the skin. He also avoided looking at the pig's eyes and the gaping wound across its neck. As he rubbed off the hairs, he felt he'd betrayed Chacky.

Young Mary was in her element; she'd heard them talk of chopping the pig's head open next. Her father took a hatchet and split it in half, and then Uncle John helped him prise it open like a book. Curious, she approached one half and gave the ear a pinch. Then she stroked the stiff, white eyelashes. She examined an eye and, half-afraid, prodded it gently with her finger; it was more solid than expected.

Her brother was appalled. He turned away as the men cut through the tendons of the back legs and shoved a wooden pole through. The pig was then hoisted up and hung from the beam in the open shed. William scattered sand on the floor and slit open its belly to pull out the stomach and intestines. He shared the organs out among the helpers and, when the bladder was removed, he called out to his son.

'Francis! Come and take this – we can make a football for you.' The boy shook his head in disgust. William sighed, disappointed. 'Right then, I reckon there'll be some other lad who'll be glad of it.'

Francis stared down at his feet. His sister would probably end up with the bladder and she'd wave it in his face and gloat.

Young Mary was too engrossed for the moment. She was now down at the bottom of the garden helping the women wash out the chitterlings. Tomorrow, she was told, they'd be used for sausage skins. Sarah Ezard had already gone indoors with Ben and the pail of blood to make the black pudding, and left the women to their filthy task. They all stood round a large tub of water well away from the others. Young Mary soon realised why – the chitterlings stank. Up to her elbows again, she helped untangle the tubes and slide off the fat. Then she swished and squeezed the intestines between her fingers and thumbs to get all the mucky stuff out. The first lot of water soon turned black. She hated the smell, though it was nice to feel the thin tubes slip through her fists. Jane and her mother argued as to which person had last fed the hog.

'Just look at all this muck coming out!' her mother complained. 'No one in their right mind would feed a hog the day before it's butchered.'

'It wasn't me,' Jane assured her. 'I only gave it water yesterday. It's what we always do.'

'I believe you, but someone has fed it.' She glanced up the garden at Francis. 'Ugh!' she shouted in his direction. 'It stinks to high heaven!'

Francis heard his mother and edged away sheepishly. The women clicked their tongues, guessing he was the culprit. They continued with their dirty job, and turned the intestines inside out for more rinsing. For the final task, Jane got a smooth piece of wood and began to scrape off the slimy coating from the tubes.

Francis stood out of the way to one side with his two-year-old brother while the men halved the pig and cut the backbone into pieces for roasting. The chunks of backbone were put to one side for salting. William took the brains from the head and parted the meaty jowls from the bone. He called out for help.

'One of you women come here – take these jowls to make into chap hams. And take these brains to the kitchen for poaching.'

Young Mary lifted her head from the tub of intestines. She wanted to see what her father was doing.

'Can I go?' she asked her mother.

'Oh, go on then, and after, you can help in the kitchen.'

Young Mary wiped her hands on the grass and ran back to her father. She watched, full of admiration, as he cut off the pig's ears and chopped the head into smaller pieces for the cauldron beside him. He also cut off the tail, the trotters and the hocks, and passed them along to be added to the pot.

'That's it done then,' he said and picked up a clump of straw. He wiped his hands and beckoned to her. 'I'm going to carry this cauldron to the kitchen. Come with me and you can help.'

Young Mary followed him indoors and kept her distance while he hung the pot over the fire and filled it with water. Sarah Ezard added the brains. William turned to his daughter and winked.

'That's for the brawn. It needs to boil for a long time. We want all the lovely meat to fall off, and then you and Jane can get the skin and bones out.' He rubbed his hands together. "Mmm, fatty brawn! Just what you want on a cold winter's day!'

At the bottom of the garden, the women had finished rinsing the intestines. They tipped the water away and packed them in salt, ready for when they made the sausages.

Nothing more was to be done that day except salt the meat joints and jowls. They took off their blood-stained aprons and scrubbed their hands and nails clean. Then they separated, some to do the salting, others to help in the kitchen.

The men gathered together. They lounged around the top of the garden and lit up their pipes. Soon, Jane fetched them a mug of beer each. As the day grew darker, they moved into the kitchen to keep warm by the now simmering cauldron. Young Mary sat on the floor between her father's legs with her head against his knee. She yawned, desperate to keep awake and not miss anything.

'What are we doing tomorrow?' she asked, tilting her head. 'Will I help at home, or will I be at my lessons?'

'Seeing as you've been such a help, it's up to you. Do you want to stay and finish off the pig?' She nodded. 'Then tomorrow you can watch us dress it.' She looked puzzled and her brother grinned.

'Father doesn't mean they're going to dress it up in a gown!' he sneered with a superior air.

William laughed and kissed the top of her head. 'No, Mary – not that kind of dressing. You'll see.'

Chapter 41

The next day, young Mary woke early and coaxed everyone else up. She was eager to get back to the pig, but her mother was cross.

'Oh, Mary – I've just got the baby off to sleep again. I'm tired. I haven't the energy to deal with that pig.' She continued to complain as she dished out the porridge. 'It's all right for you – it's nothing but fun, isn't it?'

William nudged his daughter. 'I bet your mother will want to join in later,' he hinted. 'She'll enjoy making the sausages – you'll see.' He winked at his wife. 'I'm right, am I not?'

'Go on with you!' She managed a smile in spite of her poor temper.

Francis glanced from one to the other and shuddered. It was no fun for him. It was going to be a long day – another day of dealing with a lot of raw meat, bone and fat. On top of that, his portion of porridge seemed to get less every day.

As soon as breakfast was over, young Mary was the first to rush outside and be ready to help. Before long the others joined her. The men sliced the white fat out of the pig while the women chopped it into smaller pieces to render down. Young Mary put the pieces into a large pot.

Francis grew more accustomed to the sight of the dead animal. It hardly looked like a pig anymore and was certainly nothing like Chacky, the pet he'd fed for most of the year. Without a head or trotters, and hung open in two halves, it was just what it was – a carcase. He determined never to name another hog. He stood holding his young brother's hand as his father dealt with one half. First, a ham was cut off, and then the belly and the shoulder.

'Come on, Jane,' William ordered, 'trim some lean meat off this ham and shoulder.'

While the women began their task, the ribs were cut out and shared amongst the helpers. Mary carried the belly indoors and laid it on a thick layer of salt. Then she covered it with even more salt, thankful for the supply from Bridlington. As soon as the others had finished trimming the ham and shoulder, she laid them on top. The same was done with the other half of the pig. By this time, Mary had had enough, and the baby needed a feed. She remained indoors while the women fetched the guts.

Francis took the chance to go inside as well. He told his father he'd be more useful there.

Young Mary stayed in the garden and was shown how to cut the guts into lengths and rinse off the salt in different tubs of water. Before long, her hands were cold and sore, and she whined to be allowed a different job in the kitchen.

'Not yet,' warned Jane. 'There's one more thing you can do before you disappear. As we rinse these chitterlings, I want you to see if there are any holes anywhere. Fill them up with water and see if any comes out.' She showed her how to do it. 'See? The good ones you can put over there in that bowl of water and vinegar. We'll leave them to soak and they'll soften up ready for the sausages.'

Young Mary did as she was told. It was more fun, but her hands were still cold and wet. She kept glancing at the back door. The smell of pork cooking in the cauldron was wafting out, making her hungry. She thought, if she helped the women take the meat off the bones, she could sneak some mouthfuls.

'Can I go in now?' she pleaded. 'I can help mother and Sarah in the kitchen.'

'Go on then,' said Jane, 'you've done enough for now.'

Young Mary ran back indoors. Sarah Ezard was busy stirring the cauldron and getting the meat to separate. The smell made Mary's mouth water. She stood on tiptoe and peered into the pot. There was an eye half afloat among the gristle.

'Hey, Francis,' she called, 'have you seen in here?' He walked across to have a peek. As soon as she pointed out the greasy eyeball, he retched and backed off.

'Oh, Francis!' cried his mother. 'You need to be tougher than this. You'll be glad of the brawn before long. You mark my words.'

He cowered away and mumbled that he'd tend to young William – keep him away from the fire.

Young Mary stayed beside the pot to watch Sarah Ezard. The meat was so tender it fell off the bones with the slightest stir. Sarah fished out the meat and bits of brain and put them in the waiting row of pots. When no one was looking, young Mary slipped a piece of fatty meat into her mouth. She gave away no telltale signs of chewing, and let it dissolve instead on her tongue.

Once the meat had been removed, Jane came in to help Sarah strain the liquid and pour it into the pots. They pressed the meat down to get rid of any air bubbles. Young Mary saw how they did it and joined in. It was soft and warm between her fingers and it smelled so good.

'That's all done then,' said Jane as they finished. 'It's always a busy time with a pig, but we'll be needing that brawn come Christmas.' She tucked a stray lock of hair back under her bonnet. 'Now we can start on the sausages.'

The other women came indoors and sat wherever they could, glad to be warm and have a brief rest. All too soon they'd be back at work. The men outside had cleaned up and were free for the rest of the day. As they wandered off to drink and smoke at the forge, Jane took out a huge chopping board and began to scrub it. The women took the hint. They washed their hands, put on clean aprons and prepared to make sausages.

All the lean meat and fat had to be chopped into smaller pieces. As they cut up the meat, young Mary was the one to scoop it off the board into an enormous bowl. It took a while to prepare, but everyone was happy now, even her mother. Sarah Ezard brought in some bags of herbs and set them out for the women to choose from.

'There,' she announced, 'I've powdered thyme, rubbed sage, marjoram, parsley an' nutmeg.' This led to a heated discussion. Each family had its own preferences and secret recipes it was not keen to divulge, and they argued about the relative merits of the different combinations. Since it was Mary's pig, she had the last say. She decided on a compromise.

'Let's mix different batches. I have some garlic and fennel seeds put by.'

Knowing that Mary liked to experiment, the women groaned and resigned themselves to making some strange sausages.

'Come on,' Mary coaxed, 'put plenty of pepper and salt in all the bowls while I fetch my flavourings.'

They did as they were told and were surprised when she agreed to have at least one traditional herb mix.

'Sarah, you put in your sage,' she ordered, 'and Jane, you chop these onions up finely. Another bowl can be thyme and marjoram, and we can put in the rosemary I have lying about somewhere. And I'll throw in some sugar as well.'

They added all the ingredients and kneaded the mixtures. Every so often Mary took samples. She flattened them into tiny discs and sent Jane to fry them. After tasting them, more herbs were added until she was satisfied. Soon it was too dark and cold to work anymore. Their fingers ached and they were relieved to leave the bowls overnight for the meat to absorb the flavours. Tomorrow they'd make the sausages. Sarah Ezard winked at them and gave a dirty laugh.

'Who's ready for a good stuffin' i' mornin'?' she asked. Young Mary didn't know why they all grinned so much. Even her mother was smiling.

That evening, thanks to the pig, Mary prepared a different meal. 'I saved a pig's ear and a couple of trotters to make a stew,' she informed them. 'It'll be tasty. Mind the gristle though.'

As a tired young Mary sucked the ear, her father put an arm around her. 'It's like your grandmother says – nowt's wasted with a pig. We eat all but the squeak.'

The next morning the women arrived to make sausages. They nudged each other and giggled as they pushed through the door. First, they washed their hands in hot, soapy water.

'Where's young lass put chitterlin's?' asked Sarah Ezard. 'I know she was last one to rinse 'em.'

'Mary!' shouted her mother. 'Where are they?'

'Outside – somewhere,' the girl answered vaguely. She was just about to go and fetch the bowl when her mother grabbed her.

'No – don't. You'll go and drop them and then we'll be in a right mess with dirty skins again. Jane – you fetch the bowl.'

Young Mary stuck out her bottom lip in a sulk. Francis smirked as he spied on them from the doorway.

The intestines were given one last rinse. Jane had quite a job to untangle them before she could fill them with water. She eased out any twists as the water drained through.

'They're clean and soft now,' she declared at last. 'They're ready to be stuffed.'

Mary brought the bowls of sausage meat to the table, and the women edged up to each other on the benches to work in pairs. They began to giggle again as they were handed the hollowed out bones and wooden rammers. It was their chance to be as bawdy as they pleased, with a man nowhere in sight. The crude jokes began almost at once.

'It's a pity tha sister, Lizzie, isn't 'ere,' chuckled Sarah Ezard. 'She'd be envious o' yon rammer! I bet she'd swap it for Robert given 'alf a chance.'

Mary and Jane grinned at each other. The fun was just beginning. First, the bones were oiled and then, while one woman held the hollow bone, the other chose a long, thin skin from the bowl of intestines. Young Mary watched as they fiddled with their fingers and thumbs to prise open one end. It looked very difficult as the skins were so thin. She didn't know why they laughed so much as they struggled to slide the skins over the ends of the bones and then push them on, bunching them up into white wrinkles. Jane was helpless with laughter and crossed her legs, afraid of wetting herself. This made them laugh all the more. They tried to concentrate on their job and wiped the tears from their eyes with their sleeves.

Somehow they managed to tie one end of the skins. Then they began to stuff the bones with the sausage meat. Mary pushed the meat through the bone with her thumb. Then she used the rammer to force it out the other end into the skin held by Jane. Trying not to laugh, Jane used both hands to mould the emerging sausage. She crossed her legs again as the white-veined skin in her hand bulged suddenly with pink meat.

'Twist it, quick!' shouted Mary, as Jane found herself with a length of sausage. All at once, young Mary saw how funny it looked. She started to laugh though she didn't understand their jokes. She was soon lying on the floor, rolling about and laughing until her stomach ached. Her brother kept sneaking to the doorway to see what all the fuss was about.

'Shoo! Shoo!' they cried. 'Go away! We want no lads in 'ere!'

Eventually, the job was finished. With aching sides and tears still in their eyes, they surveyed the links of sausages piled up. It was a good job done. All they had to do now was prick them with a pin to get rid of air pockets, and then hang them up to dry out. Jane and Mary discussed ways to preserve them.

'I thought to leave some raw, just as they are,' said Mary. 'They can dry out over a few months. What do you think? We could hang some up in the kitchen rafters to smoke.'

Jane agreed and assured her the smoked ones would keep. 'And I could boil some and put them in tubs of lard,' she suggested. 'That way, you'll have sausages right until spring.'

Mary looked at the pile and reviewed what other foods she had in the larder. Spring seemed a long way off.

Three days of work on the pig left William and Mary tired yet satisfied. They spooned together in bed for warmth, knowing that other houses in Reighton would also have their pig-killing days, and they'd be expected to help. It was some relief to know the extra meat they'd get would eke out their own rations. As William fell asleep, Mary listened to the wind getting up. If the coming winter proved long and harsh, they still might not have enough food for the family's survival.

Book Three

Whisper to the Bees

1714 to 1720

Young Mary continues to be a challenge, especially when she finds a friend and ally in her brother, William. While the children are thrilled with the snow and ice of the exceptional winters, a major death in the family will change everything. Drinking, smuggling and clashes with the law will test the Jordan family to the limit.

About the Author

Joy Stonehouse's father came from Filey. He moved to Hornsea before the war and married Gladys Jordan, a descendant of the Jordans of Reighton. Joy writes under her maiden name. She is known locally as Mrs Gelsthorpe.